ADAM'S RIB

ALSO BY ANTONIO MANZINI

Black Run

ADAM'S RIB

A Rocco Schiavone Mystery

ANTONIO MANZINI

Translated from the
Italian by Antony Shugaar

HARPER

NEW YORK · LONDON · TORONTO · SYDNEY

HARPER

Originally published as *La costola di Adamo* in Italy in 2015 by Sellerio Editore, Palermo.

The publication of this volume has been supported by a translation grant of the Italian Ministry of Foreign Affairs. Questo volume ha beneficiato di un contributo alla traduzione assegnato dal Ministero degli Affari Esteri italiano.

FIRST U.S. EDITION

Designed by Jamie Lynn Kerner

Library of Congress Cataloging-in-Publication Data

Names: Manzini, Antonio, 1964- author. | Shugaar, Antony translator.
Title: Adam's rib : a novel / Antonio Manzini ; translated from the Italian
    by Antony Shugaar.
Other titles: Costola di Adamo. English
Description: First edition. | New York : Harper, 2016.
Identifiers: LCCN 2016013385 | ISBN 9780062354679 (pbk.) | ISBN 9780062354693
    (ebook)
Subjects: LCSH: Murder--Investigation--Fiction. | Detective and mystery
    stories. | GSAFD: Mystery fiction
Classification: LCC PQ4913.A69 C6713 2016 | DDC 853/.92-
-dc23 LC record available at https://lccn.loc.gov/2016013385

ISBN 978-0-06-235467-9 (pbk.)

16 17 18 19 20   OV/RRD   10 9 8 7 6 5 4 3 2 1

To Uncle Vincenzo

A man has every season while a woman only has the right to spring.

—JANE FONDA

CONTENTS

ADAM'S RIB

FRIDAY

They were March days, days that bring splashes of sunshine and hints of the springtime to come. Shafts of sunlight, warm, not yet hot, and fleeting, but still: light that colored the world and kindled hopes.

But not in Aosta.

It had rained all night long and pellets of watery snow had pelted down on the city until two in the morning. Then the temperature had plunged by many degrees, handing defeat to the rain and victory to the snow, snow that continued to flake down until six, covering streets and sidewalks. At dawn, the sun came up diaphanous and feverish, illuminating a city washed white while the last straggling snowflakes fluttered lazily down, spiraling onto the sidewalks. The mountains were swathed in clouds and the temperature sat several degrees below freezing. Then a malevolent wind sprang up unexpectedly, charging into the city's streets like a raiding party of drunken Cossacks, rudely slapping people and objects.

On Via Brocherel, the wind had only objects to slap, given the fact that the street was deserted. The NO PARKING sign tossed and wobbled while the branches of the small trees planted along the road creaked like the bones of an arthritic old man. The snow, which hadn't yet been packed down, whirled through the air in little wind funnels, and here and there a loose shutter banged repeatedly. Gusts of icy powder swept off apartment building roofs.

As Irina rounded the corner of Via Monte Emilus onto Via Brocherel she was caught by a punch of cold air straight to her face.

Her hair, gathered in a ponytail, swung out behind her; her blue eyes squinted slightly. If you'd taken a close-up of her and knew nothing about the context, you might think she was a madwoman without a helmet riding a motorcycle at 75 miles per hour.

But that sudden icy slap in the face actually felt to her like a gentle caress. She didn't even bother to tug closed the lapels of her gray woolen overcoat. For someone who'd been born and raised in Lida, just a few miles from the Lithuanian border, that blast of wind was nothing more than a mild spring breeze. While it might still be winter in Aosta in March, back home in Belarus they were dealing with ice and temperatures around 15 degrees, well below freezing.

Irina was walking briskly, her feet clad in a pair of knock-off Hogan sneakers that sparkled with every step; as she walked she sucked on a piece of honey-flavored hard candy she'd bought at the café after enjoying her breakfast. If there was one thing she loved about Italy, it was breakfast at the café. Cappuccino and brioche. The noise of the espresso machine steaming the milk, churning up the frothy white foam that the barista then blended with strong black coffee and finally sprinkled with cocoa powder. And the brioche, hot, crunchy, melt-in-your-mouth sweet. Just the memory of the breakfasts she used to eat in Lida . . . those inedible mushy gruels made of barley and oats, the coffee that tasted like mud. And then, the cucumbers—that bitter taste first thing in the morning. Her grandfather used to chase them down with a glass of schnapps, while her father used to scoop the butter directly off the butter dish into his mouth as if it were some caramel dessert. When she told Ahmed about that, he'd laughed so hard he'd come dangerously close to vomiting. "Butter? By the spoonful?" he'd asked in disbelief. As he laughed, he displayed the gleaming white teeth Irina so envied. Her teeth were a dull gray. "It's the climate," Ahmed had told her. "In Egypt the weather is hot and so people's teeth are whiter. The colder it is, the darker the teeth. It's the exact opposite of skin color. It's all because of the sunshine you don't have. Plus, on top of that, if you start eating butter by the spoonful!" and he laughed some more. Irina loved him. She loved the way he smelled when he came home from the market. The scents of apples and new-mown grass floated off him. She loved it when he prayed to Mecca, when he baked apple cakes for her, when they made love. Ahmed was sweet and considerate and he never got drunk and his breath always smelled of mint. The only drinking he did was a beer every now and then, and even then he would say, "The Prophet wouldn't approve." But he did like beer. Irina would look at him and think about the men back home, the way they guzzled hard liquor, their foul breath, the stink on their skin. A mix of stale sweat, vodka, and cigarettes. But Ahmed had an explanation for this stark difference too. "In Egypt, we wash more often, because you have to be clean when you pray to Allah. And as hot as it is, we dry off very fast. Where you're from, it's cold, and you never really get dry. This too is because of the sunshine," he told her. "In any case, we'd never eat butter by the spoonful," and he was bent over laughing again.

But now her relationship with Ahmed had come to the crossroads. He'd made his declaration.

He'd asked her to marry him.

There were a few issues, strictly technical ones. If they were going to get married, either Irina would need to embrace the Muslim religion, or he'd have to convert to Eastern Orthodoxy. And that was easier said than done. She could never become a Muslim. Not for any real religious reasons: Irina no more believed in God than she believed in the likelihood of hitting the Powerball jackpot. No, it was the thought of her parents that kept her from converting. Up north in Belarus, her family was Orthodox and faithful—to them God was "Bog." Her papa, Alexei, and her mama, Ruslava, her five brothers, her aunts, and most of all, her cousin Fyodor, who had married the daughter of a metropolitan. How could she tell them: "Hi all! Starting tomorrow I'm going to be referring to Bog as Allah"? For that matter, it wasn't as if Ahmed could call his father down south in Faiyum and say: "You know what, dad? Starting tomorrow, I'm Eastern Orthodox!" Aside from the fact that Ahmed seriously doubted his father even knew what being Orthodox meant: he'd probably think it was some kind of infectious disease. So Irina and Ahmed were considering a civil union. They would grit their teeth and stick to the plan. At least as long as Aosta remained home to them. Then Bog, Allah, or the Lord Almighty would look out for them.

SHE'D REACHED THE APARTMENT BUILDING AT NO. 22 of Via Brocherel. She pulled out her keys and opened the street door. What a fine big building that was! With its marble steps and wooden handrails. Not like her building, with its chipped terra-cotta floor tiles and damp patches on the ceiling. And no elevator, not like here. In her building you had to trudge up the stairs to the fourth floor. And every third step was broken, the next one was loose, and then one would be missing entirely. To say nothing of the heating, with the kerosene stove that hissed and whistled and would operate properly only after you gave a good hard bang on the door. She dreamed of living in an apartment building like this one on Via Brocherel. With Ahmed and his son, Hilmi. Hilmi was already eighteen and he didn't know a word of Arabic. Irina had done her best to show him love, but Hilmi didn't give a damn about her. "You're not my mother! Mind your own fucking business!" he'd shout at her. And Irina would take it in silence. She'd think of that boy's mother. The woman had gone back to Egypt, to Alexandria, where she was working in a shop run by relatives; she had never wanted to hear from her son or her husband again, as long as she lived. The name Hilmi meant calm and tranquility. Irina smiled at the thought: never had anyone been given a less appropriate name. Hilmi seemed like a flashlight that never turned off. He went out all the time, he didn't even come home to sleep, he was a disaster at school, and at home he bit the hand that fed him.

"You miserable loser!" he would say to his father. "You'll never get me to go sell fruit from a stall like you! I'd rather have sex with old men!"

"Oh really? So what are you going to do instead?" Ahmed would shout back. "Get the Nobel Prize?" It was a sarcastic reminder to his son of how catastrophically bad his grades were. "You'll just be unemployed and homeless, that's what you'll be. And that's not much of a future, you know that?"

"Better than selling apples out on the street or cleaning other people's apartments like this scrubwoman you've taken in," and he'd point at Irina in distaste. "I'll make plenty of money and I'll come visit you the day they put you in a hospital bed! But don't you worry. I'll pay for a nice big coffin to bury you in."

Usually those arguments between Ahmed and Hilmi ended with the father taking a swing at his son and his son slamming the door as he stormed out of the apartment, extending further the crack in the plaster wall. By now it reached practically up to the ceiling. Irina felt certain that the next time they had a fight, both wall and ceiling would collapse, worse than what happened during the Vilnius earthquake of 2004.

The elevator doors swung open and Irina turned left immediately, toward Apartment 11R.

THE LOCK OPENED AFTER JUST ONE TURN OF THE KEY. Strange, very strange, thought Irina. All the other times, she had to turn the key three full turns. She went to the Baudos' three times a week and never once in the past year had she ever found either of them at home. At ten in the morning, the husband had long ago left for work, though on Fridays he actually left home at dawn to go ride his bike. The signora, on the other hand, only came in after doing her grocery shopping at eleven: Irina could have set her watch by it. Perhaps Signora Esther had caught the intestinal flu that was felling victims in Aosta worse than a plague epidemic in the Dark Ages. Irina walked into the apartment, bringing a gust of snowy cold air with her. "Signora Esther, it's me, Irina! It's nice and cold out . . . are you home, Signora?" she called as she put her keys away in her purse. "Didn't you go grocery shopping?" Her hoarse voice, a result of the twenty-two cigarettes she smoked every day, echoed off the smoked glass of the front door.

"Signora?"

She slid the pocket door to one side and walked into the living room.

ANTONIO MANZINI

The place was a mess. On the low table in front of the
TV sat a tray with the remains of dinner still on it. Chicken
bones, a squeezed lemon, and greenish scraps. Spinach,
maybe. Crumpled up on the sofa was an emerald-green
blanket and in the ashtray were a dozen cigarette butts. Irina
decided that the signora was most likely in her bedroom
with a fever, and that last night her husband, Patrizio, had
eaten dinner alone and watched the soccer game. Otherwise
there would have been two trays, his and Signora Esther's.
The pages of the *Corriere dello Sport* were scattered all
over the carpet, and a drinking glass had left two distinct
rings on the antique blond wood table. Shaking her head,
Irina walked over to clear up: one foot kicked an empty wine
bottle and it went rolling across the floor. Irina picked up
the bottle and set it on the low table. Then she took the ashtray and dumped the butts into the plate with the stale food.
"Signora? Are you in there? Are you in bed?"

No answer.

With both hands occupied by the tray and precariously
balancing the bottle of merlot, she bumped the kitchen door
open with one hip. But she didn't walk through the door.
She froze and stood staring. "What on earth . . . ?" she half-
muttered to herself.

The pantry doors swung open. The floor was covered
with dishes, utensils, and glasses alongside boxes of pasta
and cans of tomato paste. Tablecloths, dish towels, silverware, and paper napkins were strewn everywhere. Oranges
had rolled to the base of the half-open refrigerator. Chairs
were knocked over, the table was shoved almost against the

8

wall, and the handheld electric mixer that lay shattered on the floor tiles spewed wires and electric gadgets out of its belly.

"What happen here!" Irina shouted. She set down the tray and turned toward the hallway.

"Signora Esther!" she called again. No answer. "Signora Esther, what happen here?"

She hurried into the bedroom, hoping to find the signora there. The bed was unmade. Sheets and duvet heaped in a corner. The armoire thrown wide open. She backed away, cautiously, toward the kitchen. "But what . . . ?" Then her foot hit something on the floor. She looked down. A cell phone, shattered.

"Burglars!" she shouted and, as if someone had placed a cold, menacing blade against her back, she stiffened, turned, and ran. The antique afghan carpet that lay rumpled on the floor tripped her up. Irina sprawled headlong and banged her knee on the floor.

Chunk!

The muffled sound of a kneecap cracking, followed by a stabbing pain penetrating directly into her brain. "Aahh!" she screamed through clenched teeth, and holding her knee with both hands she got to her feet. She aimed straight toward the sliding pocket entrance door, certain that behind her lurked a couple of scary-looking men, their faces concealed by balaclavas, black, and with the sharp teeth of ferocious beasts. She banged her shoulder against the panel of the sliding door, and it quavered, shivering the smoked glass. Now another stab of pain sank its fangs deep into

her clavicle. But this one she felt less. Irina mustered all
the adrenaline she had in her body and limped out of the
Baudos' apartment. She hastily slid the door shut behind
her. She was panting. Now that she was on the landing she
felt a little safer. She looked down at her knee. Her stocking
was torn and drops of blood stained her pale white flesh. She
licked two fingers and ran them over the wound. The pain
had shifted from keen to dull and throbbing, but it was now
a little easier to take. Then it dawned on her that she was
not even remotely safe on the landing. If the burglars were
inside the apartment, how hard would it be for them to open
the door and slaughter her, to stab her with a knife or beat
her to death with a crowbar? She started limping gingerly
down the stairs and shouting: "Help! Burglars! Burglars!"

She pounded on the doors facing the third-floor landing, but
no one came to answer. "Help! Burglars! Open up! Open up!"

She continued downstairs. Given her preferences, she
would have been taking the steps two at a time, but her knee
wouldn't let her. She held tight to the handsome wooden
handrail and thanked God that she'd put on the counterfeit Hogan sneakers that morning, sneakers that she'd purchased at the flea market near her house: at least they had
rubber soles. If she'd been wearing leather soles on those
marble steps, she could easily have slid down two or three
flights flat on her ass. She tried knocking on the second-floor
doors. She pounded with her fists, pushed the doorbells, and
even kicked, but there was no one home. No one came to the
door. Only from one apartment did she hear the hysterical
yapping of some tiny dog answering her knock.

A building full of dead people, she thought to herself.

Finally she reached the ground floor. She tugged open the front door and lurched out into the street. It was deserted. Nothing in sight, not even a shop or a bar where she could ask for help. She looked at the buildings lining Via Brocherel. No one at the windows, no one entering or leaving. The sky was leaden and gray. There were no cars. At ten in the morning it seemed as if the world had ground to a halt, at least in that street: as if it were paralyzed, as if she were the only living creature in the whole neighborhood. "Help!" she screamed at the top of her lungs. Then, as if by some miracle, an old man appeared at the corner wrapped in a heavy scarf with a little mutt dog on a leash. Irina ran straight toward him.

Retired army warrant officer Paolo Rastelli, born in 1939, lurched to a halt in the middle of the sidewalk. A woman with no overcoat, her hair standing straight up, and limping with a badly bloodied knee was galloping straight at him, her mouth gaping like a new-caught fish. She was shouting something. But the warrant officer couldn't hear what it was. All he saw was her mouth wide open, as if she were chewing the chilly air. He decided to turn on the Maico hearing aid he wore in his right ear, which he always kept off when he took Flipper out for his walks. Flipper was a mix of Yorkshire terrier and thirty-two other breeds. The dog was more volatile than a flask of nitroglycerine. A dry leaf in the wind, water gurgling down a runoff pipe, or just Flipper's diseased imagination was enough to set that fourteen-year-old mutt off, yapping in an irritating high-pitched bark that sent shivers up and down Rastelli's spine, worse than fingernails on a blackboard. As soon as he switched it on, the hearing aid shot a burst of electric static into his brain. Then, as he expected, the white noise sharpened into Flipper's shrill yapping, until he could finally hear words with some meaning pouring out of the woman's open mouth: "Help, help, somebody help me! Burglars!"

Flipper had lost most of the vision in his right eye, and his left eye had been useless for years. The dog wasn't barking at the woman, he was barking at a traffic sign tossing and clattering in the wind on the other side of the street. Paolo Rastelli had only seconds to make up his mind. He looked behind him: there was no one in sight. There wasn't time to pull out his cell phone and call the police; by now the woman was just yards away, galloping toward him as if demonically possessed, shouting all the while: "Help! Help me, Signore!" He could turn and run from that latter-day fury with her straw-blond hair, but first he'd have to reckon with the pin in his hip and his wheezing lungs, already on the verge of emphysema. And so, just as when he was a raw recruit, a private standing guard at the munitions dump, he remained rooted to the spot, standing at attention, waiting for trouble to wash over him with all the ineluctability of malicious fate, cursing Flipper and the dog's midmorning walks, cursing at the constant need to take a tiny yapping dog out to piss and break off work on his crossword puzzles.

It was 10:10 on the morning of Friday, March 16.

● ● ●

WHEN THE ALARM WENT OFF, IT WAS TWENTY TO eight. Deputy Police Chief Rocco Schiavone had been stationed in Aosta for months now, and as he did every morning he walked over to the bedroom window. Slowly and intently—like a champion poker player fanning open the hand of cards that's going to determine whether he wins or folds—he pulled open the heavy curtains and peered out at the sky, in the vain hope of a glimpse of sunlight.

"Shit," he'd muttered. That Friday morning, as usual, a sky as oppressive as the lid of a pressure cooker, a sidewalk white with snow, and natives walking hurriedly, bundled up in scarves and hats. Now even they feel the cold, Rocco had thought to himself. Well, well, well.

The usual daily routine: shower, coffee pod in the espresso machine, shave. Standing in front of his clothes closet, he had no doubts about how to dress. Same as yesterday, and the day before that, and the day before that, and the same as tomorrow and so on for who knows how many days yet to come. Dark brown corduroy trousers, cotton T-shirt underneath, wool T-shirt over that, wool blend socks, checked flannel shirt, V-necked light cashmere sweater, green corduroy jacket, and his trusty Clarks. He'd done some rapid mental calculations: six months in Aosta had cost him nine pairs of shoes. Maybe he really did need to find a good alternative to desert boots, but he couldn't seem to. Two months ago he'd bought himself a pair of Teva snow boots, for when he'd had to spend time on the ski slopes above Champoluc, but wearing those cement mixers around town was out of the question. He'd put on his loden overcoat, left the apartment, and headed for the office. Like every morning, he left his cell phone powered down. Because his daily ritual still wasn't complete when he got dressed and left for the office. There were still two fundamental steps before really starting the day: get breakfast at the café in the town's main piazza and then sit down at his desk and roll his morning joint.

The trip into police headquarters was the most delicate phase. Still wrapped in the dreams and thoughts of the night before, his mood as bleak and gray as the sky overhead, Rocco always made a muted entrance, as darting and slithery as a viper moving through the grass. If there was one thing he wanted to avoid, it was running into Officer D'Intino. Not at eight thirty, not first thing in the morning. D'Intino: the police officer, originally from the province of Chieti, a place the deputy police chief despised, possibly even more than he hated the inclement weather of Val d'Aosta. A man of D'Intino's ineptitude was likely to cause potentially fatal accidents to his colleagues, though never to himself. D'Intino had sent Officer Casella to the hospital just last week by backing his car into him in the police parking lot, when he could perfectly well have just put the car into first gear and driven straight out. He'd crushed one of Rocco's toenails by dropping a heavy metal filing drawer on his foot. And he'd come terrifyingly close to poisoning Officer Deruta with his mania for cleanliness and order, by leaving a bottle of Uliveto mineral water around—only filled with bleach. Rocco had sworn he'd fix D'Intino's wagon, and he'd started pressuring the police chief to transfer the officer to some police station in the Abruzzi where he would certainly be much more useful. Fortunately, that morning no one had come cheerfully out to greet him. The only person who'd said good morning was Scipioni, who was on duty at the front entrance. And Scipioni had limited his greeting to a bitter smile, and then lowered his eyes back to the papers he was going over. Rocco made it safely to his desk, where he smoked a nice fat joint. His healthy morning dose of grass. When he finally crushed the roach out in his ashtray, it was just past nine. Time to turn on his cell phone and begin the day. The phone immediately emitted an alert that meant he had a text message.

Are you ever going to spend the night at my place?

It was Nora. The woman he'd been exchanging bodily fluids with ever since he'd moved from Rome to Aosta. A shallow relationship, a sort of mutual aid society, but one that she was steering straight toward the breaking point—a demand for stability of some sort. Something that Rocco was unable and unwilling to face up to. He was perfectly fine with things the way they were. He didn't need a girlfriend. His girlfriend was and always would be his wife, Marina. There was no room for another woman. Nora was beautiful and she helped to alleviate his loneliness. But he didn't know how to resolve his psychological difficulties. People who go to an analyst do it because they want to get better. And there was no way that Rocco would ever set foot in an analyst's office. No one walks a woman to the altar just for the exercise. If they go to the altar, it's because they want to spend the rest of their lives with another person. Rocco had already taken that walk once years ago, and his intentions really had been sincere, the very best intentions. He was going to spend the rest of his life with Marina, and that was that. But sometimes things just don't go the way you expect them to, they break, they unravel, and you can't stitch them back together again. But that was a secondary problem. Rocco belonged to Marina, and Marina belonged to Rocco. Everything else was an afterthought, branches that could be pruned, autumn leaves.

While Rocco was thinking about Nora's face, her curves and her ankles, a sudden crushing realization hit him square in the forehead. He'd just remembered the words she had whispered to him the night before, as they lay curled up in bed. "Tomorrow I turn forty-three, and on my birthday I'm the queen. So you have to behave like a good boy," and she had flashed him a smile, with her perfect white teeth.

Rocco had continued kissing her and squeezing her large luscious breasts without a word. But even while he was enjoying Nora's nude body, he understood that tomorrow he'd have to buy her a gift, and maybe even take her out to dinner, and certainly miss the Friday peek-ahead to Sunday's Roma-Inter match.

"No perfume," she'd warned him, "and I hate all kinds of scarves and plants. I'll buy my own earrings, bracelets, and necklaces, and the same goes for books. To say nothing of CDs. There, at least now you know what kind of presents *not* to get me, unless you're actually trying to ruin my birthday."

What was left to bring as a gift? Nora had thrown him into a state of crisis. Or really she was forcing him to think, to reflect on what he should do. Giving presents, whether for birthdays or at Christmas, was one of the things that Rocco detested most intensely. He'd have to waste time on it, think of something, wander around from store to store like an asshole, and he didn't feel like it in the slightest. But if he wanted to slip between the sheets and go on banqueting off that splendid female body, he'd need to dream up something. And he'd need to come up with it today, because today was Nora's birthday.

"What a pain in the ass," he'd said under his breath, just as someone knocked at his office door. Rocco had lunged to yank open the window to air out the room, then like a bloodhound he'd sniffed at the ceiling and four walls to make sure you could no longer catch a whiff of cannabis, then he'd shouted "*Avanti!*" and Inspector Caterina Rispoli had walked in. The first thing she did was wrinkle her nose and make a face. "What's that smell?"

"I'm applying rosemary plasters for this cold I have!" Rocco had replied.

"But you don't seem to have a cold, sir."

"That's because I use rosemary plasters. Which is why I don't have a cold."

"Rosemary plasters? Never heard of them."

"Homeopathy, Caterina, it's serious stuff."

"My grandmother taught me how to make plasters with eucalyptus nuts."

"What?"

"Eucalyptus PLASTERS."

"My grandmother taught me how to make plasters too."

"With rosemary?"

"No. With my own fucking business. Now, are you going to tell me what you're doing in my office?"

Caterina fluttered her long eyelashes for a moment and then, after regaining control of her nerves, she said: "There's one crime report that might bear closer examination . . ." holding out a sheet of paper for Rocco to see. "In the park by the train station, somebody called to say that every night there's a tremendous ruckus until three."

"Hookers?" Rocco had asked.

"No."

"Drugs?"

"That's what I'm thinking."

Rocco gave the report a quick scan. "We ought to follow up on this . . ." Then a magnificent idea occurred to him that all by itself gave a brand-new meaning to the day. "Get me the cretins, right away."

"Get you the what?" Caterina asked.

"D'Intino and Michele Deruta."

The inspector had nodded quickly and hurried out of the room. Rocco took that opportunity to close the window. It was freezing. But his excitement about the idea he'd just had made him forget about the chill that filled the room. Not five minutes later, D'Intino and Deruta, escorted by Caterina Rispoli, walked into his office.

"D'Intino and Deruta," Rocco said in a serious tone, "I have an important job for the two of you. It will require your utmost attention and sense of responsibility. Are you up to it?"

Deruta had smiled and rocked back on his heels, balancing his 245 pounds of weight on his size 8 shoes. "Certainly, Dottore!"

"Most assuredly, no doubt about it!" D'Intino backed him up.

"Now listen carefully. I'm going to ask you to do a stake-out. At night." The two officers were all ears. "In the park by the station. We suspect there's drug dealing going on. We don't know whether it's smack or coke."

Deruta glanced at D'Intino in excitement. At last, an assignment worthy of their skills.

"Find yourselves a place where you won't be noticed. Requisition a camera, so you can take pictures and record everything you see. I want to know what they're doing, how much narcotics they're dealing, who's doing the dealing, and in particular I want names. Are you up for it?"

"Certainly," D'Intino replied.

"Well, though, I have to work at my wife's bakery," Deruta had objected. "You know that I often help her out, and we work until sunrise. Just last night I—"

Snorting in disgust, Rocco stood up and cut off what the officer was saying. "Michele! It is a wonderful and admirable thing that you help your wife out at the bakery, and that you break your back with a second job. But first and foremost, you're a sworn officer of the law, for fuck's sake! Not a baker!"

Deruta nodded.

"You'll both be reporting to Inspector Rispoli."

Deruta and D'Intino had swallowed the news unwillingly;

it was clearly a bitter mouthful. "But why her? We always have to report to her!" D'Intino had the nerve to say.

"First of all, Rispoli is an inspector and you aren't. Second, she's a woman and I'm not going to send her out into the field to do a challenging stakeout like the one to which I've assigned the two of you. Third, and this is a fundamental thing, you will do exactly what I tell you to do, D'Intino, or else I will kick your ass from here to Chieti. Is that quite clear?"

D'Intino and Deruta nodded their heads in unison. "When do we start?"

"Tonight. Now get out of here. I need to have a talk with Rispoli." The inspector had said nothing, standing off to one side. As the two male officers filed out of the room, they'd glared angrily at her.

"DOTTORE, NOW YOU'RE PUTTING ME IN AN AWKWARD position with those two."

"Don't worry, Rispoli, this way we've got them out from underfoot. What I need now is some advice. Sit down."

Caterina did as she was told.

"I have to get a gift."

"Birthday?"

"Exactly. I'll give you the information. It's a woman, age forty-three, in good shape, sells wedding dresses for a living; she's from Aosta, she has good taste, and she's quite well-off."

The inspector took a moment to think it over. "Personal friend?"

"That's my fucking business."

"Understood."

"Rule out flowers, scarves, plants, jewelry, books, perfume, and CDs."

"I need to know more about her. Is this Nora Tardioli? The one with the shop in the center of town?"

Rocco nodded, without a word.

"Congratulations, Dottore, nice get."

"Thanks, but as per aforementioned comment, my own fucking business."

"How far out on a limb are you interested in going?"

"Not far. Just consider it a tactical move, keeping the status quo. Why?"

"Because, otherwise, you could give her a diamond ring."

"That's not going far. That's handing yourself over to the enemy bound hand and foot."

Caterina smiled. "Let me think it over. Does she have any hobbies?"

"As far as I know? She likes to go to the movies, but I'd avoid DVDs. She goes swimming twice a week, and works out three times a week. She's a cross-country skier. And I think she bikes too."

"Who are we talking about here? Lindsey Vonn?"

"Right now it's . . ." Rocco glanced at his watch. "Ten fifteen. Do you think you can come up with an idea by noon?"

"I'll do my best!"

Just then, Officer Italo Pierron threw open the door and strode into the room. Along with Rispoli, Pierron was the only other officer Rocco considered worthy of being on the force. He was allowed to walk into the deputy police chief's office without knocking and address him by his first name outside the four walls of police headquarters. He glanced briefly at Caterina and nodded hello.

"Dottore?"

The young officer's face was pale and alarmed. Rocco asked: "Italo, what's wrong?"

"Something urgent."

"Go on."

"A call came in. Apparently a gang of burglars have barricaded themselves in the apartment of Patrizio and Esther Baudo on Via Brocherel."

"Barricaded themselves?"

"That's the term used by Paolo Rastelli, a retired warrant officer who's also half-deaf. That's what I managed to piece out, but in the background I could hear a woman screaming: 'They're inside! They're inside! They've turned the place upside down!'"

Rocco nodded. "Let's go . . ."

"Can I come too?" asked Caterina.

"Better not. I need you here. Stay close to the telephone."

"Roger."

AS THEY ZIPPED THROUGH CITY INTERSECTIONS WITH their siren off, Rocco pulled a cigarette out of Italo's pack and looked out at the perfectly plowed streets. "The city government does its job up here, eh? In Rome you get a couple of flakes of snow and there are more deaths than from the start of the August vacations." Then he lit the cigarette. "Why don't you buy Camels? I think Chesterfields are disgusting."

Italo nodded silently. "I know that, Rocco, but I like Chesterfields."

"Make sure you don't drive into a wall or run over any old ladies."

Italo turned into Corso Battaglione Aosta, downshifted, passed a truck, and accelerated sharply.

"If you weren't a cop, you'd be a perfect getaway driver for an armored car robbery."

"Why do you say that, Rocco? Are you planning something along those lines?"

They both laughed.

"You know something, Italo? If you ask me, you ought to grow a goatee or a beard."

"You think? You know, I'd thought about that myself. I don't have any lips."

"Exactly. You'd look less like a weasel."

"I look like a weasel?"

"I never told you that? I've met lots of people who look like weasels. But never on the police force."

After a six-month acquaintance, the two men understood each other clearly. Rocco liked Italo. He trusted him after what the two of them had done some time ago, intercepting that load of marijuana on a Dutch semi and splitting a nice big haul of several thousand euros. Italo was young, and in him Rocco glimpsed the same motivation that had led the deputy police chief to undertake his police career: pure chance. At the fateful moment when the deputy police chief's classmates were starting life on the streets, working with blades and bullets, he just happened to put on the law-man's uniform. Nothing more than that. For people who were born in Trastevere at the start of the sixties into blue-collar families, with neighbors who were on a first-name basis with prison, there were only two paths available. Like the game they used to play at the parish after-school when they were kids, a little game of tag known as police and thieves. In fact, Rocco had become a cop, and Furio, Brizio, Sebastiano, Stampella, and all the others had become thieves. But they'd remained the best of friends.

"How on earth is a gang of burglars going to barricade themselves in an apartment, Italo? It's not as if it's a bank, with hostages and everything."

"I don't get it either."

"I mean, if the people reporting them are a half-deaf old man and a woman, then what's to stop them from coming out of the apartment, clubbing them senseless, and taking off in less than a minute?"

"Maybe the old man's armed. He is a retired army warrant officer, after all."

"Absolutely crazy," said Rocco, looking out the window at the cars screeching to a halt and honking furiously as the BMW with Italo at the wheel zoomed past.

"Listen, Rocco, don't you think we should use the siren?

At least that way people would know it was the police and we'd be less likely to crash into someone!"

"I hate sirens."

So, racing at 75 miles per hour through the city streets, they pulled up in front of no. 22, Via Brocherel.

ROCCO BUTTONED UP HIS LODEN OVERCOAT AND, followed by Italo, walked over to the two people waving their arms outside the front door.

An elderly man and a woman in her early forties, with straw-blond hair, a large run in her stocking, and blood on her kneecap.

"Police, police!" the woman was screaming, and her Slavic accent was echoing down the deserted street. The street might have been deserted, but a few inquisitive faces appeared behind the glass of windows here and there. The old man immediately stopped the woman with a wave of his hand, freezing her in place, as if to say, "Better let me handle this, man to man." At the old man's feet, a tiny pug of a dog, its eyes bulging out of its head, was barking furiously at a NO PARKING sign.

"Police?" asked the man, eyeing Rocco and Italo.

"What do you think?"

"Normally the police have a flashing light and a siren on top of their squad cars."

"Normally people are a little bit better at minding their own fucking business," Rocco replied, seriously. "Are you the one who called?"

"Yes. I'm Warrant Officer Paolo Rastelli. The signora here is certain that a gang of burglars have barricaded themselves in the apartment."

"Do you live here?" asked the deputy police chief.

"No," replied the warrant officer.

"Then this is your house?" Rocco asked, turning to Irina.

"No, I just come here to clean, every Monday and Wednesday and Fridays too," the woman replied.

"Shut up!" the old man shouted at the dog, jerking at its leash until the little critter's already blind eyes seemed to bulge out of their sockets. "Forgive me, Commissario, but this dog just won't stop barking and it really gets on my nerves."

"It's typical of dogs, you know?" the deputy police chief said calmly.

"What is?"

"Barking. It's in their nature." He squatted down and with a single pat on the head silenced Flipper; now the dog was wagging its tail and licking his hand. "And anyway I'm not a commissario. The rank of commissario no longer exists. Deputy Police Chief Schiavone." Then he looked over at the woman, who still had a frightened look on her face and her hair standing straight up, held in place by some electrostatic force, probably emanating from her light blue nylon sweater.

"Give me the keys!" Rocco said to the woman.

"To the apartment?" the Russian woman asked naively.

"No, to the city. Certainly, to the apartment, for the love of Jesus!" the retired warrant officer barked. "Otherwise how are they supposed to get in?"

Irina dropped her gaze. "I forget inside the keys when I run away."

"Oh hell," muttered Rocco under his breath. "Okay, let's do this: what floor is it?"

"There . . . fourth!" and Irina pointed at the apartment building. "You see? Window up there with curtains is living room, then there is other room next to it, with shutters pulled down: that is den. Then there is last on left, the half bath, then—"

"Signora, it's not as if I want to buy the apartment. All I need to know is where it is," the deputy police chief brusquely interrupted her. Then he jutted his chin and directed Pierron toward the fourth-floor apartment. "Italo, what do you say?"

"How am I supposed to climb up there, Dottore? What we need is a locksmith."

Rocco sighed, then glanced at the woman, who seemed to have regained her composure. "What kind of lock is it?"

"There are two keyholes," Irina replied.

Rocco rolled his eyes. "Sure, but what kind? Pick-proof, lever tumbler, drum lock?"

"No . . . I don't know. Apartment door."

Rocco pulled open the street door. "Do you know the apartment number, or not that either?"

"Eleven," Irina replied with a broad smile, proud that she could finally provide the police with some actionable intelligence. "Eleven R."

Italo followed the deputy police chief.

"What should I do?" asked the retired warrant officer.

"You stay here and wait for reinforcements!" Rocco shouted. And he almost had the impression that the old man promptly clicked his heels in response.

AS SOON AS THE METAL ELEVATOR DOORS SWUNG open, Rocco went to the right, Italo to the left.

"Apartment 11R is right here," said Italo. The deputy police chief caught up with him. "It's an old Cisa lock. Excellent."

Rocco put his hand in his pocket and pulled out the keys to his own apartment.

"What are you doing?" asked Italo.

"Hold on." On his key ring, Rocco had a little Swiss Army knife, the kind that has about twelve thousand blades and clippers. He carefully pried open the little screwdriver. He bent over and started working on the lock. He removed the two screws that held the plate, then extracted the fingernail file. "You see? If you can just open a space between the wood and the lock mechanism . . ." He slid the file into the opening. He applied pressure, once, then a second time. "It's a hollow-core door. In Rome, you don't find front doors like this anymore. Nobody has them."

"Why not?"

"Because they're so damned easy to get open." And with that the deputy police chief popped the lock open. Italo smiled. "You really picked the wrong line of work!"

"You're not the first person to tell me that." And Rocco swung open the door. Italo stopped him with one arm. "Shall

I go first?" he asked, as he unholstered his pistol. "I mean, what if there really is someone barricaded in there?"

"Who do you think is barricaded, Italo? Come on, let's not talk bullshit." And he strode in.

They walked through the sliding door and found themselves in the living room. Italo headed for the kitchen. The deputy police chief continued down the hallway and took a look in the bedroom. The bed was unmade. He kept walking. At the end of the hall was another room. The door was shut. Italo caught up with Rocco just as his hand closed around the door handle. "No one in the kitchen. The place is a mess, but no one's there. It looks like a tornado hit the place."

Rocco nodded, then threw open the door.

Darkness.

The wooden blinds were lowered, and it was impossible to make out anything in the shadows. But the deputy police chief caught a whiff of something ugly. Sickly sweet, with hints of puke and piss. He found the light switch and flipped it on. A bright glare lit up the room for a second. Then a short circuit knocked out power as a handful of sparks showered down through the dark like so many party streamers. The room was plunged back into shadow. But that flare of electric light, like a photographer's camera flash, had seared a hair-raising image into the deputy police chief's retina. "Shit! Italo, call the main switchboard. And tell them to get Fumagalli right over here."

"Dr. Fumagalli? The medical examiner? Why? What is it? Rocco, what did you see?"

"Just do what I told you!"

Italo backed a few steps out into the hallway, pulled out his cell phone, and did his best to punch in the main number for the hospital, but with the Beretta in his hand, it was no simple matter.

Rocco groped his way forward and ventured in warily, one hand on the wall.

His fingers brushed the edge of a bookshelf, then the wall again, then the corner of the room. He ran his hand over the wallpaper, pushed the curtain aside, and finally grasped the strap to raise the wooden roller blind. He gripped hard and gave it a first hard tug. Slowly the gray light of day filtered into the room. From below. As he hoisted the blind, the light first covered the floor, revealing an overturned step stool. With the second tug, daylight illuminated a pair of dangling bare feet; with the third, two legs, a pair of arms dangling alongside the body; and finally, once the roller blind was fully raised, the scene appeared before his eyes in all its macabre squalor. The woman was hanging from the lamp hook on the ceiling by a slender cable. Her head slumped forward, her chin rested against her chest, while her curly chestnut hair covered her face. There was a stain on the hardwood floor.

"Oh Madonna." The words came out of Italo's mouth like a hiss, as he stood there with his phone pressed to his ear.

"Call Fumagalli, I told you," said Rocco. He moved away from the window and walked over to the woman's body. Her bony, skinny feet reminded him of the feet of a Christ on the cross. Pale, faintly greenish. All that was missing were the nail holes; otherwise those feet could have come straight out of a painting by Grünewald. The knees were scraped, like the knees of a little girl coming home from her first bicycle ride. She wore a nightgown. Sea green. One of the shoulder straps had torn free. The stitching had come unraveled under the armpit and a small gap revealed a patch of flesh and the rib cage beneath. Rocco avoided looking her in the face. He turned on his heel and left the room. As he went past Officer Pierron, he grabbed the packet of Chesterfields out of his pocket and yanked out a smoke, just as Italo finally managed to get the hospital on the phone. "This is Officer Pierron . . . put me through to Fumagalli. It's urgent."

"Come smoke a cigarette, Italo; otherwise the sight will get etched into your retinas and you won't be able to see anything else for the next two weeks."

Italo followed Rocco like a robot, the cell phone in his left hand, his pistol in his right. "And holster your piece," Rocco added. "Who the fuck are you planning to shoot, anyway?"

ESTHER BAUDO AND HER HUSBAND WERE THE SUBJECT of every framed photograph arranged on the top of an upright piano. There was a wedding picture, pictures on a beach, pictures under a palm tree, and even a picture in front of the Colosseum. In a single glance Rocco saw it had been taken from the corner of Via Capo d'Africa, where there was a seafood restaurant that he and Marina inevitably chose when they had something to celebrate. The last time—and it had been more than five years ago—was when they'd completed the purchase of the penthouse in Monteverde Vecchio. Esther Baudo was smiling in every picture. But only with her mouth. Never with her eyes. Her eyes were always lackluster, dead, dark, and deep, never sparkling with laughter. Not even on the day of her wedding.

Her husband was just the opposite. He always smiled into the lens. Happily. The hair had vanished from the top of his cranium and now adorned only the sides of his head. White, straight teeth gleamed in his small, rosebud mouth. He had small jug ears.

Rocco left the living room and went to look at the kitchen. Right at the threshold of the kitchen door was a shattered cell phone. He picked it up. The screen was chipped, the battery was missing, and who could even say where the SIM chip had wound up. Then he looked around the rest of the room. Italo was right. The place really was a mess. It looked like a herd of buffalo had trampled through. The ground was a crazy hodgepodge of boxes, tin cans, packages of pasta, silverware, and a bread knife. He placed the shattered cell phone on the marble countertop, next to a plastic scale.

He turned to look toward the room at the end of the hall: the den. And slowly, inexorably pulled toward it, as if by a magnet, he walked back to it. The woman still hung there. Rocco was tempted to lower her to the ground. To see her dangling there like a butchered animal was more than he could take. He bit his lip and stepped closer. The first thing that caught his eye was the swollen face. It was puffy, with a split lip from which the blood had flowed. One eye was open, staring; the other was shut and swollen to the size of a plum. The cable around her neck was a metal clothesline. The woman had run it over the hook that held up the ceiling lamp and then anchored it to the floor, tying it to the foot of an armoire. Like a ten-foot guywire, to make sure it would support the weight. Actually, though, it hadn't—her weight had torn loose the electric wiring and caused a short circuit. There was a stool lying on the floor. A three-legged stool, like a piano stool. When it overturned, the cushion had torn loose. Maybe Esther kicked it in the last instant of her life, when she made up her mind that her time on this planet Earth had come to its logical conclusion. The skin on her neck was pale, but not around her throat. There a purple band ran, a little less than an inch across. Purple like the stain on the hardwood floor.

"It's the third damned suicide this month," said the medical examiner from behind him, snorting in annoyance. Rocco didn't even bother turning around, and both men, faithful to the routine they'd developed over the months, exchanged no greeting.

"Who found her? You?"

Schiavone nodded. Alberto stepped closer and stood, surveying the body. They looked like a pair of tourists visiting MoMA, admiring an art installation.

"A woman, about thirty-five, probable cause of death strangulation," said the doctor. Rocco nodded: "And they gave you a medical degree for that?"

"I'm just kidding."

"How can you kid about this?"

"With the work I do, if you can't kid around, you're done for," and Alberto tilted his head toward the corpse.

Rocco asked, "Are you going to take the corpse down?"

"I'd say so . . . I'll wait for a couple of your people and then we'll take her down."

"Who was coming upstairs?"

"The young woman and a fat guy."

Which meant Officer Deruta and Inspector Caterina Rispoli.

Rocco left the room and went to meet the two of them.

DERUTA WAS ALREADY IN THE FRONT HALL, SWEATY and panting. Caterina Rispoli, on the other hand, was still out on the landing. She was talking to Italo Pierron and twisting her police-issued gloves.

"Did you come up the stairs, Deruta?"

"No, I took the elevator."

"Then why are you out of breath?"

Deruta ignored the question. "Dottore, I was just thinking—"

"And that right there is a wonderful piece of news, Deruta."

"I was thinking . . . don't you feel the sight of all this is a little too harsh?"

"For who?"

"For Inspector Rispoli?"

"The sight of what, Deruta? The sight of you at work?"

Deruta grimaced in annoyance. "Of course not! The sight of the dead body in there!"

Rocco looked at him. "Deruta, Inspector Rispoli is a police officer."

"But Rispoli's a woman!"

"Well, she can't help that," said the deputy police chief as he walked out onto the landing.

The minute he walked out the door, Caterina took a look at him. "Deputy Police Chief . . ."

"Go on in, Rispoli. Don't leave me alone with Deruta; next thing you know, he'll hang himself too." Caterina smiled and walked into the apartment. "Ah, Dottore?"

"What is it, Rispoli?"

"I did come up with an idea for that gift."

"Perfect. Let's talk in ten minutes." As Caterina disappeared into the living room, Rocco turned to look at Italo. "Let's go get ourselves a cup of coffee."

"If you don't mind, Dottore," said Italo, moving from a first-name basis to a more official term of respect, "I'd just as soon stay right here. My stomach's kind of doing belly flops."

Shaking his head, Rocco Schiavone went down the stairs.

VIA BROCHEREL WAS CROWDED WITH PEOPLE. PEOPLE looking out their windows, people rubbernecking outside the front door. There was a muttering of conversation that sounded like a kettle on the boil. "A corpse? . . . There weren't any burglars? Who is it? The Baudos . . ."

There was a brief moment of silence when the front door swung open and Rocco Schiavone, wrapped in his loden green overcoat, emerged. Officer Casella alone was keeping the rubberneckers at bay. "Commissario," he said, saluting.

"It's deputy police chief, Casella, deputy police chief, Jesus fucking Christ! You at least, seeing that you're on the police force, ought to try to remember these things, no?"

He looked around but there was no sign of a café or a shop anywhere in sight. He went over to the retired warrant officer. "Excuse me! Could you tell me if there's a café anywhere around here?"

"Say what?" asked the old man, adjusting his hearing aid.

"Café. Near here. Where."

"Around the corner. Take Via Monte Emilus and go about a hundred yards, and you'll see the Bar Alpi. Do you have any news, Dottore? Is it true that they found the lady hanging by a rope?"

Irina too stood gazing at him apprehensively.

"Can you keep a secret?" Rocco asked in an undertone.

"Certainly!" Paolo Rastelli replied, puffing his chest out proudly.

"I can too!" Irina chimed in.

"So what do you think, I can't?" Rocco retorted and walked away, leaving them both openmouthed.

As was to be expected, the retired warrant officer's dog, Flipper, promptly began barking again, this time at the NO PARKING sign. The former noncommissioned officer glared down at the yappy little mutt and brusquely switched off his hearing aid. At last, the world turned silent, muffled and cottony once again. A giant aquarium he could gaze at with detachment. With a smile and a slight forward tilt of the head, he bade farewell to Irina and resumed his daily stroll, heading for home and the crossword puzzle.

AS THE WIND BLEW, PUSHING CHILLY GUSTS OF AIR under his loden overcoat, Rocco decided that all things considered, it could have gone worse. A suicide just meant a series of bureaucratic procedures to get out of the way, the kind of thing you could take care of in an afternoon's work. His plan was simple: leave the bureaucratic details to Casella, talk to Rispoli and find out what idea she'd come up with for Nora's present, go home, get a half-hour nap, take a shower, go back out and buy the present, go out to dinner with Nora at eight, after an hour and a half pretend he had a crushing migraine, take Nora home, and then hurry back to his place to watch the second half of the Roma-Inter game. Acceptable.

Just as the wind died down and a fine chilly drizzle began to pepper the asphalt, cold as the fingers of a dead man's hand, Rocco stepped into the Bar Alpi. A strong smell of alcohol and confectioner's sugar washed over him, like a warm, welcome hug from a friend.

"*Buongiorno.*"

The man behind the counter gave him a smile. "Hello. What'll it be?"

"A nice hot espresso with a foamy cloud of milk . . . and I'd like a pastry. Do you have any left?"

"Sure . . . go ahead and take what you like, right there . . ." He pointed to a Plexiglas case with an electric heater where breakfast pastries were on display. Rocco grabbed a strudel while the barista ratcheted the porta-filter into place and punched the button that applied pressure to the boiling water. He heard the clack of billiard balls from the other room in the bar. Only now did he notice that the walls were covered with pictures of Juventus players and black-and-white team scarves. Rocco went over to the counter and poured half a pack of sugar into his coffee. It took awhile for the sugar to sink into the hot dense liquid. A clear sign that this was a good espresso. He took a sip. It really was good. "You make a first-rate espresso," he told the barman, who was busy drying glasses.

"My wife taught me how."

"Neapolitan?"

"No. Milanese. I'm the Neapolitan in the family."

"So, you're saying that you're a Neapolitan who roots for Juventus and that a woman from Milan taught you how to make espresso?"

"Plus I'm tone deaf," the man added. They both laughed.

Another sharp clack from the next room. Rocco turned around.

"You want to play some pool?"

"Why not?"

"Look out, those two are a pair of professional sharks."

Rocco slurped down the last of his espresso and strode

into the next room, finishing off his strudel in a shower of crumbs down the front of his loden overcoat.

THERE WERE TWO MEN. ONE WORE THE JUMPSUIT OF a manual laborer, the other a suit and tie. They'd just set the cue ball down on the table and were about to begin a game of straight pool. When they saw Rocco they both smiled. "Care to play?" asked the man in the jumpsuit.

"No, you guys go ahead. Mind if I watch?"

"Not at all," said the one who looked every bit the realtor. "Just watch me dismantle Nino, here. Nino, today I'm not taking prisoners!"

"Ten euros on the best out of three games?" asked the manual laborer.

"No, ten euros a game!"

Nino smiled. "Then I've already made my end-of-year bonus," he said, and shot the deputy police chief a wink.

The realtor took off his jacket while the laborer chalked his pool stick with a vicious grin.

Clack! And the three ceiling lamps that illuminated the green felt of the billiards table went dark simultaneously.

"Well of all the damned . . . Gennaro!" shouted the realtor. From the bar the proprietor called back: "The power always goes out when it's windy like this!"

"Try paying your electric bill, and maybe that'll stop it from happening!" called the man in the jumpsuit, and he and his friend shared a hearty laugh.

But Rocco remained straight-faced, leaning against the

wall, lost in thought. "Holy shit!" he said, between clenched teeth. "I'm an idiot! Why didn't I think of it? What a shitty profession this is!" Cursing, he left the game room before the astonished eyes of the two pool players.

"ALBE', TELL ME THAT WHAT I'M THINKING DOESN'T hold up!"

"Run it by me again, Rocco," said the medical examiner, as he leaned over Signora Baudo's corpse.

"When I walked in, I switched on the light. And it short-circuited. So that means it was turned off before, right?"

"Okay, Rocco, I'm with you."

"Obviously, when she fell the poor woman yanked loose a couple of wires. When I flipped the switch I caused a short circuit. What does that mean? That she hanged herself in the dark. How did she do it? She lowered the blinds, fastened the noose, and let herself drop?"

"That doesn't make any sense at all," said Fumagalli, "and so?"

"So it must mean there was someone there with her. Whoever it was must have lowered the blinds after she hanged herself. Jesus fucking Christ!" Rocco cursed through clenched teeth.

"And listen," Fumagalli said, "as long as you're here, I have something else to point out. Look at this." He pointed to the victim's fair skin.

They walked over to the corpse, which Deruta and Rispoli had lowered to the parquet floor. "The cable is too thin to leave a bruise like that. You see it?" Alberto Fumagalli pointed to the purple stripe on Esther's neck. It was a couple of finger widths wide. "When the cable dug into the flesh, it just left a narrow stripe; you see it? In other words, it wasn't this cable that strangled her. That much is clear. And did you get a good look at her face?"

Rocco sank into the leather armchair in the den. "Of course. She was beaten up. Do you know what that means?"

Fumagalli said nothing.

The deputy police chief continued with a low rattle, from the chest, a distant sinister gurgle like a rumble of thunder, warning of an oncoming storm. "That means this isn't a suicide. It means I'm going to have to deal with this thing, and it also means a series of pains in the ass unlike anything you can even imagine!"

Fumagalli nodded. "So now I'm going to take this poor creature to my autopsy room. And you'd probably better call the judge and the forensic squad."

Rocco suddenly jumped out of his chair. His mood had shifted as quickly as a wind at high elevation suddenly bringing black rain-heavy storm clouds where minutes before the sun had been shining.

As he left the room Rocco glanced at Deruta and Caterina. "Rispoli, call the forensic squad in Turin. Deruta, go do what I told you and D'Intino to do this morning."

"But we're supposed to do the stakeouts at night," the cop shot back.

"Then go get some rest, go make bread with your wife, just get the hell out of my hair!"

Like a kicked dog, Deruta shot out of the apartment. Caterina asked no questions. Unlike Officer Deruta, she had learned that when the deputy police chief's mood turned sharply black, the best thing was to shut up and obey.

"Pierron!" Rocco shouted, and Italo's face appeared immediately at the door to the living room.

"Yes, Dottore."

"Scatter the people who are rubbernecking out in the street. I want the names of the Russian woman who was the first to enter the apartment and that half-dead warrant officer. Tell Casella to get busy and make sure nothing comes out in the newspapers. Question all the neighbors, and have someone call the district attorney's office. This is another pain in the ass of the tenth degree, Rispoli, you understand?" And though he had used her name, he was no longer speaking to the unfortunate inspector who was busy talking on the phone to someone in Turin. Right now Rocco was talking to everyone and to no one, waving his hands as if he were perched on the edge of a cliff and trying desperately to regain his balance. "This is definitely a pain in the ass of the tenth degree, no doubt about it!"

Italo nodded, sharing his boss's opinion wholeheartedly. In fact, he knew that the deputy police chief had cataloged the sources of annoyance or pains in the ass in life by degrees, or levels. From level six on up.

In Rocco's own personal hierarchy of values, the sixth level of pains in the ass included children yelling in restaurants, children yelling at swimming pools, children yelling in stores, and just in general, children yelling. Then there were salespeople calling with special offers of convenient bundled contracts for water, gas, and cell phone, blankets that come untucked from under the mattress leaving your feet to freeze on winter nights, and the *apericena*—Italy's latest trend in dining, a blend of aperitif and dinner. The seventh level of pain in the ass included restaurants with slow service, wine connoisseurs, and colleagues at the office with garlic on their breath from dinner the night before. The eighth level included shows that went longer than an hour and fifteen minutes, giving or receiving gifts, video poker machines, and the Roman Catholic radio station, Radio Maria. At the ninth level were wedding invitations, baptism invitations, First Communion invitations, or even just party invitations. Husbands complaining about wives, wives complaining about husbands. But the tenth level, the highest ranking of all possible pains in the ass, the very maximum degree of annoyance that life—that old bastard—could possibly stick him with to ruin his day and his week, towered high above the rest, unequaled: an unsolved case of murder. And Esther Baudo's death had just turned into one, right before his eyes. Hence the sudden mood shift. For anyone who knew him, this was a mood swing to be expected; for anyone who didn't, it was an overblown reaction. It was a case of homicide, and it sat there, useless and relentless, wordlessly demanding a solution that only he could provide, asking a mute question that he and no one else would have to answer. To get that answer he'd have to delve into a filthy well of horrors, plunge down into the abyss of human idiocy, scrabble around in the squalor of some diseased mind. At times like this, when a case had just blossomed like a flower of sickness among the underbrush of his life, in those very first few minutes, if Rocco had chanced to lay hands on the guilty party, he would have gladly and ruthlessly canceled him from the face of the earth.

He found himself sitting at the center of the living room. In the adjoining room, Alberto Fumagalli was working silently on the victim. The other officers had melted away like snow under bright sunlight, each to carry out specific instructions. He rubbed his face and got to his feet.

"All right, Rocco," he said in an undertone, "let's see what we have here."

He pulled on the leather gloves he had in his pocket and ran his eye around the apartment. A chilly, impersonal eye.

The mess in the living room was, all things considered, the ordinary mess of everyday life. Magazines lay scattered, sofa cushions shoved aside, a low table across from the television set covered with kibble of all sorts— cigarette lighters, bills to pay, even two African carved wooden giraffes. What didn't add up, on the other hand, was the unholy disarray in the kitchen. If there actually had been burglars in the apartment, what would they have been looking for in the kitchen? What valuables do people keep in the kitchen? The cabinet doors had all been thrown open. All except the doors under the sink. The deputy police chief pulled those doors open. There were three receptacles for sorted waste: garbage, metal, and paper. He peeked inside. The garbage was full; so was the bin for metal cans. But the container for paper and cardboard was .

almost empty. There was only an empty egg carton, a flyer for a trip to Medjugorje with a special offer on pots and pans, and a fancy black shopping bag with rope handles. At the center of the bag was a sort of heraldic crest. Laurel leaves surrounding a surname, "Tomei." Rocco thought he remembered a shop by that name in the center of town. Inside the bag was a gift card. "Best wishes, Esther."

On the well next to the fridge was a flyer from the city government. It was a map listing trash days. Rocco took a look at it. They picked up paper recycling on that street on Thursdays. The day before. That's why the bin was half-empty.

The deputy police chief shifted his attention to the cell phone that he himself had placed on the marble countertop. That was another question mark. Who did it belong to? Was it the victim's? And why had it been shattered? Where was the SIM card?

The bedroom looked like it had been gone over with a fine-toothed comb. The burglars had concentrated here, working carefully. While the kitchen looked like the aftermath of an earthquake, in the bedroom you could see the careful hand of someone conducting a surgical investigation. Only the sheets had been tossed roughly aside and, to the attentive eye, it was clear that the mattress had been shoved a couple of inches over from the box spring beneath. The front doors of the armoire swung open, but the dresser and side tables were undisturbed. Under the window, half-hidden behind the floor-length curtains, was a dark blue velvet box. Rocco picked it up. It was empty. He left it on the dresser, next to another framed photograph of the couple. In this one, they were sitting at a table and embracing. Rocco stared at the woman's face. And he silently promised her that he'd catch the son of a bitch. She thanked him, responding with a halfhearted smile.

THE DEPUTY POLICE CHIEF HAD DECIDED TO HEAD home on foot, in defiance of the wind that had started to buffet the powdery snow off the roofs and tree branches, kicking it up in small whirlwinds off the blacktop of the streets. He strode briskly, his hands buried in the pockets of his light loden overcoat, which did little to keep him warm in that chilly weather. He looked up, but heavy dark clouds had covered both mountains and sky. Looking past the apartment buildings, all he could see were fields covered with snow or dark with mud. The last thing he wanted was to head straight back to police headquarters: he didn't want to talk to the chief of police, much less explain to the judge exactly what they'd found, partly because he didn't actually know. People on the sidewalk went past him without a glance, absorbed in their own affairs. He was the only one out without a hat. The wind's icy fingers massaged his scalp. He was bound to pay for this walk with a sinus infection and a backache. The air was a blend of wood smoke from the chimneys and carbon monoxide from the tailpipes. He walked briskly into the street at crosswalks, defying death. In Rome, someone would have certainly run him over, crushing him to jelly on the asphalt. But this was Aosta, and the cars screeched to an unprotesting halt. He thought about what awaited him, what lay ahead of him. Aside from the Fiat 500 that stood patiently waiting for him to cross, nothing but work. And life in a city that was alien and distant. There was nothing here for him, and there never would be, even if he stayed for the next ten years. He'd never be able to bring himself to chat with old men in the bars about the high points of the local wines or the upcoming soccer draft picks. And for that matter his hesitant, wavering efforts to construct an affair with Nora looked thinner than a piece of onionskin typing paper. He missed his friends. He knew that at a time like this they'd rally to his support, and help him get over that intolerable pain in the ass. He thought of Seba, who had at least come up to see him. Furio, Brizio. Where were they now? Were they still out on the street, or had his colleagues in the Rome police sent them for an extended stay at the Hotel Roma, as the Regina Coeli prison was called? He'd have given a frostbitten finger of his hand for an ordinary Trastevere pizza, a good old cigarette at night, high atop the Janiculum Hill, or a game of poker at Stampella. Suddenly he found himself at the Porta Pretoria. At least the wind couldn't gust so freely through those ancient Roman gates. How had he wound up there? It was on the far side of town from police headquarters. Now he'd have to retrace his steps to Piazza Chanoux and continue straight from there. He decided that he'd stop in the bar on the piazza. He slowed his pace, now that he had a destination. Then he heard Beethoven's "Ode to Joy" issuing from his overcoat pocket. It was the ringtone he'd put on his cell phone for personal calls.

"Who is it?"

"Darling, it's me, Nora. Bad time?"

"Yes."

"So am I bothering you?"

"Why do you insist on asking questions that practically demand a rude answer?" he asked.

"What's going on? Something wrong?"

"You want to know? Then I'll tell you. I've got a murder on my fucking hands. Satisfied?"

Nora paused for a moment. "Why on earth would you take it out on me?"

"I take it out on everyone. First and foremost myself. I'm heading back to the office. Hold on half an hour, and I'll call you back from there."

"No, you'll forget to call anyway. Listen, I just want to tell you that I've arranged a party at my place. A few friends are coming over."

"Why?" Rocco asked. The recent events in Via Brocherel had run over the blackboard of his memory like an eraser.

"What do you mean, why?" asked Nora, her voice getting louder.

The deputy police chief simply couldn't remember.

"It's my birthday today, Rocco!"

Oh, shit, the gift, was the thought that flashed through his brain. "What time?" he asked.

"Seven thirty. Can you make it?"

"I will if I can. That's a promise."

"Do what you like. See you later. If you can make it."

Nora hung up. The woman's closing words had been colder than the sidewalk around Piazza Chanoux.

It's a chore to maintain human relations. It takes commitment, determination, and willingness: you have to face life with a smile. None of these things were in Rocco Schiavone's toolkit. Life dragged him rudely from one day to the next, yanking him by the hair, and whatever it was that drove him to live from one day to the next, it was probably the same force that was making him put his left foot, shod in Clarks desert boots, in front of his right foot, similarly shod. One step, another step, as the Italian Alpini used to say to themselves as they marched through the Ukraine in temperatures of 40 degrees below zero in the long-ago winter of 1943. One step, another step, Deputy Police Chief Rocco Schiavone kept saying to himself—he'd been saying those words ever since that day, that distant July 7, 2007, the day his life had been snapped in half once and for all, when the boat had overturned, and he had been forced to change course.

A hot, sticky Roman day in July, the seventh of July. A day that took Marina away from him forever. And with her, everything that was good in Rocco Schiavone. He'd spend the rest of his life with nothing to guide him but his instinct for survival.

THE MAN WALKED UP TO THE FRONT DOOR OF THE apartment building on Via Brocherel. Streamlined helmet and high-impact sunglasses, pink and blue skintight bike shorts and jersey in power Lycra, covered with advertising slogans, white calf-length socks, and shoes with the toe higher than the heel, making him walk like a circus clown.

Click clack click clack, went the iron plates on the toes of his shoes, as Patrizio Baudo walked his bike, stepping awkwardly to accommodate the padding in the seat of his bike pants. He observed the apocalyptic scene on the street outside his building. The police, rubberneckers, and even some guy with a TV camera.

What's happened? he thought as he kept walking.

He walked up to a petite blond policewoman with a sweet face and big beautiful eyes, and expressed his thoughts aloud: "What's happened?"

The policewoman sighed: "There's been a murder."

"A . . . what?"

"Just who are you?" asked the policewoman.

"Patrizio Baudo. I live here," he said, and raised one hand with a fingerless glove to point at the windows of his apartment.

Inspector Rispoli focused on the man's face, so that she could actually see her reflection in his sunglasses. "Patrizio Baudo? I think that . . . come with me."

HE HADN'T HAD TIME TO CHANGE YET. SITTING IN HIS cycling jersey and shorts across from the deputy police chief, Patrizio Baudo had however taken off his sunglasses and helmet. He'd handed his bike over to a police officer;

you don't leave a piece of fine equipment like that, easily worth six thousand euros, out on the street, even if you do live in Aosta. His face was pale, and there were two red stripes beneath his eyes. He looked like someone had been slapping him around for the past ninety minutes. He sat there in a daze, slack-jawed, staring blankly across the desk at Rocco. He was trembling, hard to say whether in fear or from the cold, and held his hands between his legs, still clad in leather cycling gloves. Every so often he'd raise his right hand and touch the gold crucifix that hung around his neck. "Let me get you something warm to put on," said the deputy police chief as he picked up the receiver of his desk phone.

Phascolarctos cinereus. Commonly called the koala bear. Patrizio Baudo resembled nothing so much as the little Australian marsupial, and that was the first thing that had come into Rocco's mind when the man walked into the room and shook his hand. The second thought was to wonder why he hadn't already detected that resemblance from the photographs scattered throughout the apartment. The proportions, he replied inwardly. You can see them much better in person. The eyes are so much better than a camera lens at judging space and units of measurement. All it took was a quick glance at the jug ears, the small, wide-set eyes, and the oversize nose square in the middle of the face, practically covering the small, lipless mouth. To say nothing of the weak, receding chin. Every detail of that face shouted *koala*. There were, of course, differences. Aside from the differences in diet and habitat, what distinguished the animal from Patrizio Baudo was the hair. The little marsupial had lovely, cottonball hair, while Patrizio was bald as a billiard ball. This was a habit of Rocco's, to compare human faces to the features of a given animal. Something that dated back to his childhood. It all started with a gift his father had given him when he turned eight: an encyclopedia of animals that had a section full of wonderful illustrations done at the end of the nineteenth century, depicting lots and lots of birds, fish, and mammals. Rocco would sit on the carpet in the family's little Trastevere living room and spend hours poring over those drawings, memorizing names, amusing himself by finding resemblances with his teachers at school, his classmates, and people in his neighborhood.

Casella walked in with a black jacket and gave it to Patrizio Baudo, who immediately wrapped it around his shoulders. "How . . . how did it happen?" he asked in a faint voice.

"We still don't know."

"What's that supposed to mean?" Patrizio's dead, dark little eyes suddenly flamed up, as if someone had lit a torch in the pupils.

"It means we found her hanged in your den."

Patrizio put his gloved hands over his face. Rocco went on. "But the situation isn't entirely clear."

The man took a deep breath and looked at the policeman, his eyes filled with tears. "What do you mean by that? What isn't clear?"

"It's not clear whether your wife killed herself or was murdered."

He shook his head and ran his hand over his weak chin.

"I don't . . . I don't understand. She hanged herself . . . how could someone else have possibly killed her? Are you saying someone hanged her? Please, I don't understand . . ."

Caterina Rispoli came in with a cup of tea. She gave it to Patrizio Baudo, who thanked her with a half smile but didn't drink any. "Please explain, Dottore. I don't understand . . ."

"There are details concerning the death of your wife that just don't make sense. Details that make us think it might have been something other than a suicide."

"What details?"

"We're strongly inclined to think that it's been staged somehow."

Only then did Patrizio Baudo gulp down a mouthful of tea, which was immediately followed by a shiver. He once again touched the crucifix with his gloved right hand. Rocco shot Officer Casella a look. "I'll have you taken home now. Please, take anything you'll need. But I'm afraid you won't be able to stay in your apartment. The forensic squad is conducting an examination. Do you have somewhere you can stay?"

Patrizio Baudo shrugged. "Me? No . . . maybe at my mother's?"

"All right. Officer Casella will accompany you to your mother's house. Here in Aosta?"

"Not far. In Charvensod."

Rocco stood up. "We'll keep you informed, don't worry."

"But who was it?" Baudo suddenly blurted. "Who could have done such a thing? To Esther . . . to my Esther . . ."

ANTONIO MANZINI

"I promise I'll do everything I can to find out, Signor Baudo. I assure you."

"I don't believe it. I can't believe it. Just like that? From one moment to the next? What is this? What's happening?" He looked around in bewilderment. Caterina had dropped her gaze, Casella was fixated on some indeterminate point on the office ceiling, while Rocco stood there, chilly and detached. Deep inside him a rage was burning that wasn't all that different from what the other man felt. Patrizio finally burst into tears. "I can't take this . . ." he murmured under his breath, crumpled up on his seat like an abandoned rag.

Rocco put a hand on his shoulder. "Tomorrow I'm going to need you, Dottor Baudo, once you feel a little stronger. We believe that there was a theft from your home."

Patrizio went on sobbing. Then the emotional tempest subsided as quickly as it had come. He sniffed and nodded to the deputy police chief. "Not tomorrow. Now."

"Right now you're too—"

"Right now!" said Patrizio, leaping to his feet. "I want to see my home. I want to go home."

"If nothing else, you can get changed, no?" said Casella, inappropriately. Rocco incinerated him with a single glance. "He can't go around dressed like a clown, you know," Casella added under his breath, justifying his comment to Rispoli.

"All right, Dottor Baudo, let's go," said Rocco, taking the cup still full of tea and setting it down on the desk.

"Don't call me *dottore*. I never went to college." He strode briskly out of the room, followed by Rocco and Inspector Rispoli.

ITALO DROVE THE POLICE BMW WITHOUT REVVING THE motor, carefully avoiding the worst potholes. It was easy to avoid the worst potholes in Aosta. Because there weren't any. At least not compared with the streets of the Italian capital, where the native Romans had given a name to every lurch and jolt and where trying to accelerate on the *sanpietrini*—the Romans had named their cobblestones after St. Peter—was an excellent way of procuring a spontaneous abortion. Patrizio Baudo looked out the passenger window. "I'm starting to hate this city," he said.

"I can understand that," replied the deputy police chief from the backseat.

"I'm from Ivrea. But you know how things are, right? I found a job here and then . . . Esther's from here, from Aosta. We were great friends, you know? I mean, before we got married. I don't even know how it happened. First we were friends, then we fell in love. Then all the rest."

Patrizio's pale legs were trembling slightly. He clutched at his thighs with both hands. He'd loosened the Velcro wrist fastenings of his bike gloves, but he still wore them.

"Signor Baudo, how was your wife this morning?"

"I didn't see her. On Fridays I only work afternoons, so I

get up at six and go out for a nice long ride. Do you ever ride a bike, Dottore?"

"No. Not me. I played soccer."

"When I was twenty I was on a team. I wanted to become a professional cyclist. But that world is just too hard, too dirty. You might just wind up being second banana, in the middle of the pack during the final sprints, nothing more than that. Maybe I wasn't really all that good. Every now and then I go out for amateur races."

Italo stopped at the light. Patrizio sniffed, but with his face turned to look out at the street, so Rocco couldn't tell if he was crying or just coming down with a cold.

"You're the last person to have seen Esther. So last night . . ."

"Right, last night. The usual. She went to bed around ten, maybe ten thirty. I stayed up to watch a little television. There was a movie about some guy who brought salmon to Yemen. So that people could fish for them. Have you seen it?" Rocco said nothing. He knew that Patrizio was just giving voice to a jumble of disconnected thoughts. He was concealing behind words the pain and grief that hadn't yet clearly surfaced in his heart, and in his head. "It wasn't bad. The movie, I mean. What I can't understand is why a person would sit in front of the television set channel surfing without actually watching anything. Do you do that?"

Patrizio sniffed again. But this time his shoulders were trembling. And this time Rocco understood that he was crying.

● ● ●

WHEN THEY GOT TO VIA BROCHEREL, THE VAN OF THE forensic squad was already parked outside. Two officers were unloading equipment. A third officer, fair-haired and short, was putting on his white jumpsuit. Italo had double-parked the car and the deputy police chief was walking toward the street entrance, followed by Patrizio Baudo. The press wasn't there yet, which struck Rocco as odd. But evidently the meeting of the regional assembly to decide on an amateur bicycle race was considered hot news. Just one less pain in the ass, thought Rocco.

The young fair-haired officer went over to Rocco. "Dottore! Special Agent Carini, forensic squad . . ."

"Welcome to the crime scene. Is your boss with you?"

"No, Dottor Farinelli will join us later. He's working on a murder down in Turin."

This was the first time that Rocco had ever heard the expression "down in Turin." As far as he was concerned Turin had always been "up." I'm going up to Turin. But "down to Turin"—that's the way they said it in Aosta. Sort of like when you're south of the equator, where the water goes down the drain spinning counterclockwise.

"We need to enter the apartment, Carini. This is the victim's husband."

The special agent looked at Patrizio Baudo, still dressed in his biking gear. "I should actually talk to my boss . . . let me call him right now and—"

"You don't need to talk to anyone. Give us some shoe protectors and latex gloves and stop busting my chops."

The special agent nodded. "Certainly. Wait here, I'll

bring you everything you need." He walked over to the van, where his colleague was all ready with briefcase and biohazard suit.

Patrizio looked at the building as if this were the first time in his life he'd seen it. "Is . . . is my wife still upstairs?"

"I don't think so, Signor Baudo." Rocco turned to a young officer standing guard outside the ground floor entrance. "Has the morgue truck been by already?"

The young man nodded.

"Who's up in the apartment?"

"Scipioni, I think."

Rocco looked at Patrizio. "Are you sure you're up for this?"

"Certainly. It's my home."

PATRIZIO COULDN'T SEEM TO MAKE UP HIS MIND TO enter the apartment. He just stood there, with the paper cap on his head, wearing latex gloves and plastic overshoes, looking at the front door from the landing while the policemen readied their gear. Officer Scipioni, who was standing sentinel outside the apartment, was engaged in a conversation with a very elderly woman, pale as a sheet with blue hair that matched her dressing gown. There were punks on the King's Road in the late seventies who wouldn't have dared to try out her look, Rocco mused as he considered her hair. The woman was nodding her head, holding both hands to her face.

"Shall we go in?" asked Rocco.

Patrizio opened the door and the hinges creaked.

"There's been a break-in!" exclaimed Officer Carini as he studied the lock.

"No. That was me, the first time I went in," Rocco replied. Next came the master of the house.

Baudo walked slowly, unspeaking, his eyes focused and sad. He shot a glance at the French door that led onto a small balcony. Someone had put his bicycle out there. The first thing he did was bring the bike in and lean it against the credenza in the living room. Rocco's alert eyes caught every detail: the man seemed to be caressing a daughter, not a piece of athletic equipment. "It's a Colnago . . . more than six thousand euros," he said, as if that was justification enough. "Where . . . where did you find her?" Rocco pointed to the den. Patrizio silently moved toward the room, softly as a shade. He opened the door. The cable dangled from the lamp hook. He stood in the doorway, gazing silently. It seemed as if he was sniffing the air. Then he heaved a deep sigh and went back to the bedroom. "We only have one thing of real value in the apartment," he said as he walked by the deputy police chief.

As soon as he saw the room, he jerked in alarm. "They've been in here too . . ." He went to pull open the drawer of a small side table under the window. Then his eye lit on the blue velvet box that Rocco had set on the tabletop. He looked inside, with a bitter smile. "So they found it."

"What was in it?"

"It's where we kept our gold."

"Your gold?"

"Yes. Nothing much. A watch, a few bracelets, my cuff links, and a brooch that my mother had given Esther. A pretty pin, with a peacock. With green and blue stones. It belonged to my grandmother, just think." He sat down on the bed. Tears poured from his eyes like an open faucet. "Is that all my wife's life was worth?"

"You did all right, my wife's wasn't even worth a euro. Just the price of a nine-millimeter round," Rocco felt like saying to him, but he said nothing.

"Esther always was unlucky," Patrizio said, looking at the floor and stroking the bed as if his wife were lying on it, fast asleep. "She always had bellyaches. You know what I used to call her? *Estherichia coli,*" and he started chuckling under his breath. "*Estherichia coli* instead of *Escherichia coli . . .* but all she needed was a massage and she'd get over it. It was a nervous disorder, if you ask me." He dried his tears. Then he looked up at Rocco. "I'm a believer, Commissario, but I swear to you that right now I just couldn't say. Where was God when someone was killing my wife? Can you tell me where God was?"

There was probably no question that Rocco Schiavone was less suited to answer.

"Please, take me to my mother's place. I just can't take this anymore . . . I can't take it anymore."

THE DEPUTY POLICE CHIEF HAD BEEN SITTING IN THE district attorney's waiting room for more than half an hour, looking at the wood grain on Judge Baldi's door. Funny how he managed to see different shapes in it every time.

On that chilly March day, what popped out of the grain was a dolphin and a rose, though the rose actually looked more like an artichoke than a rose. But if he looked at it the other way around, it became an elephant with just one ear. The door swung open and the imaginary wood-grain fresco disappeared, replaced by Judge Baldi's face. "Well hello there, Schiavone! Have you been waiting long?"

Rocco stood up and shook hands.

"Come in, have a seat."

Standing next to the bookshelf, a young man in jacket and tie was gathering a series of enormous file folders full of documents. "Let me introduce you to Judge Messina. Aldo, this is Deputy Police Chief Schiavone, who's been working with us for just a few months but has already solved one case brilliantly. Am I right?"

Judge Messina was obliged to set down his armful of folders so he could shake hands with Rocco. "I've heard a lot about you," he said, with unmistakable emphasis.

"And you still shake my hand?"

Messina smiled. "I wouldn't refuse to shake anyone's hand. If you'll excuse me." He gathered up his folders again and left the room. The first thing that Rocco Schiavone noticed was that the photograph of the judge's wife was now gone from the desktop. The last time he'd seen it, the picture had been lying facedown. Now he felt certain it was tucked away in one of the desk drawers. That's always a bad sign.

The magistrate's marriage was on its way out. The eve of the final breakup. Baldi swept his blond bangs out of his eyes with a quick flick of the hand and sat down at his desk. "Now then, what news do you have for me about what happened on Via Brocherel?"

"It was a murder. I'm sure of it. Esther Baudo—that's the victim's name—was beaten and then strangled. The hanging seems to me to have been staged. Plus, the room where we found the corpse was dark, with the shutters down. But when I walked in and I turned on the light, there was a short circuit. Which means that the woman hanged herself in the dark . . ."

"Or else, after she hanged herself, someone lowered the blinds. Right?"

"Exactly."

"So what's your theory?"

"I don't have one, Dottore. I'm still just sniffing around."

Baldi stretched both arms in the air. "And do you like what you smell?"

"Smells like shit, as usual."

"The husband?"

"He's a sales representative, works in athletic equipment. Clean record, no run-ins with the law, a traffic ticket or two. But something was stolen."

The judge nodded, thoughtfully. "Burglars caught in the act who then decided to stage the whole thing?"

Rocco shrugged. "Why not? Maybe they did it just to throw us off the trail. Still, there's something about it I don't like."

"Do tell."

"Actually, two things. The first thing, you see, is that we have a kitchen that was turned literally upside down, like there'd been a tornado. A real authentic mess. But the bedroom, where the valuables were hidden—in a small velvet box containing the family gold—was searched scientifically. They might have opened a couple of drawers, at the very most."

"As if they knew where to look. So what about the mess in the kitchen?"

"Exactly. It doesn't add up. Plus, I think the burglars had been in that apartment before."

"Why do you say that?"

"There was no sign of breaking and entering on the door or on the windows. If they got in, either it was because Signora Baudo knew them or else because—"

"Because they had the keys," concluded Judge Baldi, getting to his feet. He was hyperactive: he couldn't sit listening for more than five minutes at a time. He walked over to the window and stood drumming his fingers on the glass. "I'm afraid you're going to have to work solo, Schiavone. I've got some problems on my hands." Immediately an image flashed into Rocco's mind: the wife's picture dumped into a drawer, if not actually tossed in the trash. Baldi stopped drumming and started whistling softly. Rocco recognized the Toreador song from Bizet's *Carmen*. "We are on the trail of one of the biggest tax evasion cases I've ever worked on, me and the finance police and the Carabinieri. There's just an endless supply of tax evaders, you know that?"

"I can imagine. I can't do a lot of tax evading with my paycheck."

Baldi turned around and smiled. "If we all just paid our taxes, the tax burden would be much lighter. You know that, I know that. But it seems as if the Italians aren't interested in the fact. This really is a strange country, isn't it?"

Rocco braced himself for another pearl of wisdom from Judge Baldi, who always seemed to have some solution for the nation's political and economic problems on his mind. His notions ranged from drafting cabinet ministers and secretaries from other countries, more or less the way that soccer teams are assembled, in order to have serious, well-trained, honest people running the government, to the elimination of banknotes so that all transactions would have to be conducted through credit cards. This would make all purchases traceable and make it impossible to conceal one's income and evade taxes. "It's a strange, deeply wasteful country," Rocco said, encouragingly.

Baldi didn't have to be asked twice. "True. Let me give you an example. Public funding of the political parties. Right now, they take the money as an electoral reimbursement, right?"

"Right."

"And I don't actually disagree with the idea. Better for them to receive public money than get funds from some powerful, manipulative lobbyist or other. But follow me closely here." He turned away from the window and went back to his seat at his desk. "I say what we do is take parliamentarians, cabinet ministers, and undersecretaries off the state payroll, because that's clearly a waste of public money. Instead, we should have deputies, senators, and everyone else paid directly by the parties that run them for office. In that case, politicians would get the proper salaries. And just think of how much money the treasury would save. What do you think? Wouldn't it be a great idea?"

"But that would mean finally just giving up and bending over to take it from behind, and admitting that this country is in the hands of the political parties."

"Well, are you saying it isn't? Deputies and senators, commissioners and outside consultants, none of them are civil servants, Schiavone. They're servants of the parties they belong to. And in that case, let the parties pay them!"

Rocco raised his eyebrows. "I'd have to give that some thought."

"By all means, Schiavone. Think it over. And please, help me understand what happened to Esther Baudo. I leave that case in your hands. After all, it's clear that I can rely on you."

Baldi's expression had changed. Now a sinister light glittered in his eyes.

"Of course I can rely on you."

The magistrate's mouth stretched out in a false, menacing smile. "And since I want to rely on you, look, I'd really like to get your version."

"My version of what?"

"Of what happened in Rome."

Oh my God, what a pain in the ass, thought Rocco, but he kept it to himself. "You know everything that happened;

there are reports and documentation. I'm sure you've read them. Why dig into it again?"

"It seems to be an occupational hazard with me. I'd just like to hear your version. You've been here for six months now. You can tell me, can't you?"

"All right then." Rocco took a deep breath, got comfortable, and began. "Giorgio Borghetti Ansaldo, age twenty-nine, had a bad habit: he liked to rape young girls. I followed him, I stopped him, but there was nothing I could do about him. It just so happens that his father, Fernando Borghetti Ansaldo, is the undersecretary for foreign affairs. You may have seen his name in the news."

Baldi nodded, brow furrowed in concentration.

"Okay. Giorgio didn't shake his bad habit, and he kept it up until one day he practically killed a certain Marta De Cesaris, age sixteen, who lost her sight in one eye; a hundred years of therapy will never turn her back into the pretty, carefree high school student who attended the Liceo Virgilio in Rome. So I finally had my fill, I went to see Giorgio, and I gave him a serious beat-down."

"Translate beat-down."

"I beat him up. I beat him up so bad that now the guy has to use a cane to get around. But he's still the undersecretary's son. And the undersecretary made me pay for what I did. There, that's the story."

Baldi nodded again. Then he looked Rocco Schiavone in the eye. "That's not the kind of law enforcement we're in the business of delivering."

"I know. And my answer is I don't give a shit."

"You seem to be overlooking the subtle but undeniable difference between a policeman and a judge."

"And again, the aforementioned answer."

"Fine. I thank you for your sincerity. But now let me tell you something. Listen up and listen good, because I'm only going to tell you once. If you go on being a good cop, you're not going to have any problems, neither with me nor with the regional government. But if you start stepping over the line into my jurisdiction, I'll turn your life into a living hell, even if you're all the way up here in the snowy mountains. You'll have a bad case of hemorrhoids from all the kicks in the ass I'll give you. *Arrivederci.*" And he leaned over his documents again. Rocco said good-bye and left the office, deciding as he went that the right position for a manic depressive wasn't in the district attorney's office, but a nice quiet home somewhere, where he could take plenty of medicine and relax by taking long meditative walks.

Outside, night was falling. As Rocco walked he kept getting the distinct sensation he'd forgotten something. Something important, something fundamental. He lit a cigarette and went back over everything that had happened that day. He thought about Esther Baudo, her husband, the apartment turned upside down, Irina, the retired warrant officer. Nothing. He was scorching his neurons to no avail. He decided to stop at the bar in Piazza Chanoux for an espresso. Maybe that would help.

It was nice in there. It was warm, and there were lots of people sitting at the tables and chatting. Chatting in a language that Rocco didn't understand. He shot a glance at Ugo, who was busy pouring tonic water into a customer's glass of gin. Ugo replied by pointing with his chin to the table by the plate glass window, Rocco's usual place.

The deputy police chief sat down and Ugo came right over. "Sorry, there's a bit of a rush this evening. But then, Fridays are always like that. What can I bring you?"

"A cup of coffee, American-style."

"If you like, I'd be glad to let you sample a Blanc de Morgex that is out of this world."

Rocco thought it over. As he watched Ugo's lips moving and smelled the fumes of alcohol spreading through the bar, he decided it was a good idea to try that wine. Ugo, as delighted as if Rocco had done him some great favor, went back to the counter. The deputy police chief looked around. Next to him, on his left, sat two students, deep in an intense conversation in low voices. They kept their hands on their glasses of beer and looked each other in the eyes. On his right were two women. Blond, short hair, fresh from the beautician, already on their third glass of red. They laughed frequently, elegant and carefree. They were both well over fifty. They spoke in Italian and Rocco caught an occasional snatch of their conversation.

The one with blue eyes said: "I'll tell you what I think. You're doing the right thing. He's handsome and he loves you." Then she raised her glass ever so slightly and took a sip of wine. "Plus, and this is fundamental, he's rich. You know what my mother always used to say?"

"No, what did she say?"

The woman lowered her voice, but Rocco heard her all

the same. "She used to say, when your tits stop pointing at the stars and start pointing at your feet instead, that's the time to make sure you have some very expensive shoes on those feet!" They both burst out laughing and took another gulp of their wine. Rocco too joined in the laughter, and it was at that exact moment that his mind grasped the detail that he sensed he'd overlooked and that he'd been trying to remember so unsuccessfully as he walked: Nora!

HE THREW OPEN THE DOOR TO INSPECTOR RISPOLI'S office.

"Give me some good news!"

Caterina was at her computer. She leaped to her feet. "About what, Dottore?"

"The gift."

Caterina smiled, pulled open a desk drawer, and extracted a magazine. "Take a look."

Rocco grabbed the weekly. On it was the logo of a hotel in Chamonix, France. Pictures of a swimming pool and a girl lying half-naked on a massage bed, with an Asian woman rubbing her back. "What's this?"

"Three days of total relaxation at the romantic Hotel Aiguille du Midi . . . ayurvedic beauty treatments, shiatsu massages, three heated pools, chromotherapy, all in the magnificent setting of the French Alps."

"You talk like a travel agent." The deputy police chief laid down the magazine. "And you're suggesting I give her this for her birthday?"

"It's a romantic hotel. You'd have three wonderful days, Dottore. And you'd definitely make her happy."

"I don't have three days to spare."

"A long weekend."

"Thanks, Caterina, but it's too big a deal. Believe me. Too much. Shit, it's six o'clock and I'm back where I started from."

Caterina nodded.

"What do you say to a pair of shoes?"

Caterina made a face. "If you put it like that, it seems like a consolation prize."

"But not just an ordinary pair of shoes. Tell me, as a woman, what kind of shoes would any woman be happy to receive?"

"Personally? Prada. Or Jimmy Choo. Though I wouldn't rule out Manolo Blahniks either. But you have to try shoes on. Do you at least know the lady's shoe size?"

"Thirty-eight," said Rocco.

"Are you certain? Because I can tell you that it's no simple matter with shoes, there are half sizes, different foot widths, in other words—"

"Worst case, she can exchange them. Now, tell me what shop to go to here in Aosta."

"In the center of town; otherwise you won't get there in time."

"We're late as it is. In fact, put on your jacket and come with me."

Caterina walked around the desk. "Actually, any minute

now D'Intino and Deruta are going out for their stakeout and I'm supposed to be—"

"They'll do fine without any help from you."

"Ah, and then there are all the interviews that Scipioni and Pierron did with the Baudos' neighbors."

"Not now, Caterì, not now, or the stores will close!"

OFFICER CATERINA RISPOLI AND DEPUTY POLICE Chief Rocco Schiavone strode briskly down Via de Tillier, the broad shopping street in central Aosta, lined with boutiques and restaurants. A few pedestrians glanced at them in alarm, convinced they must be on the trail of some particularly urgent case.

"Where is this shop, Caterì?"

"We're almost there!"

They narrowly avoided colliding with a couple walking out of a pub flying the Irish tricolor and other green flags with emblems of shamrocks and the Celtic harp. As the two policemen veered around them, a Yorkshire terrier covered with a Scotch tartan coat yapped madly at them.

"Couldn't we just have driven here?"

"It's a pedestrian area, Dottore."

"But we're the police, and that's got to be good for something, don't you think?"

Then Rocco came to a sudden halt like a stubborn mule, and stood gazing at the sign outside a shop.

"This isn't the place, Dottore!"

But Rocco wasn't listening to her anymore. "Just wait for me, I'll be right back," he said, and hurried off toward a menswear boutique called "Tomei."

It was an "English-style" shop, with faux antique paintings of golfers, horsemen setting out on fox hunts, cricket gear mounted on the walls, and the inevitable canvas Union Jack behind the cash register. They sold suits in tweed and glen plaid, lots of colorful cashmere sweaters stacked on wooden shelves. The place was wallpapered with something resembling a Scotch tartan. Set on the blue-green wall-to-wall carpeting were pairs of Church's English shoes, and hanging on pegs along the shop's long wall were Burberry jackets. A man in jacket and tie came over to the deputy police chief. From the way he walked, he clearly believed he resembled some member of the Spencer family. But to Rocco he was reminiscent of a night porter in a seedy, two-star hotel. "Can I be of any assistance?" said the counterfeit English lord, dry-washing his hands.

"Maybe you can. I want to see your sacks."

The man didn't seem to understand. "What do you mean, our sacks?"

"The sacks you put the things you sell in, for the customers to carry out of the store."

"Ah, our shopping bags. But we don't sell those."

"And I don't want to buy one. I just want to see one."

"It's a rather odd request, don't you think?"

"Certainly, *mister*, but it just so happens that I'm the deputy chief of the mobile squad of the Aosta police force, and I'm in the middle of an investigation."

"Are you a policeman?"

"I suppose I am, since a deputy police chief does work for the police."

The proprietor looked stunned. "Oh Jesus . . . Of course, of course . . . please come with me, right this way."

He rushed over to the cash register. He bent down and finally pulled out two lovely red shopping bags, big enough to accommodate a heavy sweater.

"No, smaller. The smallest one you have."

The man smiled, bent over again, rummaged around a little more, then pulled out another shopping bag. It was black, with rope handles, and the Tomei logo enclosed in laurel branches. "Like this?"

"Exactly! That's it. Now let me ask you to concentrate for a moment. You might be very useful to me."

"Of course. Ask away." Signor Tomei leveled his pale blue eyes at Rocco's.

"Yesterday or sometime in the past few days, a woman came to see you, perhaps you know her, Esther Baudo? About thirty-five, with curly hair?"

The man looked up. "No . . . I don't remember. A woman, you say?"

"Yes."

"Certainly, if you had a photograph . . ."

"Try to remember."

"Look, right here and now? I couldn't say, nothing comes to mind. And I'm not always present in the store. Sometimes my wife takes over for me, or my son . . . and mornings there's a salesclerk . . . and she works *part-time*." The way he pronounced the English word in Italian, rounding his *r*'s and hitting his *t*'s especially hard, was clearly meant as a proud display of his splendid and hard-won Anglo-Saxon pronunciation.

"Shall I leave you the number of my *mobail*?" drawled Rocco, cocking an eyebrow and twisting the English word into a mockery in Italian.

"Yes."

"Here, I'll write it down." And he stepped over to the briarwood table where the cash register stood, between the electronic credit card reader and two baskets piled high with cotton lisle socks. Rocco was almost tempted to buy a pair, but twenty-three euros seemed too high a price, no matter how nice they might be. Any market stand would sell you three pair for ten euros. Sure, they might not be made of cotton lisle or cashmere, but as long as he was wearing his Clarks desert boots, those socks weren't going to last long anyway. After he jotted down his phone number he turned to look at the proprietor of the shop. "I'll arrange to send over a picture of the person who might have been here."

"All right. I'll show it to my wife and son and my *part-time* salesclerk," he replied, once again with the impeccable English pronunciation.

"Just to get an idea, what could you fit into such a small shopping bag?"

Signor Tomei turned the bag over again in his hands. "Well, I'd say a necktie, or possibly a pair of suspenders.

Or even a pair of socks. If you wear Church's shoes, maybe a pair of shoelaces. I can't think of anything else. Oh, yes, cuff links. Brass cuff links, you see? They're on display in the window." He pointed at a small set of wooden shelves full of shiny buttons. "They have replicas of all the flags of the British navy. They're made of brass and enamel; do you want to take a look?"

"No, thanks. Now, this is important: call me if anything occurs to you."

"Well, tonight we're about to close. And tomorrow I only work a half day. It's a holiday, you know?"

"A holiday?"

"Yes, it's a holiday because my wife is Irish and we celebrate it. It's March seventeenth."

"I'm still not following you."

"It's St. Patrick's Day!" And once again, he uttered the name of the saint in perfect English pronunciation.

"Ah, I see. That's why the pubs have flags with shamrocks on them downtown," said Rocco.

"Sure, it's a holiday now in Italy too. But you know why? It's just an excuse to drink, not for any other reason . . ." He laughed long and loud. And alone.

"Just another piece of information: do you sell women's shoes?"

"No, we sell only clothing for men, strictly *Made in England*." Again with the accent.

"Elementary, I daresay. Thank you very much."

And he exited the shop.

• • •

CATERINA WAS OUTSIDE, CHECKING HER WATCH. "YOU were inside forever."

"I know," Rocco replied, resuming the forced march. "But you know that I have the bad habit of mixing business with pleasure."

"Which was the business and which was the pleasure?"

"The business was doing my job and buying a gift for Nora."

"And the pleasure?"

"Doing it with you."

Caterina blushed but Rocco didn't notice because he was half a yard behind her.

HE KNOCKED ON NORA'S DOOR, THE GIFT-WRAPPED shoe box with the ribbon on it under his right arm and two bottles of Blanc de Morgex purchased from Ugo cradled in his left arm. The wine had cost practically nothing; the shoes had cost a month's salary. Nora opened the door. Beaming. "My love . . ." She planted a kiss on his lips. She tasted of cigarettes and sugar. "You came to my party . . ."

"You do have a certain spirit of observation." He immediately put the gift into her hands. "For you. Many happy returns of the day." He'd finally rid himself of that burden.

Nora's large eyes gleamed. It was a nice big box, and she

turned it over and shook it, trying to guess what it contained. "What is it? A dust buster?" she asked, laughing.

"No, it's a steam iron."

"Too light."

"Carbon alloy construction. Very high tech. Can I come in or are we having the party here on the landing?"

Nora stood aside but gave Rocco another kiss; at last the deputy police chief was able to enter the apartment. While she eagerly unwrapped the present, Rocco set down the bottles and took off his overcoat. "You know what, Rocco? There's another person here you know. I thought you'd be happy to see him here tonight."

"Who's that?"

"The chief of police."

Rocco's eyes opened wide. "You invited Corsi?"

"Yes. I sold him his daughter's wedding gown. It just seemed . . . oh *Madonna*! Jimmy Choo?" she cried with a little scream. She sat right down on the chair by the front door and opened the box.

Caterina had selected an elegant pair of plum-colored shoes with five-inch heels, insisting that these were the epitome of sexy footwear. "Oh my God, they're beautiful!"

Nora wasted no time. She took off the shoes she was wearing and immediately tried on the new ones. She looked at them, admired them in the mirror, and walked back and forth. "My love, they're wonderful."

They really did look good on her. They slimmed down her legs, showing off her narrow ankles. And now that he looked closer, even her ass looked better in those shoes.

"How do they fit?"

"Excellent, my exact size. You want to know something? I made a bet with a girlfriend of mine. And I won. Come on into the other room; everyone's already here."

And striding across the parquet floor in her new shoes, she led Rocco into the living room.

She'd prepared an aperitif, a pre-dinner cocktail party. Two ice buckets with champagne, bottles of Aperol and tonic water standing nearby, finger sandwiches with caviar and smoked salmon, and a Spanish *pata negra* ham to be sliced on a side table. There was a little lounge music in the air, which would have gone just as well in an elevator or a first-class airport waiting room. "Everyone, I'd like you to meet Rocco."

Rocco looked around at the other guests. He immediately counted them. Three men, four women. Police Chief Corsi wasn't among them. He shook hands all around, forgetting each name the minute he heard it; as he did, Nora walked over, showing off her new shoes to Anna, a very nicely put-together woman in her early forties, with wolfish eyes, skinny muscular legs, and a buttery white bosom that peeped out of the low neckline of her black T-shirt. "What do you think?"

"Oh, oh!" said her friend, "they're wonderful."

"I won my bet!" Then she turned to Rocco. "Anna bet that you'd give me a weekend's worth of massages. I told her you'd do much better than that."

Rocco smiled slyly. "Massages? Well, that wouldn't have

been a bad idea . . ." he said ironically. "But your friend must not have a very high opinion of me."

"Am I wrong?" Anna replied, winking at him and crossing a pair of legs sheathed in black stockings. Her defiant half smile and her half-lidded gaze were adorned with dark eye shadow, giving her dangerously alluring eyes an even more exotic look and making the police officer ridiculously horny. He'd have gladly thrown her on her back right there on the hardwood floor and licked her like a lollipop for a couple of hours at least. But that image of cheap and decadent sex was dispelled by the delicate touch of a hand on his shoulder. "Hello, Schiavone."

He turned around. It was Police Chief Andrea Corsi. Corsi looked at him, beaming, through his titanium-frame spectacles. "How nice to see you here."

They shook hands.

"I know this is a celebration, but maybe at dinner you can fill me in on what's happened. That way I won't have to pursue you for the rest of the day tomorrow."

"Certainly." And the deputy police chief shot a furious glare at Nora, who returned a gleaming, pearly whitetoothed smile. "And afterward, Rocco, we'll go to dinner in a new restaurant that's just opened in the center of town. All of us together. Happy?"

"Overjoyed, Nora," the deputy police chief replied, grimly.

He had just realized that even the second half of Roma-Inter, the Friday night game, had gone up in smoke. The most he could hope to see was the postgame highlights.

● ● ●

SITTING AT A DINNER TABLE FOR MORE THAN AN HOUR
was the sort of thing that irritated him, giving him a slight
intermittent shiver mixed with sudden surges of heat. Rocco
had long ago cataloged restaurants with slow service as a
seventh-degree pain in the ass. And this new trattoria with
the highly imaginative name of "La Grolla," after a local
drinking technique, couldn't even really qualify as slow—it
was dead in the water. At well past ten thirty, after a grueling two hours and fifteen minutes, they were still there, just
finishing their entrées.

Anna was across the table from him, and she'd never
glanced at him the whole evening. Only once, while he was
having an amiable conversation with the police chief, ex-
plaining the details of the unfortunate death of poor Esther
Baudo, had Rocco turned suddenly and caught her glancing
at him, but she had immediately looked away, pretending to
be interested in what Pietro Bucci-something something, an
interior decorator, was telling her. Gotcha! Schiavone had
said inwardly. They were still waiting for the espressos, and
then the cake would be the final act. The waiter came over
promptly to clear the table and Rocco grabbed him by the
arm. "Listen, how long will it be for the coffee?"

"They're on their way now," the waiter reassured him.

"Let's just hope they don't get lost, though," said
Rocco, releasing the waiter's arm. He couldn't hold out

much longer. He was exhausted. He felt like throwing up and his ass was starting to feel numb and at the same time, tingle with pins and needles. The police chief was already worrying about what to say to the news vendors, which is what he always called the detested creatures of the press, and he'd started off on his usual rant. "Tell me something more, Schiavone. I'm going to have tell those people something tomorrow, no?" Rocco smiled. "Dottor Corsi, those people, the reporters, you can wrap them around your little finger as and when you please." And as his direct superior started jotting down notes for a possible press conference to be held on Saturday at police headquarters, Rocco decided that he would brave the chilly night to smoke a cigarette—he definitely needed a break. "I'm going to go have a smoke," he said in a whisper to Nora. Then, just as he was getting to his feet, he had the stroke of genius, the idea that would get him out of that tremendous pain-in-the-ass situation once and for all and give a welcome turn to the evening. He touched his jacket pocket. His cell phone was right where it ought to be.

"Oh, by the way," the chief of police said preemptively. "The regional governor absolutely requires our help. He's organizing an amateur bike race, for charity, at the end of April. A race that's called something like . . . I don't remember . . . like the Aosta–Saint-Vincent–Aosta. Later I'll give you all the details. We have to be available to help out."

"Certainly, Dottore, certainly." And with a smile and a pack of cigarettes in hand he'd left the table.

HE WALKED BACK INTO THE RESTAURANT AND, THE
minute he sat down, the lights went out. It was time for the
dessert that Anna herself had chosen, Nora's favorite, a tira-
misu. A chunk of mascarpone cheese, heavy cream, chocolate, and ladyfingers—rich enough to knock out a buffalo.
Rocco picked at it halfheartedly, but he just didn't have
room for that caloric bomb. He couldn't understand how
Nora's friends, skinny, lithe, and athletic as they were, after
polishing off pasta, entrée, side dishes, cheese, and fruit,
could still be eager to chow down. It must be lengthy expo-
sure to the cold and mountain conditions that shaped the
stomachs of Valdostans, because they were clearly like little
heat stoves, burning calories at a feverish rate. Nora blew out
the candles. A round of applause and a chorus of "Happy
Birthday." Then the deputy police chief's cell phone rang.
"Excuse me," he said, while inwardly delighting at Officer
Italo Pierron's perfect timing—Pierron was his favorite at
headquarters, and ten minutes earlier, while being buffeted
by the usual wintry wind and gulping down quick puffs of
smoke from his Camel, he'd asked him to make this very
call. "Italo," he'd told him, "in ten minutes make an urgent
call to me!"

"Oh hell's bells, it's the office," he said as he read the
display. Nora looked at him, a dessert spoon in her mouth.

"What is it, Italo?"

But it wasn't Italo calling. It was Caterina. "Dottore, I'm so sorry to bother you during your party . . . but Deruta and D'Intino . . ."

"Now what have they done?"

"D'Intino's in the hospital. But Deruta's right here at headquarters."

"Do you mind telling what the hell happened?"

"They were involved in a physical conflict."

Rocco nodded and ended the call. He threw his arms wide. "I'm so sorry . . ." he said, looking at Nora, and the whole table fell silent. "I have one officer seriously injured and another in a state of extreme confusion . . ."

The chief of police looked up quickly. "What are we talking about here?"

"Two of my best officers. They were on a stakeout, part of an investigation into heroin trafficking . . . evidently there was some kind of problem."

"But that's not fair," said Nora in a teary voice. Corsi slapped her lightly on the thigh, as if to say buck up, as if to remind her: "Unfortunately, my dear lady, this is the police-man's hard lot." But to a careful eye, the police chief's hand had then continued to linger on Nora's knee a little longer than was absolutely necessary for a pat of consolation.

All the other guests looked over at Rocco, shaking their heads in commiseration, though they continued to shovel dessert into their mouths. All but Anna, who maintained her half smile as if to say: "Don't try to bullshit me. I know you." Rocco told himself that he wasn't finished with that one.

"Excuse me, I have to go."

"Rocco, will you come to see me later?" Nora asked in a low voice.

"I don't even know what's happened. Believe me, I'll try my best."

"I don't believe you."

"I came to your aperitif, didn't I?"

"Call me. No matter how late. Remember, tonight my every wish is your command. I'm the queen and I must be obeyed."

"And you remember that I'm a deputy police chief of the Italian republic and I reject all false monarchist hierarchies." Then he said a round of good nights with a smile.

"Schiavone, don't forget," piped up the chief of police.

"Don't forget what?"

"The race. Aosta–Saint-Vincent–Aosta. The governor really cares about this."

"Duly noted, Dottore, you can count on me." He turned to go and ran straight into the waiter who was finally bringing a tray full of espressos. The tray and the coffee cups went crashing to the ground.

The waiter smiled. "It's not a problem, Signore. I'll go have them make new ones."

"Maybe you should order cappuccinos and breakfast pastries. With those, your timing might finally be perfect."

IT WAS WELL PAST ELEVEN. ACROSS THE DESK FROM Rocco sat a young man, maybe twenty years old, pimply-faced, incessantly chomping on a wad of gum. This was the kid that Deruta had managed to hold on to in the disastrous aftermath of the nighttime stakeout. The other wrongdoer, this kid's accomplice, had fractured D'Intino's nasal septum and made good his escape into the labyrinth of lanes and alleys around the train station. The young man's face had a blank expression—a dead-eyed ruminant that just kept chewing. Rocco stared at him in silence. The sound of his jaws and the clicking of teeth and slurping of saliva were an assault on his nervous system, which had already been sorely put to the test by this unbelievably shitty day that simply refused to end.

Chomp-chomp slurp, chomp-chomp slurp, chomp-chomp slurp went the juvenile delinquent's powerful jaws. He had a shaven head topped by a Mohawk held in place by hair product, in keeping with the latest fashion among soccer players. The surreal silence was broken by the noise of a solitary car going by in the street outside. Rocco had lost himself in a reverie as he gazed at the boy's red lips. His knuckles whitened as he clenched his fists on the desk. "Be a good kid and do me a favor," the deputy police chief said to the young man, finally breaking that silence. "Spit out that gum, or I'm going to have to make you swallow it."

The indolent youth gazed at him with indifference, and contemptuously went on chewing, in spite of the fact that Italo Pierron had pulled out a handkerchief and was standing there, ready to take the rubbery bolus. Rocco stood up from his chair and went over to his office window. Outside, snowflakes were spinning lazily down. He touched the pane of glass. It was ice cold. He heaved a low, hoarse sigh and then turned around to face the young drug dealer. The sound of teeth and tongue continued to fill the room. Italo opened his mouth, about to say something, but Rocco stopped him with a flutter of his hand. He took a couple of steps toward the young man. "All right, Righetti, get to your feet."

Clueless, the kid stood up. Rocco stared him right in the eyes. "Let's see if we can't get this conversation back on the tracks of mutual respect, sound good to you?" Then, in a flash, he let fly with a powerful straight punch right to the boy's midsection, and Righetti folded neatly in half. He staggered to his chair and tried to catch his breath. His eyes were glistening with pain and anger. Fabio Righetti had swallowed his gum. "You see? How easy was that?" asked the deputy police chief, and sat back down at his desk. "Now then. Fabio Righetti, born in Aosta on July twenty-fourth, 1993 . . . you're a tough character, aren't you?" The kid said nothing. He just sat clutching his belly with both hands and doing his best to breathe. "Let's summarize what we have. My officers caught you with your friend while you were selling a few baggies. Of coke."

Fabio Righetti didn't answer.

Rocco went on. "Your buddy smashed his forehead into Officer D'Intino's face, fracturing his nasal septum, and took off. You, on the other hand, strapping big chump that you are, let yourself get caught by Deruta, a police officer who weighs in at two hundred eighty-five pounds, with a serious onset of emphysema. Believe me, this isn't going to do much for your reputation."

A complicit little smile began to play over Officer Pierron's lips.

"You had four more bags of stepped-on cocaine on your person. And that will send you straight into a jail cell." No effect: the kid was tough. Not a word. "You don't feel like telling me where you got that coke and who gave it to you, do you?" Pierron went over to the kid. "Come on, Fabio, if you give the deputy police chief a little information, then we'll give you a hand, you know that."

Finally the kid opened his mouth and spoke. "Go fuck yourself!" he said.

So the avuncular approach hadn't worked. Rocco expected that, but mentally he praised Italo's effort.

"It's okay, Italo, Righetti here is a tough kid and he's not talking. Right?"

The dealer sat there, silent as a pillar of salt. Rocco looked at the hand that had punched the kid in the belly, then he pulled open a drawer. Inside were six fat joints, ready to smoke. He needed one, and without it he was pretty sure things weren't going to trend in the right direction. "If you don't mind, Pierron?"

Italo nodded, and the deputy police chief fired one up. Fabio Righetti's eyes opened wide and he just barely smiled as Schiavone took a good hard tug on the joint, held the smoke in his lungs for several seconds, and then finally exhaled and shut his eyes. "I make them at home with a rolling machine. I've never been good at rolling them by hand . . ."

The drug dealer grinned. "What, you smoke joints?"

"What's that? You forget about 'sir'?"

"What, you smoke joints, sir?" Righetti corrected himself. Underneath his pose as a two-bit neighborhood gangster, behind his Mohawk and the tattooed serpent peeking out from his neck, this was just a good, well-brought-up kid. And Rocco knew it.

He stuck the joint in his mouth and went back to looking at the notes he had on his desk. "So how far did you make it in school?"

Righetti didn't understand. "Sophomore year of high school . . ." he answered uncertainly, with no clear idea of what the cop across the desk from him was driving at.

"Then you wouldn't have studied Hegel. Listen, have you ever heard of him?"

"He's a center fielder, right?"

"No, that's Hagen, and he's a defender who even played on the Norwegian national team. No, I'm talking about Hegel, the philosopher. And what would you know about him? Anyway, to make a long story short, this guy said that reading the morning newspaper was the realist's morning prayer. You get the concept? If you're religious, you get up in the morning and you pray to God, but if you don't believe in God, you read the morning paper. But for me, this is my morning prayer." He raised the joint to his lips and took another puff. "Every morning, before I start my day, unless I smoke one of these, I'm irritable, I have a hard time thinking, and I'm pissed off at the world. And smoking one at night every now and then is good for me too."

Fabio nodded with an idiotic grin playing over his lips.

"Do you have a realist's morning prayer of your own, Fabio?"

The kid thought it over: "Francesca."

"Who's that?"

"My girlfriend."

"Good boy. You ever been behind bars?"

Fabio said nothing, and just shook his head no.

"All right, then. Let me give you a little useful information. Behind bars, you'll meet plenty of nasty people, and someone like you could become the realist's morning prayer for some guy standing six feet five and tipping the scales at close to three hundred pounds. But not three hundred pounds like Deruta, the one who arrested you. I'm talking about almost three hundred pounds of hard muscle, looking at a twenty-year sentence for murder, a guy who hasn't laid eyes on a woman for at least three years. You understand? That's no fun at all. And you're kind of cute, aside from the fucking zits you have, and I'm here to tell you that you should stop eating all that junk food. But in the slammer, behind bars, you're Miss Italy, believe me. Nope, no fun at all, no way. Trust me." And he stubbed out the joint in the ashtray. "Now, I know that you can't actually give me the names. 'Cause if you do, you'll wind up lying in a gutter somewhere, sliced open like a baby lamb at Easter. And actually I'm not interested in knowing the names of the guys who give you the shit, not from you anyway. But you could give me the name of your friend, the kid who assaulted my officer. Now that might constitute a bargain. We could bring him in, bust his ass a little, and if the two of you manage to keep from pulling any more fuckups for the next few years, you might even be able to lead a reasonably peaceful life in this town."

"I don't even know the guy I was with. This was the first time I saw him."

"Sure, and I'm a veteran of the First World War."

"Really?" the dealer asked in a serious voice. Rocco glanced over at Italo, who spread both arms wide.

"It's late, I'm sick and tired, and I'm going to bed now. Pierron, lock him up and tomorrow we'll call the DA's office. A special-priority trial, one judge, no jury, and behind bars you go. So long, Righetti, say hi to Francesca for me when she brings you a dozen oranges. Actually, as long as she's coming to see you, ask her to bring you an extra-large tub of Vaseline. It'll make things easier."

AS HE LEFT POLICE HEADQUARTERS HE RAN INTO Officer Scipioni at the entrance: "What's up, Dottore? You going to the hospital to see D'Intino?"

"Not a chance. I'm going to bed. What time is it?"

"Almost midnight."

"Shit," he said. Even the highlights of the Roma-Inter game were shot by now. "Can you tell me how the game ended?"

"Two to nothing, Inter."

"Hurrah. Take care of yourself, see you tomorrow."

"You be well too, Dottore. And if you want a piece of

advice, pick a new soccer team. At least you'll get a little more fun out of life."

"So I should take your lead and root for Juve?"

"What are you talking about? Juve? I root for Palermo."

"If I ever start rooting for Palermo, make sure you send me to an analyst. *Buonanotte*, Scipio'."

"YOU KNOW WHAT I WAS THINKING?" I SAY TO MARINA the minute I walk in the door. I don't know where she is. Somewhere in the apartment, that much is certain. "What if I gave up the apartment and just stayed in a hotel? Wouldn't that be better?"

"You've never liked hotels," she says to me. "You can't stand them, and you never could."

She's right. I don't know why, but I'm always afraid someone is going to walk in with a vacuum cleaner when I'm naked or in my underwear. There's no real privacy in hotels. They know everything about you. What time you wake up, how you like your coffee, and even who you call on the phone.

I'm freezing. I take off my jacket, my sweater, and my flannel shirt, and I start trembling from the cold. This fucking chill has gotten deep inside me, and there's no way to get it out of my bones. You can't still have snow in March. "You can't still have snow in March," I say to Marina when she appears in the door. She replies: "That's the way it is in Aosta. And if you ask me, you might still have snow in May if you're not careful."

She's holding her notebook in one hand. She's always on the hunt for new words. She looks for them in the dictionary, or else maybe she reads them in books, writes them down, and learns them by heart. Once I looked in her notebook. It's half-empty. If you ask me, she tears the pages out, like a calendar. "You want to know the word for today?" she asks.

"Sure, go ahead and tell me."

She runs toward the bed, barefoot. That's what Marina always does. She walks around barefoot at home, gets cold, and then dives under the blankets. She says it's more fun that way.

"All right then, the word for today is: hemiplegia. Paralysis of one side of the body."

"Paralysis?"

"Yes. Physical. Or paralysis of the soul."

"Am I hemiplegic?"

But she doesn't answer me. She puts her little notebook on the side table, pulls the blanket up to her chin, and says "Brrrr," with laughing eyes. This is my moment, now it's my turn. I know that she'll get angry, but I also know that she's only pretending. I slip under the covers.

And sure enough, she gets angry.

"You stink of cigarettes!" and she tries to shove me away. But I just grab her tighter.

"Come on! At least take a shower first!"

Nothing doing, what are you thinking? I stay right there. And I wrap my arms around her. After all, it's always the same story. When we get in bed at night, she's always cold and I'm always warm. Then during the night she steals all my heat and leaves me like this, frozen and alone on my half of the bed. In the morning, she's warm and I'm cold. And if I try to embrace her so I can warm up, she mutters and grumbles and turns her back on me. She always makes me laugh. Marina is possessive about her warmth.

She always has been.

I'm not possessive about mine. I'd give her every last bit of it.

I'd give her every last bit of it, if I could only wrap my arms around her again. Even just one last time. Just one last time, and after that, nothing.

SATURDAY

D'Intino was flat on his back in bed 14 in room 3 in the trauma ward at the Umberto Parini Hospital. His nose was wrapped in bandages and he had a gash on the right part of his forehead that the tincture of iodine made even more horrifying. He had both eyes closed and was breathing slowly. The physician on duty had accompanied the deputy police chief to the victim's bedside.

"Nasal fracture and a couple of shot ribs," he'd told him.

Rocco looked at the patient. He was amazed to discover that he felt something that came dangerously close to pity for the poor man. Until just yesterday, he'd have happily shipped him off to some police station in the middle of the Maiella mountains, but now the sight of him, so helpless, in that hospital bed almost stirred a sense of tenderness. "How long will he have to stay here, Doctor?"

"We'll keep him here for a couple of days, then send him on bed rest. Those ribs have to heal up."

Just then, D'Intino opened his eyes. "Deputy Police Chief . . ." he said in a faint voice, "have you seen what happened to me?"

"I sure have. At least now you can stay at home and rest up. You and Deruta were certainly on the job yesterday."

"Thanks. But did you catch them?"

"Just one. Can you remember anything about the one who attacked you?"

D'Intino tried to change his position and a grimace of pain appeared on his badly dinged-up face. "Not much, Dotto'. That guy came straight at me and gave me a head butt right to the nose. It hurt so much that I saw literally all the stars in the sky, you know that?"

"Every last one?"

"Not one was missing. Then I hit the ground, and I think that must be when I fractured my ribs. Because I broke my ribs too."

"Did you get a look at his face?"

"Just barely. It was all dark out. When it's dark out, everybody looks the same. He had a hood over his head. He was dark. I think he was part black."

"What does it mean that he was part black?"

"That he wasn't black. But he wasn't white either."

D'Intino was dragging him into a nonsensical conversation, so the deputy police chief immediately changed tactics and spoke to the doctor. "That cut on his forehead?" He pointed to a slice about four inches long.

"I dunno, what can I tell you? It's a narrow cut, and it looks like someone did it with a metal object of some kind."

"A knife blade?"

"Could be."

Rocco snapped his fingers in front of D'Intino's face to get his attention. "Hey, D'Intino, look over here! Did your attacker have a knife?"

"No. No knife. Ran away."

"I understand that part."

"Fast, he was so fast. *Teneva lu foche a li pidi*," he said, slipping briefly into dialect. "He truly had flames on his feet." And he dropped off into sleep as if a sudden bout of narcolepsy had swept over him. They wouldn't be getting any more information out of that man.

Rocco shook the doctor's hand, added "thank you very much," and then left the room that D'Intino was sharing with two young men with their legs in traction. "Break a leg!" Rocco called out to the two teenagers, and they both replied with their middle fingers held up in plain view.

As he was walking downstairs, he remembered that he still hadn't called Nora. To do that now would be a mistake, because he'd find her royally pissed off at him. But not to do it would be even worse, because it would mean putting an end to their relationship once and for all. As he was caught in that morass of Hamletic indecision, his cell phone rang. It wasn't Nora; the switchboard number from the office appeared on the display. "Hello?"

"This is Italo. We've had a piece of luck."

"What in particular?"

"There was a security camera running in a pharmacy

last night, and it filmed what happened to D'Intino and Deruta. I've got it here at headquarters."

"I'll be right there."

"Okay, but get ready."

"For what?"

"I've never laughed so hard in my life."

BLACK-AND-WHITE, WITHOUT A SOUND TRACK: THAT'S how the video recorded by the pharmacy security camera appeared on the deputy police chief's computer screen.

EXTERIOR NIGHT.

Darkness. A street. Traffic barriers surrounding an excavation site. Signs reading MEN WORKING. In the distance, a low wall, with two young men seated, chatting. A third young man sits astride a moped.

"HOLD ON A SECOND," SAID ROCCO. CATERINA STOPPED the video. "Are our guys in their car?"

"Look closely," said Caterina, touching the tip of her pen to the right side of the computer screen. "Right there, you see? Here they are, behind this bush."

"Ah, okay, right." Rocco nodded.

Behind the black shade of a leafy hedge by the side of the road, it was just possible to make out the shapes of two figures. "They look like an illicit couple necking."

"And to think, at their age . . ." added Italo.

"I told them to keep out of sight. This way they're not thirty feet away from the kids. Okay, why am I even surprised? It's Deruta and D'Intino. Go on, Caterina, start the video again."

"Now you'll see Righetti and his little friend show up."

Caterina pushed return on the keyboard and the video started up again.

STILL EXTERIOR NIGHT.

From the end of the street suddenly two shadows emerge. Wearing hoodies.

The two new arrivals go over to the trio, who turn to greet them. Fist bumps and high-fives. Righetti and his partner stick their hands into their pockets and pull out baggies.

"NOW WATCH THIS, HERE'S WHERE IT HAPPENS," SAID Inspector Rispoli.

FROM THE HEDGE WHERE D'INTINO AND DERUTA ARE hiding comes a camera flash.

"WHAT THE FUCKING HELL . . . ?" SAID ROCCO.

"They used a flash," Caterina sadly admitted.

Italo shook his head. "That's just crazy. They used a flash."

THE FIVE KIDS ALL TURN AT THE SAME TIME AND look straight at the policemen's hiding place.

The stakeout is blown.

The three kids who have been quietly talking suddenly take off like lightning bolts, two on the moped and one on foot. At last D'Intino and Deruta shoot out of concealment. Righetti and his buddy stand there, frozen on the sidewalk, staring as those two cops emerge from behind the laurel branches. Deruta levels his pistol. D'Intino, on the other hand, is brandishing the camera, as if it were a pump-action rifle.

Righetti darts to one side and goes running headlong down the street, closely pursued by Deruta, who hauls his 285 pounds with considerable effort, while the other kid heads straight for D'Intino and knocks his camera to the ground.

Righetti in the meantime suddenly trips over the construction barriers. Deruta right behind him does the same thing, twisting and twirling like a bowling pin, landing on top of the dealer and losing his weapon as he falls.

The dealer's accomplice, on the other hand, is in the middle of a fight. He delivers a hard head butt straight to D'Intino's nose. As the policeman falls to the ground, his attacker folds over at the waist and grabs his face.

He's clearly in pain. There is no sound, but he's unmistakably cursing. The head butt hurt him too.

Nothing daunted, Deruta has grabbed Righetti by his trousers and, stretched out flat on the ground, is trying to drag the kid toward him while he unleashes a hail of kicks.

In the end, Righetti's jeans with the big side pockets slide down his legs and the dealer finds himself sitting in the middle of the street, in his underwear.

Across the street, the accomplice, bent at the waist and clearly in agony from the blow to his forehead, starts to run while D'Intino squirms on the pavement like an earthworm.

Now Righetti is back on his feet, in his underwear. He's lost a shoe as well as his pants. Deruta swings the pants in a circle overhead, like an Argentine bolo, and lets fly. The pair of jeans tumble between the fugitive's legs, and he trips and sprawls headlong across the asphalt.

The police officer gets a running start, leaps into a flying tackle, wobbling through the air like Rey Mysterio, the famous American professional wrestler, and lands with his almost three hundred pounds of bulk right on top of the hapless drug dealer, who succumbs, crushed under all that weight.

Officer Deruta starts bouncing up and down, his derriere crashing down on Righetti's stomach over and over; clearly unable to catch his breath, the dealer tries in vain to get that pachyderm off his belly.

D'Intino has finally gotten back on his feet; his face is covered with blood. He's managed to pick up his camera and he walks over to Deruta and Righetti, threatening the kid with his Canon. Then, in the blink of an eye, he vanishes, swallowed up by a hole in the ground.

He's dropped into the crater of the excavation, and now there's no sign of him on the screen.

Deruta, taking advantage of the fact that the kid is half-unconscious, has managed to get his hands back on his pistol. He tosses it from one hand to the other as if it's a freshly caught fish. Suddenly, in the black-and-white of the video, a tongue of flame bursts from the muzzle of the Beretta and the glass of a front door nearby flies into a thousand shards.

Righetti freezes in terror. Now Deruta is all alone, in the middle of the street, and he's aiming his pistol at a kid in his underwear while the screen finally begins to populate with people. Various people, rubberneckers and passersby hurrying to lend a hand to the police. Behind Deruta and the boy trembling in his underwear, a pair of hands slowly emerge from the hole in the ground, behind the signs reading MEN WORKING. Connected to the hands are a pair of arms, and then at last D'Intino's head emerges, as he manages to clamber out of that urban sinkhole. Standing just on the edge of the excavation, he wobbles back and forth as if he's standing on the bowsprit of a ship, and finally he collapses to the ground.

Out cold.

Fade to black.

ROCCO, CATERINA, AND ITALO JUST SAT THERE, staring at the computer screen.

"This video is staying right here at headquarters, and it is never to leave the building, is that clear?" the deputy police chief said sternly.

"Certainly, Dottore."

"Or if it does have to leave the building, I want to make sure I have a copy. It's one of the finest things this city has given me since the day I arrived. In comparison with this, Laurel and Hardy are, I don't know, Bergman's *The Seventh Seal*."

And they all three burst out laughing.

"If you'd be so good, Caterina, go back to the point where D'Intino's attacker runs away."

Rispoli dragged the mouse and started the video again.

Once again, you could see D'Intino bent over in pain and his attacker take to his heels.

"Start it from that exact point again, Caterì, and look carefully at the shoes."

Italo and Inspector Rispoli concentrated on the screen.

"They sparkle," said Pierron.

"That's right. There, you see? D'Intino did tell me that the guy's feet were on fire, and in effect, if you will . . ."

It was true. The fugitive seemed to be wearing shoes that sparkle and glowed.

"Those are the kind that are in fashion right now," said Caterina. "They're American, you can see them in the dark, for when you go jogging in the middle of the street at night, for example."

"Right, for example." Rocco stood up at his desk. He nodded, silently. Italo and the inspector stood there looking at him.

"Very good!" the deputy police chief finally said. "All right then, let's get busy. Caterina, go have a few chats with the Baudos' neighbors. Try to understand their habits, who they see, in other words, everything you can find out about that poor woman. Take Scipioni with you; he strikes me as a solid cop."

"All right, I'm on my way."

"Do you have civilian clothing you can put on?" he asked her.

"Why?"

"Because if people see you in civilian dress they're much more likely to talk. Didn't you know that?"

"I've got a change of clothes downstairs, in the locker room."

"Get changed and go."

"You learn something new every day," the inspector said with a smile, then left the deputy police chief's office.

"So what are you and I going to do, Rocco?" asked Italo as soon as they were alone.

"You and I are going to go pay a call on Fumagalli at the hospital."

"All right. Okay if I wait outside the morgue?"

"No. You need to get used to it."

"Why?"

"Because it's part of your job, for Christ's sake. Do I really have to explain that to you every single time?"

Italo nodded his head, not particularly convinced, while Rocco went over to the window. He clasped his hands together behind his back and stood there, watching.

"Well? Aren't we going?" asked Italo, with his hand on the door handle.

"Wait five minutes."

It had stopped snowing and the wind had died down a
bit too. But the clouds still clung to the mountaintops, and
the sun had to be out there somewhere, but it just couldn't
penetrate that dense and cottony blanket. Rocco Schiavone
watched people strolling blithely down the sidewalks, with
the gait of a carefree Saturday morning. There were young
people loading skis onto the roof of an off-road vehicle, and
a man in his fifties walking an Irish setter; the dog held
its head high, sniffing at the air. Its tail was straight and
motionless: the dog had caught a whiff of something. The
deputy police chief smiled at the thought of how closely he
resembled that gundog. He'd spent most of his life identifying scents that shouldn't be there—a single sour note and
the reason it smelled.

At last, the wait was over. He saw Officer Scipioni walk
out the front door of headquarters, followed by Caterina Rispoli. Knee-length skirt and high heels in spite of the cold, a
little black overcoat, unbuttoned in front. The deputy police
chief's eyes had turned into two directional lasers. The inspector had a healthy pair of breasts that swelled proudly
from under her sweater, and a pair of slender ankles.
Shapely calves, long and tapered. He watched her get into
the car and when she swung her leg in, he caught a generous
glimpse of thigh.

He'd been right; he'd nailed it. Under her bulky awkward police uniform was hidden a highly desirable woman.
Too bad about the overcoat that covered her derriere, but
even in her uniform trousers, he'd been able to get a pretty

exact idea. Caterina Rispoli had everything she needed back there too.

"Rocco?" Italo asked. "What are you looking at?"

"Mind your own fucking business, Italo. Okay, now that life has deigned to show us a smidgen of beauty, let's descend into the depths of hell and have a chat with Charon the red-eyed demon."

"SO I HAVE TO WORK SATURDAYS TOO," ALBERTO Fumagalli had grumbled as he tied his green apron, stained with rust that wasn't actually rust. "What do you people think? That I don't have a damned thing to do all week? Two dead of poisoning plus a fatal crash in Verres, and as if that wasn't enough, Esther Baudo. You know what? On a Saturday, for instance, I could go down and visit my relatives in Livorno instead of standing here freezing my balls off."

"Alberto, do you have anything to tell me or are you just here to bust my chops?" asked Rocco, sitting down on a waiting room chair near the morgue.

"Don't sit down. Now we're going to go in and see the poor dead girl. Is he coming with us?" he asked, pointing at Italo with a smile.

"Of course," said Rocco.

Alberto walked over to the coffee vending machine and stuck in his flash drive. "Come on, let's see if he holds out this time and keeps from vomiting on himself."

"Don't make me laugh, Doctor," said Italo.

"Never been more serious in my life," replied the doctor. "You want a cup of coffee, Rocco?" He pushed a button and the machinery ground into motion. "Well, do you want it or don't you?"

"An espresso from that contraption?" said Rocco. "Have you lost your mind? Then you'd have to perform an autopsy on me too and figure out what poisoned me. I'll spare you the work." And the deputy police chief got up from the sofa. "Hurry up with that swill and let's get going."

THERE WAS THE USUAL SMELL OF ROTTEN EGGS MIXED with disinfectant and stale urine. A faucet dripped some-where in the distance, marking time, a unit of measurement that concerned no one in that place but Rocco, Italo, and Dr. Fumagalli. For all the others, wedged into their morgue caskets like winter suits put away for the summer, time had no meaning and no worth.

Lying under a sheet on the central table was the corpse of Esther Baudo. An aluminum counter ran along the perimeter of the room. On it were three stainless steel basins full of bloody clumps. The policemen were observing that array of samples on display and Alberto felt obliged to point out a detail: "That stuff doesn't belong to Esther. It's part of those two miserable wretches who died of poisoning near a purification plant. The usual things, liver, brain, lungs . . ."

Italo turned suddenly pale. "Excuse me, I can't take it." And covering his mouth he rushed out of the autopsy room. Alberto Fumagalli looked at his watch. "Twenty-three seconds. He's improving. Last time, he didn't last even ten seconds."

"Yep, the kid is making progress."

Alberto indicated the metal basins. "Should I have told him that those are just dirty rags?"

"It wouldn't have made any difference at all. He would have thrown up even if Scarlett Johansson had been lying in them naked."

"Believe me, sooner or later Scarlett Johansson *will* be lying naked in a place like this."

Rocco gazed at him levelly. "What the fuck kind of thought is that?"

"It's not so much a thought, it's more like an occupational hazard, the kind of thing I think out of force of habit."

"So let me get this straight: if you see a picture of Scarlett Johansson, tits and all, I don't know, in a magazine, the first thing you think about is the day that she's going to be stretched out on a gurney in an autopsy room?"

Fumagalli gave that some thought. "No. Not always. But to tell you the truth, there's nothing that I find less erotic than a naked body. Do you know that French poet who said that he couldn't kiss a girl's face because he was reminded that underneath that flesh was a skull that would one day lie worm-eaten in a coffin?"

"I have a vague recollection."

"Well, a naked body has the same effect on me." With that, the doctor tossed back the cup of coffee, accompanying it with a grimace of disgust. "Jesus Christ, that stuff is foul!" he muttered.

"Why do you drink it if it's so disgusting?"

"To remind myself that life is harsh and full of hardships."

"And you need that swill for that? Isn't it enough just to look around you?"

"Why, what's wrong with this place?" Alberto asked in a serious voice.

They walked over to Esther's body. The face was battered. Her lip was cut, her right eye was puffy and swollen, and on her cheekbone she had a dark bruise the size of a hand. On her neck was the unmistakable mark of the cord that had taken her life.

"All right, let's get to the point," Alberto Fumagalli began. "She didn't die of asphyxiation but from compression of the vagus nerve with resulting brachycardia and cardiac arrest." The cut down the corpse's chest showed that the medical examiner had removed the internal organs. "And we also have a dented right cheekbone and, on the same side, two missing molars."

Rocco nodded as he looked at the woman's face. Her hair spread out loose on the metal tabletop. Looking at her from above, you'd say that Esther was bobbing on the water's surface.

"She was beaten," Rocco concluded.

Alberto nodded silently. "Now listen carefully, because this is where things get interesting. Now, usually strangulation leaves a mark on the neck, from the cord or the rope, right under the trachea, but also all the way around. Practically to the nape of the neck."

"And instead here?"

"Instead here there are only marks on the front of the throat. Around the rest of the neck there's nothing but a patch of red skin. That makes me think that death was the result of hanging. Shall I make it a little clearer?"

"If you like."

"Why would you answer that question? It was a rhetorical question and everyone knows you're not supposed to answer rhetorical questions."

"I always thought that the rule was you're not supposed to ask rhetorical questions in the first place. They're less than fucking useless," Rocco retorted.

"You ask them."

"And when I do, I regret it. It's a habit I'm trying to break myself of. You want to go on? And that's not a rhetorical question."

"I'll go on. When a person is hanged, what causes the death by strangulation is the weight of the body. In other words, it's the weight that pulls down on the body, and the rope mark ought to be seen only on the front of the throat. Whereas when someone is actually choked, what causes death is the murderer's strength. The cord, the cable, or whatever is used, is wrapped all the way around the neck, and therefore it ought to leave a circular mark from the trachea to the nape of the neck."

"So what you're telling me is that she died from hanging?"

"That was the first hypothesis. But then I thought it over. And you know what I thought of? Concentrate on the scene:

Esther Baudo is being beaten. She faints. Once she's on the floor, the killer goes on working on her and strangles her. Do you see the scene, Rocco?"

"Of course I see it, it's what I do for a living."

Alberto snorted. "Talking with you takes years off my life."

"You can say that again!"

"Let's continue," Alberto went on. "So what do we have? A victim on the floor, senseless, incapable of any resistance. So the son of a bitch strangles her. And how does he strangle her? Let's just say that Esther is on her stomach. All he needs to do is jam his knee against the helpless victim's back as he throttles her esophagus and trachea with a cord and voilà! The job is done. He kills her by strangling her without leaving marks all around her neck, but only on the front of her throat, which is what we have."

"And then he stages the hanging?"

Alberto thought it over. "Look, I'm not trying to say that the murderer knew it. I'm just saying that there's a difference between the marks left by death from hanging and death from strangulation. Let's just say that he could have done what we said and as a result he lucked out. That's right, he could have lucked out, you see what I'm saying?"

"Then let's not rule out either of the two things."

"After all these years of experience, no, no, I wouldn't rule out either. Because the blows to the face that this poor woman took were serious business. I'm surprised that the beating didn't just kill her outright."

Esther's face was right there, a silent witness to the medical examiner's theory.

"What did they strangle her with?"

"Unfortunately, I didn't find any residue. No leather, no threads, no fibers, nothing. In any case, the rope must have been at least this thick." He held up two fingers side by side to show Rocco.

"That thick a piece of rope isn't something you're going to find just lying around, is it?"

"No. I'd say not."

"A belt?"

"For example, yes. Or a necktie."

The deputy police chief delicately covered the corpse back up. "And then they staged the hanging with a clothesline."

"Maybe the tie or belt were too short? One thing is certain. The mark of the belt or necktie, two finger-widths thick, is clear, then a little fainter is the mark of the plastic-coated steel clothesline."

"So you're saying they hanged her twice? That's strange, Albe'. It's all very strange."

"Well, that's your problem. As usual, I can tell you how and when they died . . ."

"I know! And the why is up to me. By the way, the when?"

"No later than seven o'clock."

"You've been a great help, as always. Take care," said Deputy Police Chief Schiavone, who then headed for the exit.

"If I were a betting man, I'd put a hundred euros on a necktie," Fumagalli added, thoughtfully.

Rocco stopped at the door. "Why?"

"Because the marks a belt would leave would be much sharper. A belt is made of leather; a tie is made of silk."

"A necktie . . . I'll have all the ties found in the Baudo apartment sent around to you. Could you take a look?"

"Certainly. If one of them was used to strangle her, there should be skin fragments on it."

"Okay, though I think that whoever did it must have gotten rid of the tie. But it doesn't hurt to try . . ."

"First-rate. Have all the ties found in the Baudo residence sent over. And the belts too; you never know, I might still lose that hundred euros. So will you let me keep her?" asked Alberto.

"What?"

"Esther Baudo? Let's say till tomorrow at the latest?"

Rocco looked at the medical examiner with a look of serious concern. "You want me to leave her with you? What are you talking about?"

"Nothing. I just want to finish doing a proper examination. Since they've just sent me two more patients from an accident up in Verres, plus the ones who were poisoned near the purification plant, I'm going to take a break and start over again tonight."

"Patients?"

"That's what I call them. And I assure you, considering what I do to them, they're very patient indeed."

"Albe', they're dead. They can't exactly complain."

"No, they can't. But if you listen carefully, there are times when you can hear them. They ask you nicely, in a tiny whisper, to take it easy on them."

Rocco bit his lip. He left without saying another word, but with the personal conviction that Alberto Fumagalli seriously needed some time off. A break, in other words, fifteen days on a sunny beach to restore his sense of proportion and re-establish the boundary that lies between life and death.

HE'D PREPARED A WHOLE SPEECH. OR, REALLY, HE'D prepared a plausible excuse to tell Nora. He tried to peer in through the plate glass window of the wedding gown shop, but the sumptuous wedding dress, its skirt embroidered with beads, blocked his view. He would have to go in and take matters head-on. Only he couldn't seem to bring himself to do it. And he felt like an idiot. He'd walked clear across town to the shop, and now he wasn't going in. But he couldn't do it. In part because, in the end, he didn't feel that guilty, really. He'd made things clear with Nora from the very outset. No questions, total discretion, and they'd see each other only when they felt the desire or the need.

Then why was he standing in front of that shop?

It couldn't have been remorse, could it? When had remorse ever made him turn back? He'd always and only followed his instincts. And his instinct the other night had told him to stay home. Even though it was Nora's birthday. Even though she wanted nothing better than to spend that night with him. He needed to apologize. And then? What would that do for him? There might be a reconciliation, perhaps. But was that really what he wanted? A reconcil-iation? Before another two days had gone by, he'd surely have mistreated her or ignored her once again, leaping flat-footed back into the doghouse. Instead, he could take advantage of the situation and leave, right now, without having to say a word. If he just stayed out of sight entirely, he could spare himself one of those breakup fights that were bound to come sooner or later—and probably sooner. One of those grueling, endless arguments, where you're as likely as not to say things you wish you hadn't. So instead of letting the thing die a gentle, painless death, he'd have to wade into a duel in which both sides were sure to come out the loser.

Better this way, he thought, better to just leave it alone. Keep your head down and your mouth shut. He turned his back on the shop and strode briskly away without a backward glance. But if he'd turned to look he'd have seen Nora, standing in the doorway of the bar across the street with a demitasse of espresso in one hand. She'd been watching him since he'd come to a halt in front of the plate glass shop window. As soon as she saw him take to his heels like a guilty thief, her eyes had filled with tears.

"THE DISTRICT IS CALLED COGNE," SAID ITALO, taking off as soon as the light turned green.

"Where is it?"

"Not far. Five minutes and we'll be there."

The wind had stopped pounding the city, and now the clouds, undisturbed, had gone to roost on the mountains, covering the whole valley. The color was a uniform gray and Rocco suspected that if the temperature dropped a couple of degrees, the snow would start falling. "If it snows again, lend me your piece and I'll shoot a bullet into my temple," he said, looking out the car window.

"Take it easy, Rocco, it's not going to snow," Italo replied. "The temperature has risen. If anything we might have a nice thundershower."

"Are we sure that the woman's at home?"

"Yes. Do you think we'll be done in time for lunch?"

"What time is it now?"

"Twelve thirty."

"No problem. At the very latest, we'll be out by two."

"Then so long lunch."

"This habit of eating lunch at twelve thirty, like patients in a hospital, is something you need to get over. In Rome, two o'clock is still prime time for lunch."

"Up here, two o'clock is teatime." And Italo downshifted.

"You know what? In March it rains in Rome too . . ." Rocco said. Italo rolled his eyes. It was time for Rocco Schiavone's nostalgic sonata. He sighed as he looked at the road ahead and started listening. He had no real alternative. "Only it's not a chilly rain. It's a warm rain. It's good for the flowers and the grass. All it takes is a little sunlight and the lawns are covered with daisies. You have to dress warm, but it's nice to walk around Rome in March. It's like when you were expecting a present as a child. You know it's coming, and the waiting is the best part. You're all bundled up but you can feel it in your bones, that things are about to change. That spring isn't far away now. Then you turn around and you can see that the women have already sensed it. Springtime. They know it long before you do. One fine day you wake up, you go outside, and you see them. Everywhere. You get a crick in your neck just from watching them. You can't say where they've been all winter. They're like caterpillars and butterflies. They hibernate and then they just explode into life, and it makes your head spin. In spring, all the ordinary categories are abolished. There are no longer skinny women, fat women, ugly women, and pretty women. When it's springtime in Rome, all you can do is stand there in silence and watch the show. And you have to enjoy it. You sit down on a park bench and you watch them go by. And you thank God for the fact that you're a man. And you know why? Because you know that you're never going to reach those levels of beauty and when you get old you won't have that much to lose. But that's not how it is for them. All those colors, one day, they'll dim and fade, they'll evaporate, like the sky over this fucking city that you can never see. And it's a terrible thing, getting old. Age is ugly people's revenge. Because it's the coat of paint that kills all beauty and reduces all differences to zero. As you watch them from your bench, it occurs to you that one day all those lovely creatures won't even recognize themselves anymore when they look in the mirror. You know something, Italo? Women should never age." And he lit himself a cigarette. Italo had braked to a halt outside the street door where Irina Olgova lived. At no. 33, Via Volontari del Sangue.

They got out of the car. Rocco flicked his cigarette away. "And this is supposed to be a deteriorating neighborhood?" he asked, slamming the car door.

"Let's just say that it's a quarter that has some problems."

Rocco burst out laughing at the thought of neighbor-hoods like Tor Bella Monaca, Laurentino 38, the Idroscalo di Ostia. Compared with those, the Quartiere Cogne was a residential neighborhood for the pillars of society.

THEY CLIMBED THE STAIRS ALL THE WAY TO THE fourth floor, where they found Irina waiting for them at her apartment door. There was a blend of odors in the stairwell but what triumphed over all others was the scent of curry, which Italo had mistaken for underarm sweat, a clear sign that this building was inhabited by immigrants from outside the European Community. "Irina Olgova, you remember me? Deputy Police Chief Schiavone."

Irina bowed her head ever so slightly, shook hands, and invited them in.

It was a small apartment. A tiny living room with a sofa that must also do double duty as a bed because there was a reading lamp clamped to the arm of the sofa and on a cubical side table there was a stack of comic books. The kitchen was carved out of a recess in the living room wall. Two doors presumably led into a bedroom and the bathroom. On the floor was a brown flowered carpet and on the wall hung a light blue tile with a phrase in Arabic and a number of pictures. The pyramids, a souk, an elderly North African couple, and a small snow-covered town that looked like it came straight out of a short story by Chekhov.

As if there weren't enough snow here in Aosta, Rocco thought to himself as he looked at the immaculate blanket of snow that covered the roof of a small wooden church in the picture. Then there was a photograph of a man and a boy standing in front of a fruit stand. The man had a jovial smile and a mustache, while the boy was serious-faced and had a piercing on his eyebrow.

Irina had brushed her hair and put a Band-Aid on her kneecap. She was on edge and kept twisting her hands.

"Now that you've had a chance to calm down, would you tell me about yesterday morning?"

Irina took a Formica chair and sat down in front of the sofa. "At ten in the morning I went into apartment and—"

"Hold on. First question. Was the door closed?"

"Yes, but not triple-locked. Strange, because I always find door triple-locked. Signora comes back at eleven after she goes shopping. Do you want to know a, what is the word . . . significance?"

"Significance?"

"Coincidence, sorry. I meant to say, coincidence?"

"Go ahead, I'm all ears."

"She does shopping at market where my husband, Ahmed, has stand and sells fruit."

"Is Ahmed this one in the picture?" He pointed to the man with the boy.

"Yes, yes. There he's with his son, Hilmi."

"Go on."

"So then I went in. I found everything in mess. Everything in kitchen, all mess. And I thought of burglars, no? So I ran. Then there was that gentleman downstairs . . ."

"The warrant officer," said Italo.

"Exactly, and then we called you."

Rocco looked at Irina: "Where are you from?"

"I'm from Belarus. You want to see visas and permits?"

"Thanks just the same, but I don't give a damn. Your husband?"

"Egyptian. But he's not my husband. We live together, but we're not married. He is Muslim, I am Orthodox. There are some problems."

"Well, understood, but as long as you have love," said Italo out of the blue, earning himself an angry glance from Rocco, who had gotten to his feet in the meantime. Irina followed him with her gaze. "How long have you been working for the Baudos?"

"I've been working for almost a year there. Monday, Wednesday, and Friday." Just as she finished saying Friday the front door flew open. A young man about eighteen came in, skinny, wearing a bomber jacket over a sweatshirt, loose trousers with big side pockets, and a pair of phosphorescent American shoes on his feet, just the thing to wear on a road repair crew late at night on a highway. On his left eyebrow was a brand new Band-Aid. The minute he saw Italo's uniform he turned pale. Rocco, on the other hand, was hidden behind the open door and could conveniently spy on him.

"Ah. This is Hilmi, Ahmed's son."

The young man swallowed and stared at Italo with his large dark eyes, hungry and wolfish.

"Pleased to meet you, Hilmi. I'm Schiavone."

As if someone had lit off a firecracker behind him, the kid flinched and swung around. At last he saw Rocco. Who was standing there, wrapped in his loden overcoat, leaning against the wall beneath the phrase in Arabic on the light blue tile, surveying him from head to foot.

"What is it? What's happened?" asked the kid. "What have I done?"

"You? Nothing. Why, have you done something?" asked Rocco.

The boy shook his head with conviction.

Italo pointed at Irina. "We're talking with your mother."

"That's not my mother. That's my father's woman," the boy corrected him.

"And didn't your father's woman tell you anything?"

Hilmi shrugged. He was slowly regaining control of his reactions. He shut the front door and walked toward the kitchen. "So just what would she have told me about?"

There he is, thought Rocco. He's just donned the mask of the pitiless gangsta again, using the American word in his thoughts. "That she found a woman's dead body in the apartment she cleans."

Hilmi looked at Irina, who nodded. "Who was it? Signora Marchetti?"

"No, Signora Baudo."

"Ah," said Hilmi, as he poured himself a glass of water.

"Did you know her?" asked Rocco.

"Me? No. It's not like I'm supposed to meet all the ladies that she slaves away for. And why would I want to? I don't give a fuck about them . . ."

"Right you are, good point. It's always best to mind your own business." At last, Rocco moved away from the wall.

"What does that say?" he asked, pointing to the light blue tile.

"It's a verse from the Koran."

"Can you tell me what it says?"

"I don't know. I don't read Arabic. I just speak it a little and that's all."

"Is written: the night of destiny is better than a thousand months," Irina broke in. "I know it because Ahmed told me."

"Do you go to school, Hilmi?" asked Rocco. Hilmi replied with a sarcastic snicker: "I try to."

Rocco answered back with a snicker of his own. "Would you rather work?"

"He doesn't like to do anything," said Irina. "He just waits for money to fall from sky."

"You'd better mind your own fucking business," said the boy, glaring daggers at her.

"And you just remember that what you eat your father and I pay for with money we earn."

"Well, fuck you!" he said and turned to grab the door handle. Rocco grabbed him by the arm and kept him from leaving. "Nobody told you you were free to go. We're not done with you yet."

"Let go of my arm!" said Hilmi.

Instead Rocco tightened his grip. "First of all, you call me 'sir,' because I'm not your dad and I'm not your friend. Second, you sit your ass down on the sofa and you listen to me. Got it?"

Hilmi ran his hand over the hair on his head, a buzz cut that was low and tight to his scalp, then jerked free of the deputy police chief's grip and went over to sit, straddle-legged, on the couch. His head hung low and he'd shut off all contact with the world around him. He kept scratching his forearm, where a Maori tattoo gleamed, probably new. He tapped one foot nervously, making his oversize orange gym shoes sparkle.

"It's murder," said Rocco, after a couple of seconds. Irina's eyes opened wide. But Hilmi just sat there, staring at the brown flowers decorating the carpet. "I wanted to tell you, because you ought to know. Signora Baudo was murdered. What can you tell me about her? Friendships? Habits?"

"Why did they kill her?" asked Irina, horrified at the news.

"We don't know that yet," Italo broke in, "but we're working on it."

"All right then, tell me something I can use. Did she have any girlfriends? Relatives? Sisters?"

"Relatives none. Signora Baudo was orphan. This I know because she told me. We didn't talk much. Basically, I cleaned and she stayed in bedroom, reading or watching television."

"She didn't work?"

"No. Only husband worked. He's salesman. Sports equipment."

Rocco went over to look out the window. "Shitty weather, isn't it?"

"You should see where I come from," said Irina.

"What's it like where you come from?" he asked Hilmi.

The boy sat with his head down, scratching his tattooed forearm. "I don't know. I went there three times when I was little. It's hot, full of people, and it smells bad."

"Wow, you're a regular patriot."

Hilmi jerked his head up and glared. "Why, would you be proud of a shitty country like mine?"

"No, not if you don't tell me which country it is."

"Egypt."

"I don't know if I'd be proud of it. But I guess when they were building the pyramids in Egypt, around here they still hadn't discovered fire. But why aren't you in school?" Rocco asked, sharply changing the subject.

"Teacher strike . . ." the boy muttered.

"So, Irina, tell me, did Signora Baudo have any female friends?"

"Often, on the telephone, she talked with Adalgisa. She was her girlfriend."

"Can you tell me anything else?"

"No, Dottore. Nothing else."

"In that case, thanks very much. Pierron . . ." The officer snapped to attention and walked toward the door. "You've been very helpful."

"I would just like to know who did this thing to Signora Baudo."

"I will be very sure to tell you the day we lay hands on him. *Ciao*, Hilmi."

Hilmi said nothing. And the policemen left the apartment. Irina took a deep breath, put the chair back in its place, and then turned to the young man: "Are you hungry? Shall I make you something?"

"No. I'm eating out."

ROCCO AND OFFICER PIERRON LEFT IRINA OLGOVA'S apartment building.

"I need to have a little chat with this Adalgisa," said Rocco.

"Who?"

"Adalgisa, Esther Baudo's girlfriend. I'm going back to headquarters."

Italo looked at him, car keys in his hand. "Aren't you coming with me?"

"No. You're not going to headquarters either. You're going to tail the kid."

"Who, the Egyptian?"

"That's right. Follow him. And tell me what he gets up to."

Italo nodded. "Mind if I ask why?"

"Did you see the Band-Aid on his eyebrow or are you blind? If instead of running your mouth and spouting bull-shit, you ran your brain, or if you looked around a little, then you'd know, like I know, that he had a piercing of some kind on his eyebrow."

"Well?"

"Just watch the video of the attack on D'Intino and you'll understand what I'm talking about."

"Do you think he had something to do with it?"

"I don't think it. I know it."

"So you see that I was right?" asked Italo as he headed for the car.

"Right about what?"

"Right about lunch. I knew we were skipping lunch today."

"Speak for yourself. I'm the boss, and first thing I'm doing is getting myself a bowl of spaghetti, then I'm going to track down this Adalgisa."

IT HADN'T BEEN HARD. ALL IT TOOK WAS A PHONE call to Patrizio Baudo and he had the address where Adalgisa worked. Even though he sensed—indeed, it was an unmistakable fact—that there was bad blood between Patrizio Baudo and Adalgisa. In fact, all he had to do was mention the woman's name to the new widower and he could sense a blast of icy air coming over the phone lines. Anyway, the woman worked in a bookshop in the center of town, not far from the piazza where the tax office building stood.

THE TAX BUILDING WAS A PIECE OF ARCHITECTURE dating from the twenties, and it was as out of keeping with the general appearance of Aosta as a pimple on a newborn's skin. In the minds of the Fascist architects, the town hall clock was meant to replace the bell tower. No longer would it be church bells in the service of Christ marking the hours of the workday and sounding alarms. Now it would be the clock, which was under the control of the top-ranking local Fascist official, the *podestà*. The geometrically shaped eyesore, though, did have one advantage. It told the correct time. Ten minutes after three. Rocco pulled open the bookshop's wooden front door. The place looked like a mountain hut. Wood-lined walls, which were stuffed to the ceiling with bookshelves lined with volumes, their spines a thousand different colors. Walking into a bookshop triggered a series of guilt complexes in him. Because time and time again, just like with a long-neglected diet, he made mental resolutions to start reading books again, one of these days. He could have read books every night when he came home to the apartment on Rue Piave, that nameless, drab place, devoid of any whiff of love, any scent of a woman. But he just couldn't bring himself to do it. As soon as he closed the door behind him, he was overwhelmed by a wave of unpaid bills from the past. The place was quickly haunted by thoughts thick as oil, thoughts that kept him from reading a book or even watching a movie with too complicated a plot. A turbulent sense of nostalgia, a yearning for the past, and the life that no longer existed took over; his books just lay there, on side tables and bookshelves, unopened: they sat there watching him as they faded and grew dustier with every passing day.

He stood by the door and noticed on the "new arrivals" counter a copy of the Turin daily, *La Stampa*, lying open to the local news page. There for all to see was the article about the mysterious death of Esther Baudo. A clear sign that the police chief had started talking with the news vendors, as he liked to call them, and also a sign that Adalgisa had already received word of her girlfriend's death, albeit in the chilly, impersonal form of a newspaper article. A woman who looked to be in her mid-thirties walked toward him. She was tall and powerfully built, with a strong nose that looked good on her face. She had shoulder-length hair.

"Can I help you?"

She had big dark eyes filled with the kind of sadness that only Russian actors in black-and-white movies seem able to project.

"I'm Schiavone, deputy police chief of the Aosta mobile squad."

The woman gulped and stood listening, saying nothing.

"I'm looking for Adalgisa."

"That's me," she said, tilting her head slightly forward. Then she extended her hand. "Adalgisa Verratti. You're here about Esther, right?"

"Yes."

Adalgisa turned and called out toward the interior of the shop. "I'm going out for a moment!" she cried. "Be back soon." Then she turned to look at Rocco. "Shall we go get a cup of coffee? Would that be all right?"

ADALGISA KEPT HER EYES LOCKED ON THE LITTLE coffee cup as she stirred her espresso. "Esther and I went to high school together. We've always been friends. Always." She sniffed. She hastily grabbed a paper napkin and dried her eyes.

"When did you talk to her last?"

"Thursday night."

"Anything odd?"

"Nothing, nothing at all. The usual conversation. I wanted to take her with me to do Pilates."

Rocco drank his coffee. It tasted like dishwater. He left the cup half-full and set it down in the saucer. "Let's get to the point. What wasn't right about Esther's life?"

Adalgisa smiled, stretching her mouth at both sides in a sort of grimace. "Aside from the fact that she was dissatisfied with her life and her marriage? That she didn't want to have children, but Patrizio was insisting on it? Nothing; everything was fine."

"Things with her husband weren't going well?"

"Things with her husband weren't going at all. Patrizio is an asshole."

There we go, thought Rocco.

"Why?" he asked.

"Jealous, possessive, he made her quit her job. Then, you want to know the thing that just made me stop speaking to him entirely? He made up his mind that I was a bad influence on her."

"In what way?"

"I'm no longer married. Let's just say that I lead my life the way I like."

"And what does that mean?"

"When I couldn't stand living with my husband anymore, I asked for a divorce and we each went our own way. Now I live as I please, free to spend time with anyone I like. My leisure belongs to me and, believe me, it's a beautiful sensation. And I've even been able to get a couple of cats, something I couldn't do with that pain-in-the-neck of a husband of mine. I love animals, books, and movies. I don't care about cars, soccer, or the newest-model cell phones."

"So Patrizio was convinced that you were trying to break up Esther's marriage?"

"You could put it that way. And if I had succeeded, then you and I wouldn't be here talking today, would we?"

"No. Maybe we'd be in the bookshop talking about books."

Adalgisa bit into a sugar cube. "Are you married?"

"Yes."

"And do you love your wife?"

"More than I love myself."

The woman popped the other half of the sugar cube into her mouth. "I envy you."

"Believe me, you shouldn't."

"Why not? You love your wife, you're happy with her, no?"

Rocco smiled, nodded quickly a few times. Then he shot a look around the store, as if making sure nobody could overhear him. But then he said nothing. In the creases around Rocco's eyes, or in his gaze, or even in his somber smile, Adalgisa glimpsed a black and bottomless well of sorrow. Her heart began to race and she decided to ask the deputy police chief no more questions. Silently she took his hand. "How did Esther die? Tell me the truth."

"Hanged, like the newspaper says."

"It was bound to happen, sooner or later."

A single tear ran quickly down Adalgisa's face. She didn't wipe it away. She let it run until it vanished over the line of her jaw.

"My poor sweet friend . . ."

"She didn't kill herself. Someone else took care of that for her."

Adalgisa's eyes opened wide. "What? Someone killed her?"

"Right."

The woman stood there, openmouthed. "I don't understand . . . by hanging her?"

"Someone staged it to cover up the murder."

"But who could have . . ."

"That's what I have to find out."

"No . . ." The word slipped out of Adalgisa's lips like a hiss. "No, no, no. Not like this. It's too horrible." And she covered her eyes with both hands.

Rocco said nothing and waited for Adalgisa to run out of tears. The barista who had brought the two espressos to their table gave the policeman a disapproving look. Rocco felt like shouting out that he was completely innocent. It wasn't his fault that she was crying. But the old man shook his head and stared at him coldly. Finally the deputy police chief waved his hand, with a gesture that suggested the old man could go to hell and mind his own business. At last, the woman got a grip on herself. She wiped her eyes one last time: they'd become two glistening black spheres. "Oh Lord, I probably look like a raccoon . . ." she said, with forced cheerfulness.

"A little bit," said Rocco. "What if I need to get in touch with you again?"

"Eh?" asked the woman, emerging from her thoughts.

"I said, if I need to get in touch with you again?"

"You can always find me in the bookshop. I'm always there, from opening time to closing. In the mornings, though, I get there at eleven. I have to go to the hospital."

"I hope it's nothing serious."

"No. My mother. Her hip is in pretty bad shape. I keep her company."

"Good luck," said Rocco. Then he picked up the check, read the total, and left a five-euro bill on the table. "Adalgisa, you aren't hiding anything from me, are you?"

"How on earth could I?" she replied, sniffing. "You're no fool, Dottor Schiavone, I can see that, and people find things out in this city. And I could never hide anything from you, believe me."

But Rocco continued looking down at her, without saying a word.

"Dottor Schiavone, do I seem to you like someone who hides things? In less than five minutes I've told you details of my life that are so personal not even my mother knows them."

"What does that have to do with anything? She's your mother. I'm just a stranger. It's much easier to open up to strangers, didn't you know that?"

HE WAS WALKING CLOSE TO THE BUILDINGS IN THE center of town, like a stray cat doing its best to shelter from the rain that had begun falling again. There were no taxis in sight; he'd have to walk all the way to police headquarters.

The Sinhalese standing under the portico appeared like a heaven-sent angel.

"How much?"

"Five euro one umbrella, seven euro two umbrellas."

"What am I supposed to do with two umbrellas?" Rocco paid and picked the least flashy one, red with black polka dots. He opened it and continued on his way to the office. He put his hand in his pocket and pulled out his cell phone.

"Hey, Farinelli? Schiavone."

"Ah, you're exactly who I wanted to talk to. Listen . . ." The assistant chief of the forensic squad was speaking in a strange voice, usually a sign that he was about to give the deputy police chief an angry dressing-down. "You guys left quite a mess here in the Baudos' apartment."

"I know, I know, but I need to ask you something urgent."

"I'm all ears."

"Can you send Fumagalli all the belts and neckties you find in the Baudo residence?"

"Mind if I ask why?"

Now this, thought Rocco. "Because I have to examine them. Likely murder weapons."

Farinelli laughed wholeheartedly. It was the first time Schiavone had ever heard him laugh. "I don't see the joke, Farine'!"

"So you're saying the murderer left the murder weapon in the apartment?"

"And you're saying I shouldn't even try?"

The laughter audibly caught in the throat of the deputy chief of the forensic squad. "No, certainly not, you're perfectly right."

"Do it fast. The medical examiner is expecting them. And you know what a temper he has."

"Him? The best thing for him to do would be take early retirement, take it from me. Now, listen carefully . . ."

"Tra . . . falgar . . . pea soup . . . grab bag in springtime?" asked Rocco.

"What?"

"No . . . tell . . . doesn't . . . anymore! *Hello? Hell?*" and he snapped his phone shut. With a smile he started walking faster.

THE DROPS OF RAIN WERE SMEARING LIKE TEARS across the window glass. If nothing else, they were bound to melt all the snow piled up on sidewalks and roofs. As he watched the rain pelt the asphalt, raising tiny jets of water, the phone on his desk rang, startling him.

"Who is it?"

"Dottore? This is De Silvestri."

De Silvestri. The old cop from the police station on the Via Cristoforo Colombo in the EUR district of Rome. The man he could always count on, the one who did things before he was told to, a crucial piece of the life he'd once had, a piece whose loss he felt keenly. "De Silvestri? It's good to hear your voice!"

"How are things going up there in Aosta?"

Rocco looked around his office, looked at the rain on the window glass. "Any other questions?"

"Dottore, I'd never have bothered you if it wasn't for something very important. Unfortunately, there's something I need to talk to you about."

"Your retirement?" asked Rocco with a smile. From the other end of the line came De Silvestri's companionable, booming belly laugh, reverberating as if in a grotto. "No, Dotto', I've still got to wait for that. A few more years. But it's clear to me by now, I'll start taking my pension the day they put me into a casket."

"Now, don't say that."

"But there's something else I need to tell you. Your replacement here, Mario Busdon, is from Rovigo."

"I'm happy to hear it."

"Yes, but he doesn't understand a thing. He doesn't know how things work down here. There's a problem that needs to be taken care of."

Rocco sat down. De Silvestri's voice had suddenly turned serious. "Do you want to talk about it over the phone?"

"No. That's not a good idea. Tomorrow is Sunday. I'm taking my son to the stadium. Juve's playing Lazio."

"Why would you take him to see a bloodbath? You're just cruel, De Silvestri."

"Not necessarily, Dottore."

"Necessarily, necessarily, take it from me . . . you'll get three referee's whistles and be heading back to Formello with your tails between your legs."

"Like the three penalty whistles you all got yesterday in Milan?"

"Don't start getting snappy, De Silvestri. Even if I'm up in Aosta, I'm still your superior officer. So anyway, you're going to Turin and . . . ?"

"And I'll make a side trip. You want to meet halfway?"

"Fine. You have any suggestion about where?"

"We're flying up. Do you know Ciriè?"

"Who the fuck is Ciriè?"

"Not who, where. It's a small town near Turin. Let's meet there. I'll drive down with a rental car from the airport."

"You want to tell me why Ciriè of all places?"

"Because I'm going to pay a visit on a close personal relation, and round-trip from the airport is just twenty kilometers. I wouldn't even have to refill the tank on the rental car."

"Do you have a place in mind?"

"Certainly. There's a bar on Via Rossetti. We'll see you there."

"At what time?"

"Let's say noon. I'll wait for you inside."

"De Silvestri, I'm not going anywhere unless you tell me the name of the close personal relation you're going to visit in this small town outside of Turin."

"Why would you want to know that, Dottore?"

"I just do. A lover?"

De Silvestri laughed once again, boisterously. "Sure, my eighty-four-year-old lover. It's my aunt, the sister of my mother, God rest her soul. The only living relative that remains to me."

"You're a man with a heart the size of a bull's."

"No, Dottor Schiavone, very simply my aunt just got remarried and she wants to introduce me to her new husband."

"She remarried at eighty-four?"

"Her husband is ninety-two."

Rocco thought it over. "Find out what it is they eat in Ciriè. It strikes me they've found the right diet for longevity."

"You can be sure of it. See you tomorrow."

"Till tomorrow."

WHAT COULD THIS PROBLEM BE? SOMETHING TO DO with old cases in Rome, maybe a friend of his was in trouble? But in that case it wouldn't be De Silvestri getting in touch with him. He would have received a phone call from Seba or Furio. Something to do with him? But he hadn't left any outstanding matters behind. He'd settled all his debts and collected anything that was owed him, and if there was something wrong with his bank account he'd have gotten a call from Daniele, his lawyer and accountant, certainly not from De Silvestri. He'd have to wait until noon tomorrow to find out the truth. The afternoon light was dying and with it the lights in Schiavone's office. He wanted to go home and turn up the heat, dropping by a *rosticceria* to get some dish of unappetizing prepared food or other, and then take a bath and watch a little television.

He'd completely forgotten about Italo Pierron; they

hadn't talked since two that afternoon, when he sent him off to tail Hilmi, Irina's Egyptian son.

He was thinking about that as he walked out of the pizzeria where he'd just bought six euros' worth of rancid mozzarella pizza. The rain had stopped, giving the city a bit of respite, but the sidewalks were a filthy morass of water and mud. He almost plowed straight into a woman walking in his direction.

"Excuse me . . ."

"Dottor Schiavone!"

It was Adalgisa. She looked good in jeans and boots, bundled up in a Moncler down coat that stretched all the way down to her knees. The bookseller glanced at the packet with the slice of pizza. Rocco turned it awkwardly over in his hands, and for some reason he felt an urge to hide that evidence of his solitude.

"I was just heading home," the woman said. "But don't think for a minute that my dinner's going to be any better than what you're holding in your hand. I imagine . . . there's no news, right?"

"You imagine right. How are you, Adalgisa?"

"I miss her. I can't even bring myself to erase her name from the contacts on my cell phone," said Adalgisa. "I'd have called her today. It's our book club tonight. Did you know? We have reading nights at the bookshop. At first Esther never missed a session; with her notebook, she'd jot things down, ask questions, argue points. Then she stopped coming. Patrizio wouldn't let her. He was certain that there was someone in the book club who was more interested in his wife than in Edgar Allan Poe."

ANTONIO MANZINI

"Why Edgar Allan Poe?"

"We like him. Don't you?"

"Well now, tell me. Was there someone more interested in Esther than in literature?"

"Sure. A seventy-two-year-old CPA who's recovering from a recent stroke and Federico, a thirty-five-year-old tango dancer, who's been living with Raul for seven years."

"Then we're done with the book club."

Adalgisa walked forward a couple of steps, her eyes on the ground. "That's right. Done with the book club. Esther wanted to write. That was her dream. To tell the truth, it was both of ours, ever since high school. She'd start a short story, but she'd always quit halfway through. Her creative drive was manic-depressive. That is, either she was inspired or she was depressed. There wasn't room for both at the same time."

"What about you, Adalgisa? Do you write?"

"Yes, since I started living alone. They may publish a novel of mine."

"Autobiographical?"

"I'm not that interesting. No, it's a detective novel. I like detective novels. Maybe, I was just thinking, if I give you my novel you might be able to give me some advice. You must have seen plenty of things in your line of work, no?"

Adalgisa smiled. Only with her mouth, though. Her eyes remained sad, veiled, as if a highlighter had run over them, leaving a patina of gray.

"Yes. I've seen plenty of things."

"My book is about a perfect crime."

"There's no such thing as a perfect crime. You know why? Because it was committed in the first place. And that's enough. If anything, there are some very lucky criminals."

Adalgisa nodded. "Do you read much?"

"I'd like to. I don't have time. Sometimes at night. The one who used to read was my wife," Rocco said.

"I don't like that past tense."

"Neither do I, believe me."

"You, sir, are a man full of regrets. How do you live with them?"

"Uncomfortably. Don't you have any regrets of your own?"

The woman did nothing but shrug, then pointed to a building entrance. "This is my place. Can I call you by your first name?"

"Sure. I started calling you Adalgisa already without even asking."

"Now you know where I live. You've been in town six months already. I hope you'll consider me a friend."

Rocco looked at the building. It was a two-story building, very nice. "How do you know that I've been here for six months?"

Adalgisa smiled again and started walking toward her front entrance, escorted by the deputy police chief. "Because I read the papers. I followed that whole case up at Champoluc, in February. I told you that I like detective novels and true crime, no? You were very good. Maybe someday you'll tell me how you wound up here, in Aosta."

"A special reward vacation."

They laughed together. Once again, Adalgisa laughed with her mouth. Never with her eyes.

"Seeing that you know so much about me, you must know where I live too."

"No. That's your private life. All I know are things about your public life. Life on the street. The things I've read in the papers. I told you, I read a lot. And I keep my eyes open."

"So do you have a book club or a hairdresser?"

"All aspiring writers, in the final analysis, are tremendous gossips."

"We have another word for people like that in Rome."

"Busybodies?"

Rocco smiled. "There was nothing you could have done for Esther. Don't feel guilty. And above all, don't feel tortured by remorse."

"It's much more complicated than that, Rocco."

"Then why don't you tell me how it is?"

"It's not worth it. It's a long and complicated story. Maybe someday, when we're better friends . . ." Then she pulled out her house keys. "See you soon, Rocco Schiavone."

"I hope I'll have better news for you."

"Find out who did it. Please."

"Don't worry. Where do you think the asshole can go?"

"Do you think it was a man?"

"Yes. To haul a body up on a cable through a lamp hook, you'd need to be good and strong, wouldn't you?"

"It wouldn't be easy," said Adalgisa, and her eyes turned sad and filmy again. She was picturing the scene to herself.

Her best friend, strung up like a side of beef in a butcher's freezer.

"Right. How do you think he did it?"

She was leaning on the small wooden door that opened in from the larger carriage door of the building. The bright light from the stairway illuminated a quarter of her face. "It's not something I like to think about."

"You say you write detective stories. So give me your take on it."

Adalgisa took a deep breath. "Maybe I'd do what mountain climbers do when they're faced with a sheer wall. With a carabiner, and then just haul her up."

"Yes, up in these mountains that strikes me as the most apt image. So you're saying he used a carabiner. Or a pulley?"

"Yes. That's the kind of thing I'd imagine."

"Very good. It's the only way."

"Is that how he did it?" the woman asked in a faint voice.

"Yes. He used a cable, anchored to the leg of a heavy piece of furniture."

Rocco's Nokia rang. The deputy police chief stuck his hand in his pocket. It was police headquarters. "Sorry, I have to take this," he said, and waved good-bye to Adalgisa. "See you later," he said.

The woman walked through the front door and closed it behind her, vanishing from Rocco's view.

"This is Officer Pierron."

"I was just thinking about you, Italo. What news do you have for me?"

"That I came back to headquarters but you weren't here. We need to have a quick chat. Can we meet at your place?"

"Are you crazy? Come into the center of town, I'll wait for you at the bar in Piazza Chanoux."

"Let me give Deruta a couple of documents, and then I'll be right there."

Then Italo hung up without completely hanging up, so Rocco was able to catch a snatch of the conversation between the two officers.

"Deruta, I have to go see the deputy police chief. Can you finish up these two documents for me?"

"Me? Why me? I don't even feel particularly well."

"This is a favor I'm asking you. We're working on a very important case."

"You and Rispoli act so snotty, all buddy-buddy with the deputy police chief, and you give me the boring jobs to do. But one of these days I'm going to walk upstairs to the chief's office and set things right."

"Do as you think best. Then you can talk to Schiavone. And if you want my advice, the less you say about Caterina the better it'll be for you."

"Go fuck yourself."

"No, you go, fat-ass."

Then he heard the sound of paper being crumpled, a door slamming, and a sigh. Clearly, Pierron had put an end to the argument and left.

Rocco stuck his cell phone back in his pocket and started off toward the bar, looking down at the package of pizza he was still holding. He tossed it into the first trash can he encountered. It would be cold by now. And if there was one thing that he didn't need, it was to sit in his apartment and gnaw on a slice of pizza with the consistency of chewing gum.

"ITALO, YOU WANT TO EXPLAIN SOMETHING TO ME?" Rocco asked the minute the police officer sat down at the table by the front window. "It's Saturday night. Where are all the kids?" He waved his hand to indicate the half-empty bar.

"I don't understand."

"We're in the center of town. What is there beside this bar, which is about to close? A pub and nothing else? What do they do on a Saturday night?"

"I couldn't say."

"What did you do?"

"I'm not from Aosta. I'm from outside of Verres, and for me it was like a burst of nightlife to come down to Aosta."

Rocco looked out the window. The rain had started pounding the streets again. There were a few people walking under the portico, a couple of umbrellas here and there; otherwise the place resembled nothing so much as one of De Chirico's metaphysical piazzas. "Maybe they go down to Turin." He got a secret thrill from being able to say *down* to Turin.

"Yeah, down in Turin there's more excitement. Clubs, pubs, discotheques, movie houses, and theaters. Oh, and speaking of Turin. Farinelli from the forensic squad called three times. He left the last message with Caterina. He's back in Turin now and I think he needs to talk to you."

"Yeah, I know. He definitely wants to crush my balls. Is that why you wanted to see me?"

Just then, Ugo brought two glasses of white. Rocco smiled in thanks and the man went back to his bar to serve retirees involved in a lively discussion in their incomprehensible language.

"No," said Italo, toying with his glass. "I followed the kid, Hilmi, just like you said to do. And I learned something interesting."

"Let's hear it."

"He stopped at a video arcade for half an hour, then he drove up to Arpuilles."

"Where's that?"

"Up above Aosta, it's a pretty good drive, four, five miles, winding mountain roads the whole way."

"So what did he go up there for?"

"He stopped in a little warehouse kind of place up there. He was in there about twenty minutes, and then he went back to Aosta."

Rocco finished his wine. Italo hadn't even touched his lips to his. "Where's the news?"

"In the warehouse. Turns out it belongs to Gregorio Chevax. Sanitary fixtures and bathroom tiles."

"I'm still not getting the news."

"Because you're not from here. Gregorio Chevax is fifty-three now, but in 1990 they sent him up for five years for fraud and receiving stolen goods. He sold three paintings that were stolen from a church in Asti."

"All right, now I see, Italo. This opens up a lovely panorama. Good work."

At last Pierron drained the glass of white wine in a single gulp. Then he smiled and wiped his lips. "So what do we do?"

"It's Saturday night," said Rocco. "Let's go have some fun."

IT WAS NINE O'CLOCK WHEN ROCCO, UNDER THE shelter of a black umbrella, rang the buzzer of a small house in the outlying village of Arpuilles.

"Who is it?" replied a harsh voice, clearly out of sorts.

"I'm looking for Gregorio Chevax."

"Sure, but who is this?"

"Deputy Police Chief Rocco Schiavone."

Silence. The only sound was the rain pelting hysterically down onto the umbrella's waterproof fabric.

"Come in." An electronic whinny and the gate swung open. Rocco walked through the front yard, a hundred square feet, following a gravel path that led to the house. A light went on on the ground floor, and a moment later the door swung open. Backlit, a figure appeared: five foot nine, in shirtsleeves. "Come on in . . ."

"Pleased to meet you. I'm Schiavone. Forgive me for the timing of this visit, but there's no time off in the work I do."

The man didn't smile. He shook hands and stood aside to let him in. He took Rocco's umbrella and placed it in a large vase by the door. Now, in the glow from three halogen can lights in the dropped ceiling, Rocco had a chance to get a good look at the man's face. The resemblance with a triggerfish was stunning. Those small, brightly colored fish that live in warm waters and coral reefs, and that have a gigantic, strangely elephantine snout and tiny eyes located in their midsections. The minuscule heart-shaped mouth was separated from the oversize nose by a distance greater than four finger widths, a space so vast that not even Magnum P.I.'s mustache would have been sufficient to cover it. The round expressionless eyes were too far from the root of the nose, as if they'd grown on the man's temples. He looked surprised, just like the little *Rhinecanthus aculeatus* fish, whose reputation as a relentless predator was well known to the other denizens of the barrier reef.

"What can I do for you?"

"It's very simple." He couldn't take his eyes off him. The monstrosity of that face, humanized by three days' growth of whiskers, hypnotized him. He had to delete the images from the encyclopedia of animals that were dancing through his head, or he'd spend the next half hour in rapt contemplation of that face. "I need a little help. Now, according to my sources you had a little trouble with the law back in 1995, am I right?"

Gregorio smiled. "I've paid my debt to society."

"Yes, I know that, but that's not why I'm here. I know that these days you're dealing in sanitary fixtures and bathroom tiles. You have a nice little warehouse and I believe you've got a pretty prosperous operation going, don't you?"

"I've got no complaints. I'm an honest businessman."

"I know that too. But still, you might be able to help me out. You may not know this, but lately there have been a large number of thefts in churches and private collections around here."

"I didn't know that."

"Now you do," Rocco replied. "And we're trying to track down the loot."

Rocco fell silent and looked him in the eye. Gregorio said nothing, waiting to hear the rest.

"You were in this line of business. So I was thinking you might be able to mention a few names and give us a hand, you know what I mean?"

Gregorio leaned against the wall, on which hung a handsome Neapolitan harbor scene. "No, I don't know what you mean. I don't know anyone and I don't have any idea of what the fuck we're even talking about."

"Why would you get so aggressive all of a sudden?" Rocco asked politely.

"Because it's nine at night, because I was just going out to dinner, because I don't have anything to do with that shit anymore, and because if you really want to have a conversation with me, you need to send me a subpoena and we can talk in your office."

"I'm sorry to have bothered you, Signor Cheval."

"Chevax."

"Whichever. But now, you see, I have to come up with

some results; otherwise the police chief is going to make my life a living hell."

"And why does that matter to me?"

Rocco laughed. And his laughter caught the reformed fence off guard. "True, very true, an excellent answer. Way too smart. But now you and I should play a little game. Do you know the game of What If?"

"No, I don't know that game. And I don't feel like playing."

"What if I were to say to you: I stole some semiprecious stones from an apartment and I need to fence them, then who would I go see? Who would I talk to?"

"Again? I already told you that I don't know anything about it and you should know you're testing my patience."

"But did you see? I was very polite." Chevax gave him a blank look. "But you keep acting like a little piece of shit. And that's not right, is it?"

"Now I'm going to—"

"Now you shut your trap and listen to me." The deputy police chief's eyes had narrowed to two slits. "I don't believe your fairy tales. I can smell a whiff of bullshit that's just befouling the air. And I'm never wrong. So now we're going to stop playing games and shift gears."

"If you think you can—"

"Shut your piehole, you talk after I'm done, you miserable shitface."

Gregorio Chevax swallowed uncomfortably.

"You refused to help me and that's a mistake, a terrible mistake. Tomorrow I'll come back up here with a search warrant and I'll take a look inside your underwear. Here in the house, in your fucking bathroom supplies warehouse, everywhere! Just one thing I don't like and back behind bars you go." The deputy police chief quickly grabbed his umbrella, so fast that he frightened Chevax, who recoiled as if to escape a punch to the face. "Starting tomorrow, it's going to be nothing but hell for you."

"I don't have anything to hide and I'm not afraid of you."

"I'm not here to scare you. I'm just here to tell you that you've made an enemy. And you couldn't have made a worse one. Believe me."

The deputy police chief opened the door, popped open his umbrella, and left the building, striding decisively. Chevax watched him cross the front yard in the pouring rain. He waited for him to go out the gate, then he shut the front door.

As soon as he had left the little detached house, Rocco pulled out his cell phone: "Italo? Are you and Caterina in position?"

"Yes, we're here. The last thing we needed was this rain."

"I know, right? Well, I'm going home now because I'm exhausted. Don't forget, keep your headlights off and stay in the car. And your blinkers off too."

"Certainly, Dottore, of course."

"I'd say, and it's just a guess, you'll probably have to stay there for a while. This asshole's not going to move until the middle of the night. Try to be patient."

"All right."

• • •

"DE SILVESTRI CALLED ME, HE NEEDS TO TELL ME SOMETHING about Rome," I say to her, but Marina doesn't answer. *"Where are you? Are you here?"* But she's not in the bedroom, not in the living room, and not in the kitchen either. The bed is made and untouched and the rain continues to drum against the windowpanes. There is one surprising thing about this city. The ability to withstand seemingly endless amounts of rain and snow. If even a tenth of this quantity of precipitation fell on Rome, can you just picture the banks of the Tiber, the lungotevere? There'd be dead bodies, wounded people, a biblical apocalypse. I threw away the pizza, and the refrigerator's so empty that if you talk into it there's an echo. There's half a lemon, a container with some junk in it—I don't even want to guess what it is, before long I expect it to get up on its own legs and take a stroll around the apartment—half a bottle of mineral water, and a bottle of Moët Chandon. What the fuck did I buy that for? What do I have to celebrate? What am I forgetting? My birthday? No, that's in August. Marina's birthday, on the twentieth? Impossible. For her birthday I promised her something, and that's a promise I have to keep. And it wasn't champagne. To commemorate Papà? Papà died in November. Mamma died at the beginning of October. And in any case, that's not the kind of thing you remember with a bottle of Moët. You don't pop the cork on a bottle of champagne to remember the dead. *"Why did I buy it, my love?"*

"What's the matter with you? Our anniversary," Marina replies. I can't figure out where she is.

"Our anni— Oh Christ! You're right! March second . . ."

"We've already missed it," Marina says helpfully.

"But didn't we celebrate?"

"Of course we did, Rocco. But you bought two bottles."

March 2, 1998. At city hall in Bracciano, the town where Marina's parents live. I've never drunk that much in my life, before or since. The party was on the lakefront. There are people who still remember it all today. But I don't. My memories of that evening stop more or less at nine. Apparently I even stole a rowboat from the lakeshore resort. "What on earth did I drink, Marì?"

"It'd be easier to tell you what you didn't drink." And now I smell the scent of her. I turn around and there she is, leaning against the door to the living room. "You need to eat something."

"I forgot to get groceries."

"Make yourself some pasta."

"Without even parmesan cheese?"

"Why don't you go to the supermarket, buy yourself something to eat, and put it in the freezer? That way at least you'll have something to eat every now and then."

"You know what I'm going to do? I'm going to smoke sixteen cigarettes, drink three espressos, down the whole bottle of champagne, and that'll kill the hunger."

"Well, that's certainly what I call a nice, balanced meal!" said Marina, with a laugh. How many teeth does she *have in her mouth? More than I do. They're too white to be believed.*

"Have you gone back?" I know what Marina's referring to. Did I go back to look for a house in Provence. Our long-time dream. To end our lives there, like old elephants bleaching their bones in the sun. "Have you gone back or not? It's not even two hours from here."

"No, I haven't gone back. And if you want to know the truth, I haven't even bothered to look on the Internet for farmhouses around Aix." I flop down in the armchair and avoid looking at her. Still, she asks me anyway. "Why not?"

"Why haven't I gone back?"

"Exactly. Why not?"

How can I break this to her? "Marì, they just cost too much."

"Money's never been a problem for you."

"And plus, it's Provence. Everyone speaks French."

"Yes, that's something you'd have to expect, what with it being in France and all. You always said you could learn it in six months. What happened? Don't you like it there anymore?"

I don't know. "I don't know, Marina. It's just not the same."

"But you need to have someplace to go, Rocco. Otherwise what are you living for?"

I turn around to look at her, but she's gone. I'm sure she's gone into the bedroom to get that notebook of hers, where she must have jotted down some hard word or other.

"And are not these, the masts inviting storms, not these / That an awakening wind bends over wrecking seas, / Lost, not

a sail, a sail, a flowering isle, ere long? / But, O my heart,
hear thou, hear thou, the sailors' song!"

I turn around. She's back in the living room. She has a
book in her hand. "Nice. Who's it by?"

"It's one of your old books. You should know," and she
shows me the cover. I can only make out the colors, not the
author. "I don't know, I don't remember."

She hides it behind her back. "I marked all these poems,
my love. They're beautiful."

I look at her. She runs her hand over her face, she flashes
me another smile, and then she vanishes. I sit on the sofa, too
depleted to go and get the champagne or even the remote control.
I feel as if I'm sinking into a bed of sand. I let myself go. And I
think. Maybe this is what dying is like. You just shut your eyes
and let go of everything, forever, you plunge into a black mass,
lightless, sweet and warm like a mother's womb, you return to a
fetal position, you close your eyes and you go back to what you
were before being born. An indistinct note that slowly goes back
into tune with all the others . . .

SUNDAY

The music came from the last movement of Ludwig van Beethoven's Ninth Symphony and it was being played by Rocco's Nokia, lying on the glass coffee table. First Rocco opened one eye, then the other. He was sprawled on the sofa, it was dark out, it had stopped raining, and his mouth was gummy and dry. He reached out his arm and grabbed the electronic device: "Who's busting my balls at this time of night?"

"Dottore, it's Caterina Rispoli. We have him here."

Rocco dragged himself up to a sitting position and rubbed his eyes: "Who do you have where? What time is it?"

"It's three in the morning. And we have Gregorio Chevax out front of his warehouse. It might be a good idea for you to swing on by, sir."

"He fell for it?"

"Like a fat chicken," she said, using a common Italian phrase.

"Would you explain something to me, Caterina? Would

you tell me why people say someone falls for it like a fat chicken? Where is it these fat chickens fall from?"

"I don't know, it's just a figure of speech."

"Well, it's bullshit." He snapped shut his cell phone and got to his feet. He uncricked his neck and took a deep breath. "Well, let's go talk to this dumb cluck. Or maybe I should say, let's go talk to this triggerfish."

The road was black and there wasn't a star in the sky. At the end of the straightaway, behind the crowns of the trees that concealed the curve, a glow of light broke the darkness, a milky white halo of illumination. It might have been a house on fire.

Instead it was the headlights of the police vehicle meeting the headlights of a Fiat panel van. The two vehicles parked outside the front gate of the bathroom supply warehouse seemed to be having a standoff, or a stare-down. Rocco stopped his car and got out. The air was chilly. It was possible to make out the black shadows of the mountains that loomed over the valley. A light breeze tossed the branches of the fir trees. The dirty slushy snow had withstood that day's rain and was piled high alongside the roadway.

Gregorio Chevax was leaning against the hood of the Fiat Ducato. Italo stood about a yard away from him, watching him and smoking a cigarette. Caterina was sitting in the car with the door open, one foot on the asphalt and the other inside the car. Rocco joined the group with a broad smile on his face. Caterina leaped out of the car. "Gregorio!" cried the deputy police chief, throwing both arms wide. "We meet again so soon!"

The man stood there without speaking. "Well, what happened?"

"Come take a look for yourself, Dottore," said Italo, leaving Caterina to keep an eye on the reformed fence.

They walked around the panel van. The rear doors swung open. Italo switched on his flashlight. Inside were a couple of plastic-wrapped sinks, two sealed cartons, and an open aluminum toolkit. Inside the toolkit, though, were plastic bags instead of screwdrivers or drills.

"You want to see some?" asked Italo, picking up one of the bags. He opened it. Rocco peered inside and by flashlight there appeared rings, bracelets, and necklaces.

"It's full of this junk," said Italo, picking up another bag and holding it up, open, in front of Rocco's face.

"Excellent."

"Lot of stuff, eh?"

"There's only one thing in particular that interests me. Let's see if I can find it." Rocco grabbed the flashlight out of Italo's hands and started rummaging through the little valise. He tossed aside coins, cuff links, and watches. Italo followed every single movement. "What are we going to do, Rocco?"

"What do you mean?" the deputy police chief replied, his face poking into a bag.

"I mean does all this go to headquarters?"

Rocco smiled. "Now, let me explain something, Italo: This is all stolen merchandise. That means it's been reported to the police. In thieves' argot you know what items like this are called? They say they're bent. That is, their value is limited to the gold or precious stones you can get by dismantling them. Because a piece of jewelry like this can't be sold as it is." He pulled out a beautiful brooch shaped like a peacock and studded with blue and green stones. "Look at this one, for instance: It's an antique. It ought to be worth, say, ten thousand euros, according to bill of sale et cetera et cetera. But if you break it up, you'd get little or nothing. No, Italo, this stuff goes straight to police headquarters."

Italo looked crestfallen. He was hoping to put a little something aside, repay himself for that Saturday night spent roughing it. "Too bad. I was counting on it," he said to Rocco.

"Now open up the boxes too. If you ask me, there's plenty more. For instance, look at those vertical ones. You'd have to guess those are paintings."

ROCCO WENT BACK TO WHERE CATERINA WAS STANDING guard over Gregorio. He was carrying the peacock-shaped brooch. "Well, well, well, Gregorio Chevax . . . I bet you feel like a bit of an asshole now, don't you?"

The man had lost all the arrogance and pride of just a few hours before. "Caterina, tell me just what happened."

"Certainly. Chevax drove this delivery van out of his bathroom supplies warehouse at one forty-five A.M. And this is where we pulled him over. He immediately showed signs of extreme nervousness."

Rocco gazed at the man with a broad smile, but Chevax stared stonily into the distance, somewhere among the trees. Caterina went on. "At that point my colleague and I became suspicious and asked if we could take a look inside the van. And we found what you just saw, sir."

Caterina had finished her story. Schiavone wasn't talking. He was staring at Gregorio Chevax and waiting for him to say something. But now the man not only resembled a fish; he also produced the same limited amount of sound. The light breeze whistled through the pine needles. Rocco lit a cigarette. "If you'd been a little more polite, Gregorio, we wouldn't be here now, at three in the morning, freezing our balls off in the cold and wasting our time interrogating you."

Finally he raised his eyes. "I want to talk to my lawyer."

"Did you call him?"

"Yes, but he didn't pick up," Caterina broke in.

"What a shitty lawyer, eh? All right, let's turn this night around. You see if you can get in touch with your lawyer, and while you go on calling him, my officers are going to take you in." Then he turned to Caterina. "Get a couple of squad cars up here. Let's take the delivery van in and impound it. And tell Deruta to draw up a list of the objects recovered, with plenty of pictures. One picture per item, that's important."

"All right, Dottore."

"Chevax, what's starting for you today is going to be an ordeal in comparison with which Our Lord's tribulations on Mount Calvary will seem like a Sunday jaunt." He held up the peacock brooch. "I even told you, no? All I wanted was this, and I would have let you go back to your fucked-up pursuits. But you wouldn't lend me a hand . . . you had to prove that your dick was longer."

"When my lawyer gets his hands on this story, maybe you're going to be the one experiencing the ordeal."

Rocco smiled. "My friend, my life has already been an ordeal for the past six years, at least. You know what we say in Rome? *Lei mi fa una pippa*, Chevax. You're nothing but a jack-off to me. You and your lawyer. Shall I summarize the situation for you? You were caught red-handed with stolen goods in a legal police search, you have a rap sheet with prior convictions for theft and receiving stolen goods, and the only thing your lawyer can plead is mental infirmity. But I don't think he can pull that off. You see, you don't exactly have mental problems. What you have are problems with your IQ and I don't think those are considered valid grounds for clemency under criminal law."

Gregorio's face had turned whiter than the headlights.

"Can we come to a deal of some sort?" he asked in a low voice.

"What did you have in mind?"

"You're interested in that brooch. What if I tell you who brought it to me and we just drop the whole thing?"

"Well, if you'd given me that information three hours ago I would have been delighted. But it's too late now. Put yourself in my shoes. How on earth can I cover all this up?" He pointed to the delivery van where Italo was unloading box after box. "And then there's something you don't know. I already knew who brought you that brooch. I just needed to be one hundred percent certain of it." He buttoned up his overcoat. "Fucking freezing out, isn't it?"

Pulling up his collar, he went back to his car.

• • •

"SCHIAVONE! FIRST OFF: I DON'T LIKE BEING WOKEN up at six in the morning. Moreover, when it's six in the morning on a Sunday, let's just say that my annoyance and irritation are elevated by a power of three. And second of all, I don't like being called at home." Judge Baldi spoke on his phone with the groggy voice of a man yanked out of a deep sleep.

"I know, Dottore, but there are two inaccuracies in what you just said to me."

"Let's hear them."

"First of all, it's not six in the morning, it's seven thirty. Second, I'm not calling you at home, I'm calling you on your cell phone. And I have no idea whether or not your cell phone is necessarily at your home."

"Normally, at seven thirty on a Sunday morning, it is."

"I just assumed you were already poring over documents, Dottore. There's nothing I can do about it. I just have this picture of you."

"Schiavone, you just can't bring yourself to be fully serious even for a moment, can you?"

"I'm completely serious, sir. And the reason I'm calling you is that I firmly believe in rules and institutions."

"Go fuck yourself, but first tell me what you want."

"Two arrest warrants. One for Gregorio Chevax and another for Hilmi Bastiany."

"You want to tell me on what charges?"

"Sure. Chevax for receiving stolen goods. Hilmi for sale of narcotics, assault and battery on an officer of the law, and burglary."

"And you call me at seven thirty on Sunday morning for nonsense like this?"

"Does it help if I tell you that Hilmi Bastiany committed the burglary in the apartment of Esther Baudo, our victim on Via Brocherel?"

Rocco heard Baldi cluck his tongue. "Fine. I'll make myself a cup of coffee . . . Are you going to send someone or come yourself?"

"I'll send someone."

"Do me a favor. Don't send me that fat officer or the one from Abruzzo."

"Don't worry. The fat guy's not on duty, and the other one is at the Umberto Parini."

"What happened to him?"

"Hilmi sent him to the hospital, Dottore."

"Let me get this straight, Schiavone. When did he do that?"

"I had sent my two intrepid officers out on a stakeout. There was a brawl. We even have it on video. The security camera in a pharmacy. In fact, I'll make a copy of it and send it to you for your information."

"I know them. They're those surveillance videos in black-and-white, all speeded up. You'd need the forensic squad to even figure out what's happening."

"Believe me, Dottor Baldi, watch this video and you'll thank me."

"Why?"

"Just trust me."

"How long is it?"

"Three minutes. When you were a kid did you watch the Saturday afternoon comedy roundup, *Oggi le comiche*?"

"Certainly, like all the other kids, Saturday at midday, as soon as we got home from school. Why?"

"In comparison with this thing, Buster Keaton was strictly an amateur."

"Schiavone, I want that video here at my home with all deliberate speed!"

HE'D SENT SCIPIONI AND ITALO TO GO PICK UP HILMI and keep him in a room where he couldn't talk to anyone else, especially not his buddy Fabio Righetti, with whom he'd dealt drugs and assaulted the two police officers. Chevax's lawyer was out of town and wouldn't be back in Aosta until the next day. At eleven o'clock, Rocco had gotten into his car, set the GPS to the address in Ciriè, and taken the highway to Turin.

As soon as he drove into the Piedmont region the sky turned blue and the sun, tepid and pale, did its best to warm up the countryside. He lost himself in a reverie, staring at the low, dark vineyards bunched up at the foot of the mountains, and the bristling Savoy outpost forts, grim and threatening and squat, set among outcroppings of rock.

Skinny black carrion crows flew in lazy circles over the stubbly fields in search of food. Now and then one would

venture to the middle of the deserted roadway if there
was roadkill to pick over. Rocco hated those birds. Even
in Rome they'd shouldered aside the other bird species.
They'd devour the eggs and ravage the nests of sparrows,
robins, and goldfinches, and their population was booming.
They were becoming the masters of the skies over Italy, and
by now the only winged creatures that could stand up to
them in Rome were the seagulls and the big green parrots
that had colonized the major city parks. Now those were
authentic birds of prey: they came from Brazil and when it
came to ravenous appetites they could certainly hold their
own with any common Italian carrion crow. Whenever he
was in Villa Borghese or Villa Ada and saw those parrots
flying overhead in formation like so many German Stukas,
green and red, with their unpleasant cawing cries, he'd
think of the first idiot who had opened a cage and let the
alpha parrot out, the pioneer of what had now become an
enormous deadly and aggressive colony that was systemat-
ically slaughtering Rome's sparrows and other small native
species. That said, when it came to looks, the parrots certainly stood head and shoulders above those mangy awkward carrion crows. Rocco waited apprehensively for the
day that some idiot in Rome decided to let an anaconda go
free. The alpha anaconda. Then things would certainly get
interesting. If nothing else, there would be a sharp drop in
the Eternal City's eternal rat population, which were now
rivaling Great Danes in sheer size. Roman cats would flee
immediately at the sight of a rat. Now he'd like to see those
swaggering rodent bullies faced with an anaconda from the

Amazon delta, thirty or so feet long, capable of swallowing a southern Italian water buffalo in minutes. This would be just one more collateral effect of globalization, and a positive one in Rocco Schiavone's opinion. Certainly, it would be a little complicated to deal with giant snakes draped over the branches of the plane trees along the banks of the Tiber, but there at least the enemy would be visible, less treacherous, handsome, and even poetic in a way. Moreover, those snakes don't carry the infectious diseases that rats do. Perhaps there'd even be a boom in the production of handbags and shoes. Who could say.

Immersed in that fanciful bestiary, Rocco pulled into the town of Ciriè and parked his car in front of the bar on Via Rossetti.

De Silvestri was already there, seated at a table all the way in the back with two glasses filled to the brim with some orange liquid and a small bowl of peanuts in front of him. He had his eyes glued to the front door and the minute he saw Deputy Police Chief Schiavone walk in, he took three long strides and met his old superior officer, embracing him like a long-lost brother. As he wrapped his arms around Officer De Silvestri's shoulders, Rocco realized that after working side by side with him for all those years, this was the first time he'd ever seen him in civilian garb. They broke out of the clinch. De Silvestri's eyes were glistening.

"You're looking well."

"You too, De Silvestri; you're in fighting trim."

"Come this way, sir. I ventured to order a couple of Aperols . . ."

"Alfre', why the 'sir'? Can't we just be on a first-name basis?"

"I can't bring myself to do it, sir. After all these years, I just can't do it."

The two men sat down and clinked glasses. Rocco downed half his glass at a single gulp. "Ahhh, I needed that . . . have you seen this lousy weather?"

"We're up north, what did you expect?"

"How's my replacement?"

"He's a good guy. He's young and he doesn't know Rome. He'll have the time he needs to get accustomed. Just think, he's only been there seven months and he already curses in Roman dialect: *mortacci vostri* and *'sticazzi*! No question, he still needs to work on his accent, but he's coming along fine."

They both laughed.

"How is my favorite protégé, Elena Dobbrilla?"

"She's getting married next month. If you ask me, she'll have lots and lots of kids and quit the police department."

"You think?"

"Her husband is an architect. That guy makes more than enough money for the two of them."

"To Elena!" They clinked glasses again.

It was only then that De Silvestri's expression changed. "I'm sorry to bother you, but there's something that's not right, down in Rome."

Rocco shifted slightly in his chair and moved several inches closer to De Silvestri, so the officer could speak a little more quietly. "What's this about, Alfredo?"

Rocco's old colleague spoke a name, "Giorgio Borghetti Ansaldo," and Schiavone's face became a mask of creases and hatred. "What's he done?"

"Same old thing. He raped two girls. One outside Vivona high school, the other one in the eucalyptus grove, near the Fonte San Paolo."

Rocco's hand gripped the little wooden table until his knuckles whitened.

"Deputy Police Chief Busdon says that we have no proof it was him. But that's not true. I'd never have taken this step if I wasn't one hundred percent positive, Dottor Schiavone."

"Just how can you be so sure?"

"The high school student from the Liceo Vivona got a good look at his face. And when I showed her an array of photographs, she immediately picked out the son of the undersecretary for foreign affairs. Plus this guy walked with a limp and wore a pair of glasses with one dark lens. Dottor Schiavone, it's him."

Giorgio Borghetti Ansaldo had raped seven girls, and one of them even killed herself, until the day his path crossed Rocco Schiavone's. Schiavone had beaten him practically to death. And because of that ruthless and feral act of vengeance, the deputy police chief had been sentenced to a grim penalty: immediate transfer. In fact, considering how powerful the rapist's father was, he'd gotten off easy, amazingly easy. More than once, as he was waiting to learn the verdict of the internal investigation, he'd imagined the sound of a cell door slamming in a high-security prison. Instead, he'd just been sent to work in Aosta. All things considered, he'd been lucky.

"What can I do, De Silvestri?"

"I don't know. We need to give your replacement, Busdon, a bit of a push, but most of all we need to stop that bastard. If you'd only seen the state he left that poor girl's face in."

Rocco stood up from the table. He took a quick stroll around the café, watched by De Silvestri and the proprietor, who glanced at him blankly and then went back to reading his copy of *Tutto Sport*. Then the policeman sat down again. "I'll have to come to Rome. Would you write down the names of the two girls who were raped for me?"

"Certainly, hard to forget them. The one from the garden is Marta De Cesaris—he'd already raped her once, you ought to remember."

"Of course I remember. And now he's raped her again. What, did he think he hadn't finished the job? What about the other one? The one who identified him?"

The old policeman looked down at the table. "Her name is Paola De Silvestri."

"De Silvestri? Like you?"

"She's my niece."

AS ROCCO DROVE, HE FELT AN INTENSE THIRST FOR blood. He felt angry, frustrated, and helpless. He could hear his heart pounding in his ears like a bass drum.

Thump thump thump.

A muffled and continuous bass drum that not even the volume of the stereo was enough to drown out. Outside the windshield and beyond the strip of asphalt, he glimpsed in the reflections off the windshield the face of Giorgio Borghetti Ansaldo, as he recalled it on the last day he'd seen him at the DA's office. Those protruding teeth, the thin untidy stands of hair on the sides of his cranium, the stupid, lifeless bovine eyes, the cadaverous white hands, and the freckles sprayed across his face like a helpless spurt of diarrhea. He hadn't even had time to go home and rest up from the injuries the deputy police chief had inflicted on him, and the psychopath was already back at work.

He had to get back to Rome. He had to stop that mental defective, the son of the powerful undersecretary; Rocco remembered one of the few meetings he'd had with the father, when he'd recommended pharmaceuticals for his son and, if that treatment failed, proceeding directly to chemical castration. But the almighty Francesco Borghetti Ansaldo had obviously ignored his advice. He had defended his son and insisted on the innocence of that slow-witted thirty-year-old who spent his days at his PlayStation and his nights between the thighs of screaming helpless minors. He picked up his cell phone, switched it on, punched in the PIN, and inserted his earpiece. He dialed Seba's phone number— one of his longtime friends, someone he knew he could always count on.

"Seba, it's Rocco."

"I know, you old swine, my eyes are still good enough to read the display on my phone. What's new?"

"Are you in Rome right now?"

"I'm sitting on the can in my apartment right now. Do you want me to tell you exactly what I'm doing?"

"That's not necessary, thanks. So tell me, what about Furio and Brizio? Are they there too?"

"You're asking if they're in my bathroom with me?"

"You idiot, I'm asking if they're in Rome."

"I think so. Now, are you going to tell me what's up? You have some nice little project to offer me?"

"There's a sour note in Rome," he said. Seba said nothing. He remained silent and listened. "And it's irritating, it's a sound we have to silence."

"Is it something that's looking to hurt you?"

"No. But it concerns me, however indirectly."

"I see. You coming down?"

"I think so. I don't know when, but I'll be coming."

"We'll be waiting for you. All I need is a couple of hours' advance notice."

"*Grazie*, Seba."

"Don't mention it, brother. What's new up in Aosta?"

"It's raining."

"Same thing in Rome, if that's of any help."

"It's no help at all."

"Just one last thing, before I let you go. I want to be clear on one thing. Are we going to need the little girls?"

Seba was talking about firearms.

"Yes. Without license plates, if you can do that," Rocco replied.

"Got it. I can't wait to see you."

"Me either. Give my best to the others. And a kiss to Adele."

"We're not together anymore," said Seba.

"Ah, no? Since when?"

"Since that slut started going to bed with Robi Gusberti."

"Er Cravatta? The shylock?"

"That's right. Crazy shit, don't you think, eh?"

"Crazy shit. But how old is the guy?"

"Er Cravatta? Seventy."

"You let a seventy-year-old man take your woman away from you?"

"According to Brizio, Adele saw him as a father figure."

"But Adele never even knew her father."

"Exactly, no? Brizio also says that its called transference. That is, she's projecting the father figure she never had on Er Cravatta and so she's fallen in love with him."

"Since when has Brizio become a psychologist?"

"Got me. These are all things that Stella's been telling him, and she's always reading magazines like *Focus*."

"You believe this thing about the father figure?"

"Rocco, all I know is that I caught them in bed together in my apartment, in the same bed my mother used to sleep in, God rest her soul!"

"You can see that Adele was interested in a threesome."

"How a threesome?"

"What I'm saying is that she was trying to arrange a transference with both the father figure and the mother figure!"

"Oh go fuck yourself, Rocco."

"And you take care of yourself, Seba. See you soon. And you just wait, Adele will come back to you soon."

"Why would you say that?"

"Because they used to call Robi Gusberti 'Pic Indolor,' the no-hurt needle. And believe me, it wasn't because he gave kids painless injections."

Seba burst out laughing. "It's true. Pic Indolor . . ."

"So you'll see, she'll come back to you and she'll beg your forgiveness."

"And I won't forgive her."

"You *will* forgive her, and I'll tell you why. Without Adele you're nothing but a grouchy old grizzly bear, and you know you'll wind up in deep trouble. In fact, from now on why don't you try to be less of an asshole. Aside from all the bullshit about Brizio and the transferences, the truth is that Adele is making you pay; she's letting you know what life would be like without her. You must have pissed her off again, as usual, and she's settling accounts with you. A woman who seriously means to break up with a man doesn't start things up with Er Cravatta of all people, much less in your own apartment, where she could be certain you'd walk in on them. If Adele seriously wanted to break up with you, she'd do it with someone handsome and smart who looks half his actual age."

"Someone like you?"

"Exactly, someone like me."

The two friends laughed together.

"Are you sure that's how it is, Rocco?"

"I'm sure that's how it is. In fact, if you want, we can put two hundred euros on it. Two hundred euros says in three days, you'll be telling Adele hello from me. Are we on?"

"Two hundred euros? You've got a bet! If I lose, I'd be more than happy to pay!"

"And I'll be happy to take it. Have a good day."

As soon as he hung up, the alerts for six voice messages rang out like a burst of machine-gun fire.

"What the fuck . . . ?"

All six voice messages were from the same number. The main switchboard at police headquarters.

"What the fuck just happened?" he said aloud, and then his cell phone rang. Another call, from headquarters.

"Who is this? What's wrong?"

"Rocco, this is Italo."

"And?"

"Hilmi . . . he's disappeared."

"What do you mean?"

"He hasn't been seen since he left home yesterday."

"I'm there. I'm coming. Let's meet at the apartment, at Irina's place."

THIS TIME THE WOMAN HAD COMPANY: AHMED, Hilmi's father, the fruit vendor. Ahmed kept twisting at his mustache and his reddened, anxious eyes darted around the room, as if in search of something he'd lost.

"Let me get this straight. Hilmi went out yesterday and never came home?" asked Rocco.

"That's not exactly right," Ahmed replied. "He came home, but we weren't here when he did."

"How do you know that?"

"He took some of his things and then left again."

"He took backpack and clothing," added Irina. "And his wooden box. Not there now. That's gone too."

"His wooden box?"

"Yes. I think he kept his money in it," said his father.

"Did Hilmi have identification papers of any kind?"

"Certainly. Passport, why?"

"And is it here?"

Ahmed looked at Irina. Suddenly he rushed to the little piece of furniture by the front door. He pulled opened the top drawer. He pulled out his passport, and then Irina's. But there was no sign of Hilmi's. He went on rummaging through the door, muttering something under his breath in Arabic, then with both hands still in the drawer, he looked disconsolately at the policemen. "It's not here. This is where we keep them."

Rocco looked at Italo. "What do you think?"

"Me? I think it's simple. A train to Switzerland, and from there a nice fast airplane. Where to? Who can say?"

Rocco nodded. "We need to put out an international alert. What a pain in the ass!"

"But what has he done? Why would he run away?" asked Ahmed, stepping closer to the deputy police chief.

"Burglary, and assault on a police officer."

"Burglary? Where did he steal?" asked Irina.

"At the Baudos', Signora. The morning of the murder."

Irina and Ahmed exchanged a glance. The father put both hands up to his face and burst into tears. "No . . . no . . . Hilmi no . . ." Irina wrapped her arms around him. The fruit vendor let his head drop onto the woman's breast, like an overwrought child. And he sobbed brokenhearted, wailing so loud that he drowned out the noise from the street, car horns and all. Irina rocked him soothingly, her eyes wet. She looked at the two policemen. There were dozens of questions in her eyes, but she didn't ask even one. The two officers of the law couldn't have given a straight yes-or-no answer to any of her questions, and Irina knew it.

" . . . at his mother's . . ." Ahmed murmured, once his tears were no longer shaking his body.

"At his mother's?" Rocco asked. "What is that supposed to mean?"

"I'm saying that he went back to his mother's house. In Egypt. In Alexandria."

"How many years could he get?" asked Irina, displaying a surprisingly pragmatic point of view.

"I don't know. At least a couple, for burglary, and assault and battery."

"But there's murder, no?" asked Irina. Ahmed was staring Rocco right in the eyes.

"That I don't know. It's why we wanted to take him in for questioning."

"My son a killer? My son a killer . . ." Ahmed broke away from Irina's embrace and slowly, head down, without another word, trudged into the bedroom and closed the door behind him.

"What can be done?" Irina asked at that point.

"Put out an international alert and warrant for his arrest, an all-points bulletin for airports and train stations. That'll bring Interpol in on this, Signora. And that's outside my jurisdiction."

"And if they find him?"

"And if they find him, as we say in Rome, *so' cazzi amari*—it's bitter dicks all around."

HE'D WASTED AN HOUR ON THE PHONE, FIRST FRUIT-lessly trying to track down the chief of police, who was up on the slopes at Courmayeur skiing, and then talking to Judge Baldi. Baldi, as was to be expected, had turned over Hilmi's case to a colleague. Only an earthquake could get the man out of his apartment on a Sunday.

He needed to meet with Patrizio Baudo, but he wasn't at his mother's house in Charvensod. His mother had suggested Rocco try at Sant'Orso, the late Gothic church, one of Aosta's main tourist attractions.

It was the first time Rocco Schiavone had ever set foot in the place. He stopped, lost in a reverie as he gazed at the lovely church nave. It was intensely cold in there, and his breath tinged the air. He heard a creaking sound and at last he glimpsed Patrizio Baudo. The man was on his knees, eyes shut, forehead resting on his begloved hands, which were clasped in prayer. Rocco sat down five pews behind him, determined to wait and not to ruin that intimate, transcendent moment. He raised his eyes to the ceiling, admiring the forest of columns that were intertwined high above. Then he looked at the triple-arched Baroque chancel screen that separated the nave and the choir. But it was clear that the stone partition had been added in some more recent period. It had nothing in common with the late Gothic style of the rest of the church.

While he was engaged in those idle thoughts, he heard a rustle behind his back. He turned around. A priest had appeared. The priest smiled at him. Rocco smiled back. The prelate sat down next to him.

"You're the deputy police chief, aren't you?" he asked.

"Do you know me?"

"From the newspapers." He had a goatee, and his hair was close cut. His eyes were clear and untroubled. "You're here to talk to Patrizio, aren't you?" He jutted his chin toward the man absorbed in prayer five pews away.

"Yes, but I didn't want to bother him. I'm actually only looking for a piece of information."

"Perhaps I can give it to you."

"No. You can't," said Rocco. And he gave the priest a level stare.

"We're going to hold Esther's funeral service here. Are you in charge of the investigation?"

"You could say that."

"Is there any news?"

"No. There isn't."

The priest gave him a half smile. "You're a vault."

"Considering that it's the priest who'll hold the funeral

service saying it, I'm not sure I should take that as a compliment."

Just then Patrizio Baudo stood up. He crossed himself and stepped out of the pew. As soon as he saw Rocco talking to the priest, he scowled. He slowly walked over to them.

"*Buongiorno*, Signor Baudo," said Rocco without getting to his feet. "I didn't want to bother you."

"*Buongiorno*, Commissario."

"It's deputy police chief, actually. They eliminated the title of commissario a few years ago, Patrizio," said the priest. Patrizio nodded.

"That's true. Ah, by the way, Patrizio, best wishes for yesterday. It was your name day, wasn't it? St. Patrick's Day? San Patrizio?"

"Yes . . . *grazie*, Dottore."

"I just wanted to show you something." Rocco pulled out a photograph of the peacock-shaped brooch. "Do you recognize it?"

Patrizio's eyes opened wide. "Of course I do. That's my mother's brooch, and I gave it to Esther." He handed it over to the priest, who was clearly dying of curiosity.

"Where did you find it?"

"A fence had it!"

"Find out who brought it to him right away!" Patrizio Baudo shouted, and his voice echoed off the vaults overhead.

"We already know who it was," Rocco replied in an exaggeratedly low voice, hoping to restore peace and quiet to the house of the Lord.

"Then that's who murdered Esther. That's got to be the one!" Patrizio was having difficulty controlling himself.

The priest looked at him. "Calm down, Patrizio!"

"What do you mean, calm down? You caught him. Who is it? Who is it? I want to know."

"Please, calm down, Signor Baudo. I was only interested in the brooch."

"I can't believe it. This is the evidence that nails him. I demand to know who it is."

"We'll tell you, Signor Baudo, don't worry about that. Right now we're in the midst of the investigation, and I'm sorry but that's strictly confidential information."

"My wife's murder is strictly confidential information too, but everyone in town is talking about it."

"Now that's enough, Patrizio!" the priest broke in. "I'm sure that Dottor Schiavone is doing his best to catch the murderer."

At the sound of the pastoral voice, Patrizio seemed to calm down a little. His breathing was labored and he kept looking down at his hands, encased in brown leather gloves. "I'm sorry, Dottor Schiavone. I'm sorry . . ."

"Don't worry about it," said Rocco. "It's over. I'm in the middle of an investigation, Signor Baudo, and it's an investigation that involves you. Please, now, stop insisting and stay out of it. If you have no objections, I'll get back to my job."

"I haven't been able to sleep since Friday. And if I do get to sleep, I always have the same dream." Patrizio sat down in the pew. "Two men break into my home, two burglars, my wife sees them, they kill her, and then they string her up like a side of beef. From the lamp hook." He put both hands over his eyes. "Is that what happened?"

"I really can't say, Signor Baudo. But it strikes me as a reasonable reconstruction."

"If you've caught the thief, then this story is over," the priest put in.

"Not exactly. There's one little problem. But those are internal matters. I really have to go," Rocco said brusquely. "There are some grueling days ahead of me. Thanks for your help, Signor Baudo. And thank you too, Padre . . ."

THE WIND WAS NO LONGER BLOWING IN THE VALLEY and the temperature had risen slightly. He had the impression that it was warmer outside than inside the cathedral.

He left the church and looked around at the lovely piazza, with its bell tower and a linden tree that was said to be more than five hundred years old. That tree must have seen things. Five hundred years. A human being would certainly lose his mind if he lived even half that long, Rocco mused, his hands in the pockets of his loden overcoat, as he strolled through the ancient streets of Aosta.

THE VISITING ROOM AT THE HOUSE OF DETENTION OF Brissogne had four damp patches, one in each corner. Looking at each other across a table, Rocco Schiavone and Fabio Righetti sat in the light cast by the one small, high window, in absolute silence. The kid was pale and his Mohawk had started to wilt. He sat there, wordlessly watching the deputy police chief, and every so often staring at the floor. Someone in the distance opened a gate. Rocco seemed to be writing notes on a sheet of paper with a pen. Actually, though, he was just scribbling a series of psychotic doodles. The pen shot along, designing spirals, letters, and names without any logical sequence. And the Bic ballpoint on the paper was the only sound in the room. Then Rocco jotted a single sharp period—full stop—and raised his eyes to look into Fabio's. The young man had been observing him. He was about to chomp down on his gum when a light glinted in his eyes. He raised one hand to his mouth and spat out the gum; then he stuck it to the bottom of the table.

"You keeping that for later?" asked Rocco.

The boy nodded.

At last the door swung open and Riccardo Biserni, Righetti's lawyer, came in. Suit and tie, about thirty-five, a ruddy, healthy face, intelligent blue eyes. He immediately smiled at the deputy police chief. "Sorry I'm late, Rocco, but in-laws will be in-laws . . ."

They shook hands. "Don't think twice, Ricca', don't worry. On the other hand, you're the one who wanted to get married."

"Me? You crazy? She bear-trapped me."

"That's the first time anyone ever caught a lawyer in a trap, instead of the other way around."

"Well, if you want to know the truth, it didn't hurt a bit. Now then . . ." The lawyer sat down next to his client.

"How are you doing, Fabio? Everything okay?" he asked as he pulled a sheaf of papers out of his briefcase. "These are things I'll need you to sign." Fabio nodded. Rocco yawned and stretched and sat back down.

"How are they treating you? All right?"

"Fine. I have a cell all to myself, and I never have to deal with the others."

Riccardo glanced at the deputy police chief. "Is that your doing?"

Rocco nodded. "I didn't think he needed to familiarize with certain people."

"In that case, I usually record my conversations, but I can skip it this time. After all, it's a friendly conversation, isn't it?" the lawyer said. Rocco nodded.

"We caught Hilmi Bastiany, Fabio," he said suddenly, scrutinizing Righetti's face. "Your accomplice."

The boy lowered his gaze.

"And he had a few things to tell us. Tell me when I go astray here, eh? The two of you sold off some jewelry to get the money to give your dealer so you could peddle drugs in the gardens outside the train station. Sound about right?"

Fabio looked over at his lawyer, who slowly nodded his head yes. "We got the coke without having to pay, at least not yet. If we did well, they were going to give us more."

Rocco didn't ask who'd given them the coke. Right now, he had a very different target. He needed to go on bluffing. So he went all in and played his ace in the hole. "What time did you enter the Baudo apartment?"

Fabio snickered. "The Baudo apartment?" he asked back.

"Hilmi told me you were there at seven thirty. Can you confirm that?"

"I've never been in the Baudos' apartment. I don't even know where it is."

"I'll tell you where it is. It's the place you burgled and stole gold and jewelry that you fenced to Gregorio Chevax to get the money for the drugs you sold."

"I already told you. We got the coke without paying a cent. We didn't need money."

"Then why did you burglarize the Baudos' apartment?"

"I've never burglarized anyone's apartment."

He could still try out the final full-on assault. "Listen, asshole . . ."

"Rocco . . ." Riccardo intervened with an avuncular tone.

"Listen, asshole," Rocco insisted, "you and Hilmi went into the Baudos' apartment, you took the gold, the lady walked in on you, and you killed her. You strangled her! Then you staged the hanging."

"Rocco, what the fuck are you talking about?" the lawyer snapped. "Are you accusing Fabio of murder?"

"I'm not, Hilmi is. He told me that it was Fabio's idea to stage the hanging."

"I never killed anyone! What are you talking about?"

"Rocco, if you're planning to charge my client with anything of the sort, I'm afraid I'm going to have to interrupt this informal conversation and elevate it to a different level."

"Riccardo, I'm just trying to help Fabio out here, because Hilmi is trying to sell him down the river."

"Don't force me to go to the judge. If I have to leave this room . . ."

"Hilmi took a picture of your client inside the apartment, Riccardo. While he was rummaging through an armoire. You realize what that means? I'm just trying to save him from a homicide charge, for Christ's sake!"

"It was nine thirty!" Fabio Righetti shouted, freezing his lawyer and Rocco too, in mid-dispute.

"Fabio, if you want to remain silent, go ahead; you and I should have a talk first."

"No, I don't have anything to hide. It was nine thirty. Not seven thirty."

Rocco leaned back in his chair. "So you're saying Hilmi is lying?"

"Of course he's lying," said Fabio. "We were supposed to go in right after seven because Signor Baudo left on his bicycle. Only that fucking moped of Hilmi's had a flat tire and we were running late."

"Did you get a new tire?"

"Yes. At the tire repair shop in front of police headquarters. He can tell you about it; his name is Fabrizio."

"Nice, Fabio. So go on."

The lawyer was breathing heavily. He was like a panther ready to pounce, but the situation was already tangled beyond repair. Rocco thought he could practically see the lawyer's brain chugging away, trying to put things back together. "It was past nine by the time we got to the Baudo place. I know because I got a text message on my phone."

"When did you make copies of the keys to the Baudo apartment?"

Fabio looked up. "Three days ago. It was Hilmi who stole them from Irina."

"Tell me how it went."

"We went straight to the bedroom. I knew they kept the gold there." Riccardo Biserni listened in silence. He was taking notes, but there'd be no getting this cat back into the bag.

"How did you know that?"

"One time Irina told Hilmi's father that Signor Baudo kept a box in the bedroom and she had told him he should get a safe because leaving valuables around like that was dangerous."

"And in fact it was. Go on."

"We found the jewel box with all the gold. We were just leaving when we heard the key turn in the lock."

"Was it Irina?"

Fabio Righetti nodded. "Hilmi and I didn't know where to hide. We beat it all the way to the back of the apartment, the room with the door closed."

Rocco looked at the boy: "And what was in there?"

"How'm I supposed to know? It was dark, and I made sure I didn't turn on the light, or else Irina would have seen me."

"And then what did you do?"

"I heard Irina calling out to the signora. And I knew that the signora wasn't at home, for sure she was out doing her shopping. That's what she always does in the morning. Then I heard Irina running away, and I thought to myself:

shit, she must have noticed something, or she saw us. How could she, though? Irina tripped on the carpet. I heard a noise; it was her screaming and slamming the front door behind her. I waited a little while and then we both snuck out of the apartment."

"How did you manage to leave the building?"

"We just went out the front door. There wasn't anybody around. We ran for it and hid behind a car. Irina had stopped a man in the middle of the street."

Rocco stood up from his chair. "Good work, Fabio. You were perfect."

"I didn't kill anyone. I've never even seen the signora in my life, Commissario Schiavone."

"Deputy Police Chief Schiavone," Rocco corrected him. "Did you know what was in that dark room?"

"No . . ."

"Esther Baudo's corpse was in that room, my friend." Rocco and the lawyer looked at each other.

"Why did Hilmi tell those lies?" asked Fabio.

"Listen to me, Fabio, I already told you this the first time we met. If you want to be a gangster, you have to be born one. And you're no gangster. I just wanted to hear what happened in that apartment, and now I'm going to compare stories and see if you told me the truth. If you did, then all you'll be looking at is a drug dealing charge . . . oh, and burglary . . . and you've got your lawyer right here, and he knows how these things work better than I do. But I'll do what I can to blame the initiative for the burglary on Hilmi, that it was his idea to pull this inside job and at the very worst, you were an accomplice. You'll do a couple of months behind bars, and then you'll be out on the street."

"Commissario, that's the truth."

"Call me commissario one more time and I'll make sure you get life without parole."

"Yes, Deputy Police Chief," Fabio promptly corrected himself.

"But if it turns out you lied and you do have something to do with this murder, then things change." And he looked at the lawyer. "Well, Fabio, we've had a really nice talk. Your cell phone, please?"

"Why?"

"It's important. You told me you received a text message at nine o'clock Friday morning. That's a little piece of evidence in your favor, you know that?"

"It's down in the storeroom," said Riccardo.

"Let me tell you again, sir: I told the truth. You can ask the guy at the tire repair shop."

"You can count on it. Thanks, Riccardo," he said as he walked toward the door. The lawyer caught up with him. Under his breath, he said: "You didn't catch Hilmi at all, tell me the truth."

"If you already know it, why are you bothering asking me?" He opened the door and left the meeting room.

"WHY DIDN'T YOU GO INTO THE SHOP YESTERDAY?"

"You saw me?"

"I was in the bar across the street."

Standing on the landing, uncertain whether to go into the apartment or continue to stand there talking, Nora and Rocco looked at each other with tired eyes.

"You put me through a truly miserable birthday, you know that?"

"Yes, I know that."

"And now you come to see me. Why?"

"To ask you to forgive me."

"Rocco Schiavone asking for forgiveness."

"You don't think much of me."

"Why should I?"

"Are you going to let me in or shall we stay on the landing?"

"Neither one," Nora replied, and sweetly shut the door in the deputy police chief's face. He stood there, gazing at the knots in the wood. Then he took a deep breath, did an about-face, and left Nora's apartment building.

Outdoors the temperature had plunged along with the setting sun and an icy hand clutched the policeman's chest. "So fucking cold . . ." he muttered bitterly between clenched teeth while buttoning his loden overcoat. Before he could take even two steps down the sidewalk the first solitary snowflake fluttered lightly before his eyes. The streetlamps were already on and in the yellowish light hundreds of flakes flew, like moths, slow and majestic. A flake landed on Rocco's cheek. He rubbed it dry. He raised his eyes to the steel-gray sky and saw them land on him by the dozen. They emerged from the darkness and took shape a few yards above him. He imagined himself as a spaceship traveling at the speed of light and all those dots hurtling toward him as so many stars and galaxies through which he was moving, into the mysterious depths of the cosmos. The lights were on in Nora's windows. And in the luminous rectangle of the living room window he saw Nora, standing there watching him as he played at letting the snow tickle him. Their eyes met once again. Then a movement in the adjoining window, the one in the bedroom, caught the deputy police chief's attention. A shadow behind the curtains. It had gone by quickly but not fast enough for there to be any doubt about its nature: it was a man. Rocco bit his lip and immediately tried to assign a name and a face to that shadowy guest. He raised his right hand as if to say hello to Nora, then he raised the left hand next to it and mimed the act of opening the window. At first, Nora didn't understand. Rocco repeated the gesture. The woman complied, opening the window and sticking her head out ever so slightly, one hand on her chest to protect herself from the chill. Rocco smiled up at her. "If you ask me, it's the interior decorator Pietro Bucci-something-or-other. Right?"

Nora made a face. "What did you say?"

"I said, if you ask me, it's the interior decorator Pietro Bucci-something-or-other."

"His name is Pietro Bucci Rivolta."

"Is that him?"

"Is who him?"

"Whoever it is that's over in the bedroom."

Nora said nothing. She shut the window and pulled the

curtains, vanishing from Rocco's sight. Not even ten seconds later, she turned off the lights.

Okay, fair enough, thought Rocco: you don't answer rhetorical questions.

Now there were plenty of snowflakes, and they no longer looked like stars he was passing as he explored the cosmos, but just what they were: icy snowflakes that were getting inside the collar of his overcoat, and were bound to turn the road into a dangerous sheet of ice.

It was time to go home.

"WHEN YOU THINK ABOUT IT, THERE IS A GOD AFTER all, no?" Marina tells me.

"What are you talking about?" I ask her.

"The guy that rapes little girls." She's making an herbal tea, I guess, because she's clattering around in the kitchen.

"Excuse me very much, but what does God and His existence have to do with that son of a bitch?"

"Nothing to do with him. It has to do with you." She comes into the living room and goes over to the table. In one hand she has a mug. Sure enough, an herbal tea.

"I don't understand you, Marì."

"I'm saying, there's a God because in the end they punished you. If you think about it, they punished you for the dumbest thing you've ever done, that is, beat that guy up."

She's right.

"Sort of like Al Capone, no? They finally put him in jail

for tax evasion, and not for littering Chicago with corpses. If you make the necessary adjustments, that's more or less what happened to you, Rocco."

"I didn't litter the city with corpses."

"No? Think back."

I don't want to think back. I don't want to think about any of it. "All right," I say to her, "there's a God. But why are you so glad that I'm exiled up here?"

She laughs prettily and pulls out her notebook. She reads the word of the day. "Diluculum. It's a Latin word. You know what it means?"

"No."

"It's the first light, the light of the new day."

"Daybreak?"

"Yes. Nice, eh?"

"The word itself, not so much. It's funny-sounding."

"But the first light is pretty. It brings hope, because sooner or later it's bound to come." And she disappears again. It's what she always does. After all, I already know what she's saying to me. It's always the same thing, even if she uses complicated phrases, words that she finds in the dictionary but that always talk about the same problem. As if I didn't know it. I just don't have the strength. I probably don't have the will, either. It takes tremendous strength. And a person doesn't necessarily have that strength. A person might not be able to muster it. I'm there, with both shoes. But you just take a look at my shoes on the radiator. Look at the pitiful shape they're in. And it's not even the end of

March yet. I wonder if springtime will ever come here. The day after tomorrow is the twentieth, and springtime arrives at midnight. But around here no one seems to have noticed. But I have. The day after tomorrow is Marina's birthday. And she was born right at midnight. Another minute and it would have been the twenty-first. But to me Marina and springtime have always been the same thing.

MONDAY

The snow had gone on falling all night long, covering the streets and piling high atop the cars. A few straggling flakes still fluttered indecisively through the chilly air, uncertain whether to land on a branch or a streetlight. Rocco had left his car double-parked all night long, next to a panel van that had been parked there for six months now without moving. By rights he should have called the traffic division and had them tow that van away, but why give up a convenient place to double-park right downstairs from his apartment? The panel van could stay right where it was.

Taking care where he set his feet, he reached his Volvo and climbed in. His warm, dense breath filled the chilly air inside the vehicle. "Fucking cold as hell," he snarled. Then he turned the key and the car's 163 horses roared immediately to life under his command. He turned on the heat, rubbing his hands together, hands that his leather gloves just couldn't keep warm. He needed to get to the office for his realist's morning prayer. But he'd made a mistake. An unforgivable oversight. He'd forgotten to turn off his cell phone, which he normally only turned on after nine. And the damned thing started ringing. Rocco leaped off the seat, in something approaching fear. "Fucking Christ . . ." he swore as he frantically felt in his various pockets. He grabbed it, holding it as if it were a hot potato.

Private number on his display. He'd need to be ready. It could be a sales call, or it could be the chief of police.

"Hello?"

"Beating Palermo two to one on their home field ain't peanuts."

It was Andrea Corsi, the police chief, who was rejoicing that his soccer team, Genoa CFC, had won an away match in Sicily.

"And so Schiavone, a splendid week stretches out before us. The weather is fine and the sails are proudly bellying!"

"Dottore, your optimism at this hour of the morning is annoying, to say the least," Rocco replied.

"All right then. Do you have any news for me on the Baudo case? Let me remind you that tomorrow there's going to be a press conference."

"Which I won't be able to attend. You know how to handle journalists; you have them wrapped around your little finger. I just don't know how to handle these things."

"Those assholes . . ." said the police chief.

"Believe me, you can hypnotize them. You could tell them the story of Hansel and Gretel and they'd be happy."

"You're flattering me, Schiavone. But you see, I still

have to have some red meat to toss those hooligans. Give me something."

"Certainly. Why don't you see if this does the trick. On Friday, in the dead woman's apartment, it was busier than an August day at Rome's Stazione Termini. Not only was the housekeeper there, but a couple of two-bit burglars happened by."

"What are you telling me?"

"That there was a burglary at the Baudo residence."

"And are they suspects in the murder?"

"No way. They're just a couple of losers. Shall I explain why they had nothing to do with it?"

"Sure. Is it very complicated?"

"Only slightly."

"Then let me get a pen." There was a pause during which Rocco could clearly hear the desk drawers opening and shutting as Corsi frantically searched for a pen. "My pens! Who keeps stealing my pens!" the police chief shouted. "Finally. I'm ready, Dottor Schiavone."

"All right, the two young men, known respectively as Fabio Righetti and Hilmi Bastiany . . ."

"Hilmi what?"

"Bastiany."

"Bastiany. Where's he from? Albania?"

"Egypt, Dottore. So the two kids just happen to be there, ransacking the place, or actually, stealing gold that they knew was in the bedroom."

"How did they know?"

"Hilmi is the son of the man who cohabits with the

housekeeper, and the boy stole her house keys, had them copied, and used them to enter the apartment. Now, according to the findings of our crackerjack medical examiner, Esther Baudo was killed no later than seven thirty. Righetti, Bastiany's accomplice, tells us that they entered the apartment at nine thirty."

"Maybe he's not telling the truth."

"I don't think that's it. I checked it out. At nine o'clock he and Hilmi were still getting the moped's flat tire fixed. Now listen. When the housecleaner, Hilmi's stepmother, came in, the two burglars hid and, according to what Fabio Righetti told us, watched the whole thing—Irina running terrified out of the apartment and then meeting a retired warrant officer downstairs, in the street; and he was in fact the man who first called us."

"So what does that mean?"

"That Irina got there at ten. And at that time of the morning, the kids were in the apartment."

"The stepmother, whatchamacallit, the housecleaner, could have told them everything afterward, couldn't she?"

"But when? No, I don't think so. Righetti actually told me that she tripped over the carpet and that down in the street she stopped to talk to a man walking a dog on a leash. You see, one thing I've learned is that when a person is in a state of panic, which Irina definitely was, they usually don't tell their stories with an abundance of details. In fact, there are details that they don't even remember. Now I wonder: if Righetti and Hilmi were caught by Esther Baudo at seven thirty that morning and killed her, what the hell reason could they have had for staying in that apartment for another three hours?"

"What about staging the suicide?"

"Three hours? To hoist up a dead body on a hook from the ceiling? Look, let's even admit the fear, the tension, the outright terror, and even the time it took to come up with the solution. But if you ask me, an hour and a half, tops, is all the time that was needed. Three hours is just too much time. Plus, we have the guy at the tire repair shop who clearly remembers the two idiots on the moped, teeth chattering with cold, who had a flat tire fixed."

"Mmm, I'm with you. The timing doesn't match up. How did you nail this down?"

"Because Hilmi took me straight to Gregorio Chevax, who's an—"

"I know who he is," Corsi interrupted. "He's back in hot water? You know, I arrested him the first time."

"Yes, he's in hot water again. Hilmi took him a batch of stolen goods from the Baudo residence. You see? Now you have something to give to the newspapers. And in any case Inspector Rispoli should be in your office shortly with a complete report. So you'll have it in writing."

"And this Hilmi? Where's he?"

"This is the one sour note. He got away. We think he made it out of the country. If you take a look at the papers that came in yesterday you'll see that there's already an international arrest warrant and bulletin out on the kid."

"Oh shit . . . but why did he run?"

"Because he assaulted a cop. Because he owes money

to people who'll stop at nothing, people that gave him the drugs in the first place. And because he knows that sooner or later we'd work our way back to him, since his accomplice is about to be subjected to a special expedited nonjury trial."

"Do you know where he might be?"

"No. He might have gone to stay with his mother in Egypt. By way of Switzerland, I think. Do we have an extradition treaty with Egypt, Dottore?"

"We'll have to ask the district attorney about that. I'd have to say offhand that they haven't signed any protocol with Italy. But, let me repeat, I'm working on memory. Thanks, Schiavone. So you work Sundays too?"

"When necessary. Because after all, there isn't a lot to do in this city; you have to face it."

"You should learn to ski. Then you'd definitely fall in love with this place."

"I'll give it some thought, Dottore."

"So aren't we going to see you at the press conference?"

"If you could see your way to letting me skip it, I'd be very grateful. I'm actually working on a pretty promising lead."

"Then stick to your work, Schiavone. And keep me informed. I'll take care of those bastards the news vendors. Ah, and don't forget the governor and his amateur bike race in late April."

"Certainly, I'm already working on it."

"Excellent. As far as I can tell those pen pushers don't have anything else on their minds. Goddamn them and blast them to hell."

A wound in the police chief's heart hadn't healed in all

these year. His wife had abandoned her home and her husband for a reporter for *La Stampa*. It was still a bleeding gash in Andrea Corsi's heart. A cut that might never heal at all.

ROCCO PARKED IN FRONT OF POLICE HEADQUARTERS, in his reserved spot. Walking gingerly on tiptoes, taking care where he put his feet, he headed for the entrance. Officer Scipioni, who was just leaving the building, smiled when he spotted him. "Dottore, are you afraid you might step on dogshit?"

"Idiot, I'm trying not to get my Clarks wet."

"When are you going to finally buy yourself a pair of suitable shoes?"

"The day you finally learn to mind your own goddamned business," Rocco replied, eyes fixed on the snow-covered sidewalk. Whereas Scipioni with his police boots comfortably strolled over the mantle of snow like an icebreaker. "I'm heading for the bar. Want an espresso?"

"No thanks, Scipio'. By the way, about Palermo . . ."

"Let's forget about it and we'll both be happier."

"No, but first you need to answer a question for me."

Scipioni stopped and turned to look at the deputy police chief: "Ask freely, Dottore."

"Are you Sicilian?"

"On my mother's side. But my dad is from Ascoli Piceno."

"And how do you like being here in Aosta?"

Scipioni thought it over for a few seconds. "I like it in terms of work. I like my colleagues and I even like the brass."

"Thanks, too kind."

"I like the weather too. I really like the cold. The one who hates it and wishes she could go live by the water is my wife."

"Is she Sicilian too?"

"No, she's from Saint-Vincent."

Rocco stood there looking at Officer Scipioni. "She was born here and she doesn't like it?"

"These things happen . . ."

Schiavone shook his head as he climbed the steps and finally walked into police headquarters. He was moving fast to avoid his morning encounter with Deruta. There was no danger of running into D'Intino; to the best of Rocco's knowledge the man was still in the hospital. He hurried down the long corridor and ducked toward his office.

When he entered the office, he found a note. Probably from Italo:

De Silvestri called from Rome. It's urgent!

Rocco didn't even bother sitting down. He picked up the phone and called the Cristoforo Colombo police station in Rome. It was actually De Silvestri who answered: he was clearly waiting for his call.

"De Silvestri, what's up? What's going on?"

"Dottore . . . he's at it again!"

Rocco slammed the receiver down hard and shouted as loud as he was able: "Italo!"

IT WAS RAINING. THE LIGHTS ON ROME'S BELTWAY, the Grande Raccordo Anulare, were gleaming off the wet asphalt. The taxi's windshield wipers were struggling to wipe away the water, while the drops on the car's roof rattled like a crazed drum solo.

"Some weather, eh?" said the cabbie.

"Completely crazy," Rocco replied.

"So I'm dropping you on Via Poerio, right?"

"What time is it?"

"Six thirty."

"Then that's right. The address is number twelve."

Rocco pulled out his cell phone. He scrolled through his directory looking for Sebastiano's phone number.

"Seba? It's me."

"Where the fuck are you?"

"In a taxi. I'm in Rome."

"Mmm. We going to see you?"

"Tonight. At Santa Maria. Tell Brizio and Furio."

"Got it. Eight o'clock?"

"Done."

He was back in Rome, his city. But even though he hadn't seen the place in months, he felt nothing. Anger. Just anger.

And plenty of it.

THE DEPUTY POLICE CHIEF OPENED THE FRONT DOOR of his apartment but didn't go right in. He stood at the threshold and looked in. There was a rumble of distant thunder. Then he turned on the light and made up his mind.

The smell of stale air. The furniture looked mournful and dreary, covered with white sheets. The refrigerator was open, empty, with dish towels on the floor. Carpets rolled up and hidden behind the sofas. In an ashtray he found a dead cigarette butt. Rocco picked it up. Diana brand smokes. A sign that Dolores, who came to clean the place once a week, had taken a break on his sofa. He went into the bedroom and opened the armoire. There was nothing in there but his summer jackets. And Marina's dresses, wrapped in cellophane. He touched them one by one. Every dress reminded him of something. Furio's wedding. The dinner in celebration of Marina's nephew's promotion. His father-in-law's retirement. The last dress was the red one. The one she wore at their wedding. He smiled. He remembered the ceremony at city hall. Marina in her red dress, him dressed in green trousers with a white shirt. Secular. Patriotic. Italian.

"How drunk was I at our wedding?" he asked aloud. He turned around. But there was nothing but the bed under a plastic slipcover. He left the bedroom and went back to the living room.

The whole apartment was reflected in the large window overlooking the terrace, streaked with raindrops on the outside. Rocco leaned his forehead against the glass. He looked out. A flash of lightning illuminated the cupolas of the churches and the silhouettes of the roofs of Rome. He felt as if he'd brought the clouds now lowering over the city of Rome with him from Aosta. The rainwater being vomited out of the downspouts was transforming the terrace into a swimming pool. He could make out the dark shapes of Marina's plants, clustered in a corner. The lemon tree, wrapped in a canvas cover, stood under the wooden shed roof, along with the rosebushes. At least the concierge was doing her job. It was crucial that those plants not die. Especially the lemon tree. He felt a stab of sorrow in his heart and a pang at the pit of his stomach. He took an umbrella from the large vase by the front door and exited the apartment, leaving the lights on behind him. Perhaps the time had come to sell that penthouse. There was nothing in it that belonged to him anymore. He was reminded of a movie he'd seen years and years ago, where the wall paintings in a Roman tomb that had just been violated dissolved in contact with the fresh air from outside, melting away entirely while the body of a mysterious handmaiden deflated on the altar, leaving behind nothing but fabric and a couple of rings. He closed the door behind him, without even single-locking it, much less double-locking it. There was nothing left to steal anyway.

IN MARCH IT CAN HAPPEN, IN ROME AT LEAST, THAT what looked like a latter-day biblical great flood suddenly dies out and dries up, leaving behind nothing but waterlogged streets, fallen trees, and an industrial quantity of car crashes and other mishaps, filling the city's emergency rooms to overflowing. The smell is a mix of bird guano, car exhaust, frying oil, and wet grass. The mopeds and Vespas start zipping through the streets again, like swallows in the spring air, and waiters appear in front of restaurants, waiting for the arrival of tourists. At least in Trastevere.

Rocco was sitting at an outdoor table underneath a patio heater, drinking a beer and waiting for his friends. It was eight o'clock and the two men showed up, emerging from the Via della Lungaretta right on time. Sebastiano was tall and strapping, enormous with his long curly hair restrained under a woolen watch cap. Furio was skinny and nervous, his hands stuffed in his pockets. The streetlamps gleamed off his bald head. They looked around. Not because they had any reason to be on the alert: it was just a habit with them. A professional habit it was hard to shake. His longtime friends walked toward him, studying the sky as if whatever danger might present itself were likely to fall from above. *Ursus arctos horribilis* and *Acinonyx jubatus*. Civilian names: grizzly bear and cheetah. A handsome pair. As soon as they reached the fountain, they'd spotted Rocco sitting at the table waiting for them. Rocco stood up. And he threw both arms open like the Christ of Corcovado over Rio de Janeiro. Seba and Furio smiled back. And the three men hugged with all the rude violence of a rugby scrum. All three at once. Rocco's heart began to beat again.

"Are you sitting outside to show how used to Nordic climes you are?" said Furio.

"I'm sitting outside because inside it's crowded as hell and after all it's not so damn cold out."

"It's not?"

"It's not. Plus also I'm sitting outside because I'm in Rome and when you're in Rome you sit outside and I want to look at the mosaics of Santa Maria. Is that a good enough reason for you?"

"You're an idiot," said Sebastiano, pulling off his woolen watch cap. His long curly hair exploded. "I'm going to get a couple of beers." He stood up, shoving the chair back as he did.

Rocco glanced at Furio. "How you doing?"

"So-so. Getting by. And you?"

"Same. Getting by. Why isn't Brizio here?"

"He's in Albano. His mother-in-law had a stroke. Now she talks all screwy."

"That's not good."

"Yeah. Not only does she talk screwy, but she can't remember a fucking thing. And since Stella went away for a week for an internship in cutting hair and doing permanents, Brizio wound up being the babysitter. Just think, yesterday his mother-in-law took him for the plumber."

"And to think that when Stella's mamma was a young thing she turned men into drooling idiots," said Rocco.

"Look," said Furio, "I'm going to tell you just so it's out there. The first times I jerked off it was thinking about her."

"You're not the only one. In the summer it was the kind of thing that could damage your health. You remember?"

"Do I remember? With those skimpy flower-print dresses and a pair of tits that looked like they were about to explode. And her hair. Her long black hair, and those lips . . . look, if you ask me, the real reason Brizio married Stella was because of a transference with her mother."

"Furio, are you all fixated on this thing with the transferences?"

"Why?"

"Because Brizio told Seba that Adele had an affair with Er Cravatta because of a transference with the father figure."

"You see? He knows what he's talking about! Look, that's the way it is, Rocco. Brizio is with Stella because of his memories of her mother. It's human; what do you think?"

"If you ask me, you're an idiot."

"One time at the water fountain in Piazza San Cosimato, it might have been in August, Stella's mother stopped to rinse her face and cool off a little. But her dress got wet too, and underneath she wasn't wearing anything at all. You could see every last thing! Her nipples, with every breath she took you'd think the whole kit and caboodle was about to explode. Brizio and I were there on our bikes, ogling her, and she noticed; she looked at the two of us with those green eyes of hers and she flashed us a smile. She even shot a wink. Then that little tramp turned around and bent over to rinse her neck. You want to know the incredible part? She wasn't even wearing panties. Brizio and I pedaled home as fast as we could and headed straight for the bathroom and we—"

"Okay, that's enough, Furio, I understand. You're getting me all worked up."

"You know what I say, Rocco? Old age is something women shouldn't have to deal with."

"True. Old age is strictly for men. Speaking of which, how is Sebastiano?"

"Did he tell you about Adele or not?"

"Yeah, but is what he says about Roby Gusberti the truth?"

Furio smiled. "He's exaggerating. He says that he caught the two of them in bed, but it isn't true. They were in the living room having a cup of coffee. Actually, Sebastiano has been embroidering on it. Still, it's true that Adele is sick and tired. Seba needs to get back in line."

"And you?"

"Still free as a bird!"

Sebastiano came back with two beers. *"Salute!"* he said, raising his beer as he let his big heavy body flop into his chair.

They raised their glasses and drank. After a healthy gulp, Sebastiano wiped his beard on the sleeve of his coat. "All right, Rocco, you want to explain?"

The deputy police chief looked at the other two. "I can tell you in three words. Giorgio Borghetti Ansaldo . . ."

"Who the fuck is that?"

"He's the guy who likes to go around raping little girls."

"Ah!" said Furio. "The guy whose father got you transferred to Aosta?"

"That's right. And he's doing it again."

Furio stuck his hand in his pocket and grabbed a cigarette. Sebastiano leaned back in his chair.

"What do you want to do about it?" asked Furio as he lit a Camel.

"He needs to be stopped."

"Who else knows you're in Rome?" asked Furio.

"No one. Only that guy Italo; Sebastiano's met him."

"Yeah, the wiseguy cop. He's all right," Seba confirmed.

Furio took a deep drag on his cigarette. "But it would be smarter for you to stay out of this, Rocco," he said, spitting out a column of smoke.

"Why do you say that?"

"Because this time if they catch you, they're not going to send you to Aosta; they'll ship you off straight to Rebibbia prison."

"And a cop in Rebibbia has a short life expectancy," Sebastiano added. "You know that better than I do."

"Are you just interested in throwing a scare into the kid? What's his name? Giorgio?"

"Maybe I didn't make myself clear, Furio. I want to stop him once and for all."

Furio nodded. "And when does this thing need to be done?"

"Tomorrow at the latest."

Furio stubbed his cigarette out in the ashtray: "Tell us more."

"I've got a person telling me everything this asshole does," Rocco began. "Finding him will be simple."

"Who is this person?"

"De Silvestri."

"Isn't he a cop?" asked Sebastiano.

"Yes. One of the best."

"And isn't it a little risky?"

"No. That piece of shit raped the man's niece. The reason I'm here is he called me."

The two friends nodded. "So explain . . ."

TUESDAY

"*Prego, señor, el café* . . ." whispered Conchita, stirring the little spoon in the demitasse. The faint, continuous ding ding ding of metal on china made Fernando Borghetti Ansaldo open his eyes wide.

"What time is it?"

"Half past *las siete*," the Peruvian housekeeper replied, leaving the demitasse on the nightstand. The undersecretary for foreign affairs rolled over in bed. His wife had already left their nuptial bed. While the housekeeper silently left the darkened room, Fernando downed the espresso at a single gulp. It was tasty, hot, and bracing. The moka pot remained and always would be superior to coffee pods, the honorable undersecretary continued to tell anyone who would listen, and if he were the undersecretary for industrial policy he'd have made sure that it was against Italian law to manufacture and sell those horrible swill-brewing coffeemakers. He got up, rubbed his face, and slowly made his way into the bathroom.

He turned on the shower. While waiting for the spray to heat up, he looked at himself in the mirror. He'd need to do something about that belly. He was turning into a watermelon. When he saw himself from the side, he looked like he was pregnant. And now his cranium was almost completely bald, a shiny dome. But he couldn't bring himself to think of getting a hair transplant. And there was no way he'd consider a hairpiece. He often spoke in public, and he knew that under the spotlights fake hair took on unlikely shapes and highlights, broadcasting to the world their complete artificiality. That would be a humiliation he'd never put himself through. Far better just to be bald. He took off his pajama pants and was about to step into the shower when he heard a voice.

"Fernando?" It was his wife, Roberta.

"What?"

"You know, Giorgio didn't come home last night either."

"What do you mean, he didn't come home? Where is he?"

Roberta leaned against the door frame and crossed her arms. "Last night he went out with his friends for a pizza."

"Well, call his friends, why don't you?"

"It's too early for that."

"Did you try his cell phone?"

"It's turned off."

"Wait and see; he's probably hooked up with some pretty girl . . . he's thirty years old, Roberta, it's perfectly normal."

"I certainly hope not."

The husband and wife locked eyes. They'd once again come to the topic that neither one of them had the strength or courage to broach. They both dropped their gazes at the same moment.

"Tea or milk?" asked Roberta.

"Milk with just a drop of coffee. Are there any pastries?"

His wife nodded and vanished. Fernando stepped into the shower.

The warm water brought him slowly back to life. Where the fuck was Giorgio? Actually, he couldn't stand the idea that his son was out and about. And he was starting to wish he could just erase him from his mind and his thoughts.

If only that boy had never been born!

He knew that a good father would have picked up the phone and kept calling until he found him. But at nine o'clock there was a very important meeting at the ministry. "I can't put my own family matters before the demands of the Italian state," he muttered under his breath. But that's not what he was really thinking. His actual thoughts were: I can't waste my goddamn time trying to find that idiot. Let his mother worry about him. She doesn't have a job, she never lifts a finger from morning to night, so there! Now she has something to keep her busy for the rest of the day.

Fernando had adopted a rather unusual habit. In the shower, or in the car, in other words, when he was alone, he'd speak aloud, as if there were a journalist with him, microphone extended, just waiting to start the interview. He had found that this was very good training for being able always to come up with a believable story. To protect his respectability. And the things he said were always politically correct, deeply rhetorical, on the verge of the ridiculous. He had to appear to be a just man, consistent, a civil servant working for the good of his country, caring about the needs and interests of the community that had elected him. In other words, even though his thoughts might veer northward, what came out of his mouth must necessarily veer to the south. It was an exercise for the TV cameras, a technique that he honed every day, more and more. "And then after the meeting I'll have a luncheon with the Malaysian delegation. Between our two nations, there has always been a profound sense of respect and reciprocal esteem. And it's going to be an important meeting, both in human and in political terms." The actual thoughts of the Honorable Borghetti Ansaldo were these, though: I'm going to have to sit there at lunch with those four colored monkeys that I couldn't give a flying fuck about and convince them not to raise the taxes on tourism but still supply the services that our resorts have requested. "The meeting will stretch out for quite a while, possibly until late at night. No, I just don't have time to worry about Giorgio's problems." Translation: After lunch with the Malaysians, which I'm hoping won't last more than an hour, I have an appointment to see Sabrina. And if you don't mind, if I have to choose between Sabrina and that brainless cabbage of a son of mine, I'm bound to choose Sabrina and her delicious thighs.

The mere thought of Sabrina's thighs had given him an erection. He could already imagine her stretched out on the leather sofa in his downtown office, the rent paid by the Italian taxpayers. Now that was an appointment he really couldn't afford to miss. And today, Tuesday, March 20, the day before the official start of spring, was a red-letter day for him and Sabrina. A date on which Fernando Borghetti Ansaldo intended to start a historic new chapter in their illicit and torrid relationship. Today, at last, he was going to ask her to let him screw her in the ass.

THE IMMACULATE BMW STATION WAGON WITH ONLY twenty thousand kilometers on the odometer turned over on the first try. He could have taken advantage of his position and requested a police escort, but then he'd have to walk all the way from the ministry to his study for his appointment with Sabrina, and that was out of the question. Plus he couldn't rule out, after the sex, the idea of a trip to a trattoria in the Castelli Romani to eat and drink until all hours. He'd need his car. The garage doors swung open, Fernando waved to Amerigo, the concierge, and turned onto Viale dell'Oceano Atlantico. There was plenty of traffic. He looked at the slow-moving cars. "The important thing is to give the citizens of this fair city a chance to travel freely by increasing the size and capacity of the public transportation network," he said under his breath. "The investments of Rome, Italy's capital, in buses and subways are in the interest not only of individual citizens but of the country as a whole. It's time to give the Romans an opportunity to get to work without necessarily taking their own vehicles, which will result in a considerable increase in outlays on fuel, insurance, vehicle taxes, and depreciation, all of which takes a bite out of a family's disposable income . . ." No, in his head he was cursing all those dickheads sitting in their cars, so many useless people who wouldn't be missed if they simply stayed home. Parasites, good-for-nothings, who get in their cars every chance they get so they can sit in traffic jams like idiots and go get a cup of coffee with their retired friends or to visit their mothers and brothers and sisters and then go window-shopping in malls. He broke into the English he'd be using later. *"It's a pleasure to meet you, Mister Joro Bahur . . . Mr. Melaka, how is your wonderful daughter . . ."* that flat-nosed fat pig who smells of fried food. *"Mr. Sibu, one of these days I'll take you to some typical Roman restaurant . . . to taste spaghetti cacio e pepe . . . wonderful!"*

"What the fuck are you yammering about?" a harsh, steely voice boomed from directly behind him, sharp as a well-honed blade. Fernando jerked in his seat. Sitting behind him was an enormous man wearing a woolen watch cap and a pair of Ray-Bans.

"Who . . . who are you? How did you get into my c—"

"Shut up and take the next right," the big man ordered him.

"I'll have you know, I am—"

"I know who you are. And I said take the next right, so quit fucking yammering."

Fernando Borghetti Ansaldo obeyed. Sweat was stream-ing down his back in rivulets. He was afraid to glance in the rearview mirror and look his guest in the eye. He was afraid to speak. He was even afraid to shift gears. He felt like a cold slab of marble.

"Put on your brakes, you moron. Don't you see the light?"

He was right. He slammed on the brakes and the car skidded to a halt just inches short of the white line. His breath was choppy and shallow, as if someone had drained the oxygen out of the car's interior. He tried to look up at the rearview mirror but just then the passenger-side front door swung open and another man, hairless, also wearing a pair of Ray-Bans, got in.

"Hello there, Dottor Borghetti. How are you doing?"

The undersecretary, his eyes wide with terror, looked wildly at the new arrival. "The light's green now," the bald man said in a calm voice. A horn honked behind him and he let the clutch out. He pulled out into the broad thoroughfare of Via Cristoforo Colombo. "Where . . . where am I going?"

"Straight ahead."

Only then did Borghetti Ansaldo notice that the man sitting next to him had an enormous pistol in his lap. And he was looking at him from behind the dark lenses of a pair of sunglasses.

Is this possible? he was thinking. Is this actually happening to me? In the middle of Rome? Where are the police? My God, what's going on here? What's going on?

"Take the beltway, heading toward the Cassia," said the man with the pistol.

"They're expecting me at the ministry," he found the courage to say. "When I fail to show up, they'll unleash the police, put out an all-points bulletin, and—"

"Don't worry about a thing," said the man with the cavernous voice from behind him. "This won't take long. Keep it under fifty-five miles per hour and do as you're told."

"Are you . . . are you kidnapping me?"

The two men didn't even bother to reply.

"Then what do you want from me?"

"You ask too many questions, fatso. Just drive and pipe down. And keep both hands on the wheel."

Fernando Borghetti Ansaldo gulped down the ball of dry dust he had in his throat, wiped his forehead, and concentrated on the road ahead of him.

"It's very likely that we'll see police cars on the beltway," said the long-haired guy in the back, "but you see, Borghetti? You just try to pull something clever, like flashing your brights, jamming on the brakes, accelerating, honking, and my friend here will shoot you. In the gut. So you'll die slowly and suffer atrociously. A gut shot hurts."

But the last thing the undersecretary was thinking about was trying to be a hero. He'd already made up his mind to obey and just hope that those two men didn't hurt him too badly.

"Do you want money?"

No answer.

"Do you want favors of some kind? I have enough influence to—"

The bald guy slapped him in the back of the head. "Shut up and drive."

He felt humiliated. Not even at school, not even as a child, had he ever been given the classic slap to the back of the head, known in Italian as a *scappellotto*. A *scappellotto* is something you give an out-of-control child, an apathetic pupil. Not a respected undersecretary, a member in good standing of the majority party, a man with institutional responsibilities, a man who always received a military salute from the Carabinieri, who snapped to attention in his presence. Then it dawned on him. Suddenly everything became clear. A horrible crudely drawn symbol appeared in his mind's eyes, a five-pointed star on a banner behind the weary, resigned face of a great statesman of the Christian Democratic Party, held captive in a Red Brigades lair, awaiting his execution. Well, so be it, he thought. "If my sacrifice is required, I'm ready. Go ahead."

"What the fuck are you talking about?"

"You're terrorists, aren't you? What are you, communists?"

The two men burst out laughing. "You're not that important, you pathetic idiot. Just take the Aurelia and shut your piehole."

No. It wasn't the Red Brigades after all.

He felt a slight pang of disappointment.

"You know that this car has an antitheft alarm system with satellite tracking, connected directly to the Carabinieri? And the minute I fail to show up at the ministry they'll know something's wrong and they'll immediately be able to find the car's location and they'll come and get us and . . ." He looked up. In the rearview mirror the big bearded man was holding up a piece of electronic equipment with dozens of snipped colored wires protruding from it in all directions. "Now," the man said, "we'd like a little silence. So shut up and drive."

Borghetti Ansaldo obeyed.

• • •

OPEN COUNTRYSIDE, NOT FAR FROM THE WATER. Abandoned farmhouses surrounded by fields run to seed, dotted with olive trees in serious need of a thorough pruning. Mud everywhere. The BMW struggled through that panorama of desolation, jerking and jolting over potholes, gears grinding and motor straining. The suspension groaned and the tires sprayed water in all directions as they churned through puddles. At the side of the road rusty tractor parts could be seen, along with old, tattered plastic bags. "Where . . . where are we?" asked the undersecretary, breaking the silence.

"Località Testa di Lepre," said the man next to him, with the flat precision of a tour guide.

"What are we doing here?" asked the politician, but he got no answer. Then he heaved a sigh. If they'd been planning to kill him, they'd have done it already, he decided.

"There . . . the warehouse," the bald guy said, pointing. Borghetti Ansaldo hit the turn signal and pulled off the dirt road onto a grassy lane that ran toward an old abandoned industrial shed.

"Get out."

Puddles and mud everywhere. Under a fiberglass lean-to roof was an old Vespa without a seat, two enormous toothed tractor tires, and heaps of stacked furniture. The glass in the warehouse windows was all broken. Someone had written on the cement wall with a marker: "Casalotti rules!"

"In you go!" said the big man, swinging open an iron gate that creaked on its hinges.

IT WAS A SINGLE BIG ROOM A HUNDRED YARDS IN length. Drops of water were dripping from the ramshackle roof: you could see the sky through the holes. Cement columns held up the rafters. The stench of stale urine and wet dirt filled his nostrils. Then, at the far end of the industrial shed, Fernando Borghetti Ansaldo saw someone squatting at the foot of a cement column. Head lolling to one side, hopelessly. He seemed to have passed out. As he got closer, the figure took shape. His hands were tied behind him. A pair of jeans, track shoes, and a sweatshirt that said HARVARD UNIVERSITY. Fernando recognized it immediately. He'd brought it back for his son, from a trip to the States three months ago. "Giorgio . . ." he said, in a small, frightened voice. The two men stopped him a few yards short of his baby boy. From behind the column, silent as a ghost, a third man emerged with a woolen cap on his head and a pair of glasses. A black jacket, a pair of gloves, and a pair of Clarks desert boots on his feet.

"This is Giorgio. Giorgio, say hello to daddy." The man grabbed Giorgio's chin and forced him to look up. Now his face was illuminated by the light streaming through the broken windows.

Blood oozed from his mouth and his nose. Giorgio barely opened his eyes. He smiled. He had blood on his teeth too.

"What . . . what have you done to him?"

"Nothing much, trust me," said the new arrival, who was clearly the leader of the pack. "But this sack of shit stuck his pee-pee where he shouldn't have. You know what I'm talking about, don't you?"

The undersecretary said nothing.

"Do you or don't you?" the man bellowed.

The honorable undersecretary nodded his head three times.

"In that case, my friends and I are giving you one last chance. Either this dickhead stops once and for all, or next time we're going to turn nasty."

"Because we know how to be nasty, did you know that?" said the big man behind him.

"What . . . what do I have to do?"

"That's something you'd need to tell us," said the leader of the band. "You see, my friends were suggesting we might do a number of things: cut his dick off, slice off his balls. All things I completely endorse, and perfectly just, no doubt about it, but in the end we're reasonable people and we thought we'd give you one last chance."

"I could have him institutionalized and—"

"Do whatever you think's best. I'm just warning you, though. If we have to come back, what happened to your son today is going to look like a stroll in the park."

"I understand," said the honorable undersecretary in a small, frightened voice.

The sound of the drops of water falling from the ceiling into the puddles below filled the silence.

"Papà, can we please go home?" Giorgio suddenly asked.

ANTONIO MANZINI

But Fernando Borghetti Ansaldo was impervious to pity.
He looked at his son, blood of his blood, flesh of his flesh,
tied up like a ham on a pole, and felt a surge of hatred and
resentment surge up his throat. "You're a dickhead, Giorgio," he said. "A complete dickhead."

"Yes, but now we're going home, aren't we?"

Beethoven's "Ode to Joy" echoed through the enormous
foul-smelling room, making the undersecretary flinch. The
leader of the trio quickly slipped his hand into his jacket
pocket. "Oh fucking Jesus . . ." He pulled out his cell phone.

"Yes?" he said, vanishing behind the cement column.

"Dottor Schiavone, of the Aosta police?"

"That's me. Who'm I speaking with?"

"What's that echo I hear?"

"Pay no attention to that. Who is this?"

"It's Tomei."

"Tomei?"

"From the Tomei menswear shop, in town."

"Ah, of course. I'm all ears."

"I told my wife, my son, and even my *part-time* sales
assistant about what you're looking for, and my wife had a
bright idea." (He emphasized the English term *part-time*
annoyingly once again.)

"Good."

"So, she'd like to speak with you. Shall I put her on the
phone?"

"No. Believe me, this wouldn't be the right time to talk."

"Are you in a meeting?"

"Good guess. I'll come see you as soon as possible."

"It's always a pleasure to be able to help Aosta's finest, after all, and . . ."

But Rocco missed the rest of what the man had to say because he'd already ended the call. He came back around the cement column. The undersecretary was still there. And also there, tied securely to the column, was the undersecretary's son.

"Now, where were we?" asked Rocco.

"The honorable undersecretary had just said that his son was a complete dickhead," said Sebastiano.

"Ah, yes, that's right. Couldn't agree more." Then Rocco walked over to Furio. "Do you mind? Let's cut through the bullshit." With a rapid move, he seized Furio's pistol. He strode straight over to Giorgio and aimed the gun at the young man.

"No!" shouted the undersecretary. Furio and Sebastiano stood motionless, watching in horror. Rocco pulled the trigger over and over again, firing into the reinforced cement just inches from Giorgio's head. The deafening gunshots blasted in quick succession while the cement, chipped to flakes by the bullets, peppered the side of the bound man's head; he flinched with every shot. Fernando Borghetti Ansaldo felt a warm rivulet run down the inside of his trouser leg. And to judge by the stain on the floor, his son too had pissed his pants. After firing all six shots, Rocco handed the pistol to Furio.

"Next time I'll aim lower." And he strode briskly out of the huge room.

Furio turned to look at the politician. "Is this clear to you?"

Fernando shut his eyes and nodded. Giorgio was whimpering softly. "I swear it. Giorgio will never hurt anyone again."

Sebastiano went over to the young man. "Borghetti? We can get in anywhere, whenever we want. Next time instead of you, we'll take your wife."

Furio laughed. "But something tells me that we're not going to be seeing each other ever again, are we?"

Then the two men left without another word. Fernando Borghetti Ansaldo stood there, looking at his son, tied to a chair. He stepped closer. The young man reeked of shit.

THEY WERE LISTENING TO A GOLDEN OLDIES SHOW ON the car radio. Right now, "Just an Illusion" by Imagination was playing.

"Ah, all the memories . . ." said Sebastiano dreamily.

"Greece. Summer, 1982," Furio began. "We hooked up with those Dutch girls, you remember, Rocco?"

But Rocco was looking out the car window. Seba and Furio exchanged a glance and then did nothing more than to hum the British hit song. Over the piece of dance music could be heard Beethoven's "Ode to Joy." Rocco answered his cell phone while Seba lowered the volume on the car radio.

"Schiavone. Who is it?"

"*Ciao*, sweetheart, it's Alberto."

It was the medical examiner from Livorno.

"What's up . . ."

"There's news. I need to speak with you. All right, first of all, I've examined all the belts and neckties from the Baudo home. No trace of epithelium, hairs, nothing."

"Mmm . . ."

"It wasn't with any of these items that Esther was strangled."

"In that case, whatever was used must now be—"

"Exactly, who knows where it is now. But I need to talk to you about something much more important."

"I'm out of town right now. When I get back to Aosta I'll call you."

"Where are you?"

Rocco didn't even reply. Alberto understood immediately. "Fine, I'll wait to hear from you. But listen: this is important." And he hung up.

Rocco put his phone back in his pocket and nodded to Seba to turn up the radio again. But "Just an Illusion" was over. Now the radio was playing Milli Vanilli's "Girl You Know It's True." Screaming, Sebastiano switched the radio off.

PRIMA PORTA IS A TOWN JUST OUTSIDE OF ROME, beyond the bounds of the Grande Raccordo Anulare, the beltway. It's on the Via Flaminia, the main artery that runs north toward Terni and the green hills of Umbria. But first and foremost, for the people of Rome, Prima Porta is the city cemetery, officially known as the Cimitero Flaminio. It covers 370 acres, with forty-five miles of roads. To get around, you either drive or take a bus. A city all its own, made up of eternal residences: graves, vaults, and two-story funerary chapels.

Sebastiano and Furio had stayed in the car. Rocco wanted to walk the last hundred yards alone. He crossed the road as the C/8 bus barreled past, heading for the Islamic section. The sky was gray, and as he strode past a fresh grave, the sickly sweet odor of flowers nauseated him. He went past a pine grove and there opened out before his eyes an expanse of headstones jutting from the soil like so many derelict teeth. Lost in the sea of graves, two women dressed in black hunched over, busy doing something to the headstones. Rocco went straight as an arrow to the third row. He walked up to the black marble slab.

Marina was there, waiting for him. There were only dried flowers on the grave. Rocco picked up those withered scraps and went back to the road. He tossed them in the trash, then went over to the water fountain and filled the vase with fresh water for his daisies. He went back to the grave. He arranged the flowers and finally looked at the headstone. He knew the dates by heart, but he read them all the same:

MARCH 20, 1969–JULY 7, 2007

He'd chosen not to put a photograph on the headstone. There was no need. Marina's face was branded into his mind's eye sharper than a rancher's mark seared into the flesh of a cow. They say that usually the faces of our loved ones gradually fade into the mist of our memories. That the features start to blur, along with the colors of the eyes and hair, their height, and especially the sound of their voices. But none of that happened to Rocco. Since July 7, 2007, Marina hadn't lost so much as a mole in his memory. So there was no need of a photograph. The image of Marina's face, clear and vivid, would be the last sight in Rocco's eyes the day it was his turn. There was no doubt about that.

"*Ciao*, Marina," he said in a low voice. "You see? I came to visit. Like I promised." He could see his reflection in the shiny, polished marble. "Look, I brought you something . . ." He stuck his hand in his pocket and pulled out a notebook. "Your words are in here. They may be useful to you." He stuck it under the vase. Next to it he left a pen. "You know what? I found a hard word for you. I wrote it right in your notebook. It describes me. You want to know what it is? *Oligemia*. But I'm not going to tell you what it means, otherwise it wouldn't be any fun for you."

One of the two women, dressed in black, had kneeled down and was crossing herself. Rocco too leaned over the grave, but only to remove a leaf that had fallen on the marble slab.

"Happy Birthday, Marina . . . see you at home," he said, and blew her a kiss.

He walked back to the little road, looked up, and saw them. They were standing about a hundred feet away, looking at him wordlessly.

He felt his heart climb into his throat. He stood stock-still. Laura and Camillo, too, seemed incapable of taking a step toward their daughter's grave. Finally Rocco made up his mind and, in spite of the fear that bolted his knees in place, he forced himself to walk toward them. As Laura watched him walk toward them, she placed her right hand on her husband's arm, as if to hold tight to the only certainty remaining to her. Rocco kept his eyes on the ground; he knew that if he looked up he wouldn't be able to make it all the way to where they were standing. If he looked at them, even for an instant, he'd change direction and head straight back to Sebastiano and Furio, who were waiting for him in the car. Then, when he was almost within arm's reach of the couple, he stopped and looked up. Laura's face was covered with wrinkles, and her lovely blue eyes had faded, as had the chrysanthemums she held in her hand. Camillo's hair, already white, had thinned, and he now wore a pair of glasses with black frames. Like his wife, he'd lost weight and looked drab, colorless. They both seemed to lack depth. A pair of cutout figurines, glimpsed through a gray veil.

"*Ciao*, Laura . . . *ciao*, Camillo."

His in-laws said nothing. Laura was having trouble breathing. Camillo was even worse off: he seemed to be in a state of waking apnea. Well, he'd come this far: he'd said hello, now what? What else did he need to say? Ask for their forgiveness? He'd done it a thousand times since that day— July 7, 2007. In the morgue, at the funeral, with dozens of phone calls, but the result hadn't changed. Marina hadn't come back to life, and they'd never forgiven him.

Not that he deserved to be forgiven. He knew that; the

blame was his and his alone. And nothing would ever alleviate the ruthless violence of those pangs of remorse that he felt in his heart, those ripping talons that lacerated him inwardly, drawing more and more blood with the passing years. He just wished they would realize one thing: he'd loved Marina. More than anything. And he loved her still. And not a day, not a night went by that he didn't weep for her. But a mother and a father have a greater right to grieve for the loss of a daughter than a husband does. They take precedence.

"I know what you want from me," said Laura, tight-lipped. "But I can't do it." Then she looked at Rocco again. "And I'll never be able to."

Rocco nodded. Her eyes were glistening now. On her weary, pale face, here and there he caught a glimpse of Marina. In the twist of the mouth, the angle of her glance, her hairline. Is that what Marina would have been like as an old woman? "I know, Laura. But I have to go on living, and I'm standing here the way I was five years ago. I just want you to know it. For what remains of my life—"

"What remains of our lives is of no importance," Camillo interrupted him. He slurred his words, and his voice was brittle as glass. "Forgiveness doesn't matter, because when hope dies, nothing matters anymore. You want to know something? I thought that dying would be the easiest thing. But it's not. Look at me. I stand here before you, I talk, I walk, and my goddamned life won't let me go, Rocco. It won't do me this favor. Don't you find that all this goes against what's natural?" he said, pointing to the flowers with a faint smile.

"I don't understand," said Rocco.

"It's supposed to be the children who put flowers on their parents' graves, no? The day you can explain to me why the opposite has happened to us, that will be the day I'll be able to forgive you and forgive myself."

He put his arm around his wife and together they walked past Rocco and started toward Marina's grave.

He watched them walk away, side by side, moving slowly. Laura had laid her head on her husband's shoulder. The C/9 bus heading toward the Jewish section of the cemetery went past, lifting the hems of Camillo's overcoat and stirring Laura's skirts. Rocco turned and went back to the car.

Only when he saw his friends leaning against the hood of their car smoking did he stop crying.

"Take me to the airport, please."

Sebastiano and Furio said nothing. And the whole way to Fiumicino they kept their mouths shut.

WHILE WAITING FOR THE BOARDING ANNOUNCEMENT, he took out his cell phone and punched in the number of his old office.

"Yes?"

"Deputy Police Chief Schiavone, please put me through to De Silvestri."

"Just a second," said the impersonal voice.

He heard a series of background noises, then the voice of Officer Alfredo De Silvestri boomed out of the phone: "Dottore . . ."

"It's all taken care of, Alfredo. The matter is settled."

He could hear the policeman's labored breathing. "If you need anything else, you know where to find me, but believe me, I only want to get a call inviting me to come down and celebrate your retirement."

"*Grazie*, Dottore."

"Don't mention it, Alfredo. Say hello to your niece from me."

And he hung up.

"Alitalia, flight AZ 123 to Turin, we're now boarding at Gate C 19 . . ."

He stood up, pulling his ID and his boarding pass out of his pocket. He was leaving Rome, his beloved Rome. But he didn't feel the same wrenching sense of loss he'd experienced the first time, just six months earlier. Could it be that just six months' time had changed his city so completely? Could you become a stranger in such a short time? Who was at fault? Had Rome changed? Or had he?

"A SHITTY DAY, ROCCO," SAID ITALO AS HE DROVE slowly down the highway from Caselle to Aosta. "The police chief called looking for you three times, and Farinelli of the forensic squad left you a box of stuff in your office."

"What did you tell him?"

"That you were in Ivrea, trying to track down someone who might have seen something."

"Excellent." The deputy police chief reached out and plucked a cigarette out of Italo's pack. "Listen, I know it won't do any good to go on pestering you about it, but why do you insist on buying Chesterfields?"

"Because I like them, Rocco. In fact, can I have one too?"

Rocco stuck two in his mouth, lit them, then handed one to Italo.

"Thanks. Did you take care of everything in Rome?"

"Yes." He said nothing more.

"Who went to Esther Baudo's funeral?" he asked after a pause.

"Me and Caterina. We did what you told us. We took pictures of just about everyone. There weren't that many people. Thirty people, more or less. I put the pictures on your desk."

WEDNESDAY

Once again, it had snowed all night long. Rocco hadn't slept a wink. He just couldn't get used to the silence in this city. There were no cars going by, he couldn't hear the neighbors' television sets, there was never anyone shouting, and there weren't even trains in the distance.

Nothing.

In the morning, when he dragged himself out of bed and pulled open the curtains to peer out, he saw that the snow had stopped falling and that the city snowplows had cleared the streets. When had they done that? Why hadn't he heard them? What did they have, silencers on their engines? As always, the sky was a quilt of gray clouds.

Another shitty day.

HE HAD JUST GOTTEN INTO HIS CAR WHEN HIS CELL phone rang. He wasn't at the top of his game. It was the

ANTONIO MANZINI

second day in a row that he'd forgotten to turn it off. An unforgivable error.

"Who's busting my balls?"

"It's Alberto. Are you in the office?"

It was the medical examiner. "No. I'm on my way in now."

"So where are you exactly?"

"What do you care? What's up?"

"What did I tell you yesterday? I need to talk to you, urgently."

"As soon as I get to the office I'll call you back."

"Listen, it's something about Esther. And I think it's something you'll be interested in."

"I swear I'll call you. You can count on it."

"You don't want me to tell you what it's about?"

Rocco rolled his eyes.

"You do know, Rocco, that dead people have stories to tell, don't you?"

"Maybe not out loud."

"Sure. But their presence is enough, and if you keep your ears pricked, they tell you stories, and how. Believe me, the other day Esther Baudo had some terrible things to tell you."

"Fine. Then let's meet at police headquarters in twenty minutes or so?"

"No. You come see me."

"Have you noticed? It snowed all night long."

"That happens quite often in Aosta, or is that news to you? What's the matter? Are you afraid of a hip fracture?"

232

"Well, at least wait until they can clean the streets, no?"

"Oh you pathetic yutz, I'm here at the hospital and have been since seven, and the streets were already perfectly clean. And explain this to me: how come I can get places with the snow and you can't?"

"You're such a pain in the ass, Alberto."

"Listen, Rocco, I worked Saturday and Sunday, because that poor woman's body had to be buried. Have you ever heard of something called a funeral?"

"Yes. Unfortunately, I attend quite a lot of them. All right, let me see if the car will start and I'll try to get over to where you are."

"You have a Volvo XC60 all-wheel drive, hundred and sixty-three horsepower, not even a year old, and you're telling me it might not start? Come on, get your ass in gear."

BUT INSTEAD ROCCO WENT STRAIGHT TO THE OFFICE. He had no intention of swinging by the hospital. He'd find some way of luring Fumagalli to police headquarters. It wasn't laziness, and it wasn't a lack of interest. Quite the opposite; he was eager to hear whatever news the Tuscan doctor had for him. But he couldn't bring himself to go to the hospital, and especially not to the morgue, one more time. To have that stench wash over him again, to look at those metal gurneys and those enormous filing cabinets that held the bodies of people who were no longer among the living.

He was starting to be sick and tired of people who were no longer among the living.

He was hurrying down the main hallway in police head-quarters, eager to avoid a meeting with a bustling, early-rising Deruta, when something in the passport office caught his attention. The door hung ajar. He tiptoed closer on his crepe sole shoes and took a peek into the room, and didn't like what he saw there, not one little bit.

Officer Italo Pierron was using his tongue to explore the oral cavity of Inspector Caterina Rispoli. They were just standing there, eyes shut tight, arms wrapped around each other like a couple of octopi. In their heads, they weren't in Aosta police headquarters: they were stretched out on some beach in the Caribbean, or maybe just in a bedroom some-where. Rocco was tempted to cough just for the fun of seeing the two lovers' blushing faces, but then he thought better of it.

Revenge is a dish best enjoyed cold. In fact, as long as we're in Aosta, freeze-dried.

HE HADN'T EVEN GOTTEN TO HIS OFFICE AND HE WAS already shouting: "Pierron!"

The sound of scurrying feet and the young officer ap-peared, panting: "Here I am. What's up?"

Rocco looked at him. His shirt collar was undone, his tie was loosened, and his lips were chapped as if someone had gone over them with sandpaper. "What the hell were you doing?" he asked.

"I was going over burglary reports."

"Get over to the hospital and pick up Fumagalli. He says he has something to tell me. Now, he's going to tell you he can't come, but you tell him I just got stuck in a meeting with the chief of police."

"Right, got it. Listen, Rocco . . ."

"At headquarters you call me sir."

"Ah right, I was forgetting. It's just that there's no one here and I thought . . . anyway, listen, sir, the head of the forensic squad, Commissario Farinelli, called you, a number of times."

"I'll call him back. You have anything else to tell me?"

"No."

"Then go do what I told you to, for Christ's fucking sake." And Rocco slammed his door right in Officer Italo Pierron's face. Who at first felt slightly hurt. And then decided that maybe his boss had just woken up on the wrong side of the bed that morning. He definitely hadn't smoked his morning joint yet, and that was probably the reason for such a bitter mood. When he got back, he would surely find Rocco as relaxed and friendly as ever.

"ONE THING YOU SHOULD KNOW, ROCCO, IS THAT THE cannabinoid receptors are in the basal ganglia, which are connected to the cerebellum, which directs nerve impulses. Also, the hippocampus, which controls memory and stress. And the cerebral cortex, and there we're talking about your cognitive activity, and such."

"What are you trying to tell me, Alberto?"

"That if you go on smoking it's going to do you serious harm. To say nothing of the tachycardia!"

In fact, the smell of grass was unmistakable in Rocco's office, and there was no point trying to conceal the truth from Alberto Fumagalli. "I don't smoke much, and only in the morning. It helps me."

"It helps you how?"

"It calms me down and it opens up my mind. I become creative and I can even stand looking at a fucked-up face like yours."

"It's a miracle."

"What is?"

"That you managed to find a wife at all, you know?"

"That's a subject I'd recommend you steer clear of. I tend to lose my sense of humor."

"You're right, sorry. Still, just between you and me, stop smoking joints. I'm telling you as a friend."

"You're not my friend."

"All right then, as a doctor."

"You're not even a doctor. Doctors cure sick people."

"Well?"

"Tell me what chances of recovery your patients have."

"Well, if you say so."

"So tell me what's so amazing."

"Can I get a cup of coffee?"

"No. The coffeemaker here is even worse than the one you have at the hospital. But just wait a second . . . why not?" Rocco got up and opened the office door: "Pierron!" he shouted.

Italo came in through a side door: "Yes, sir."

"Would you go get us a couple of espressos from the bar?"

Italo looked at Rocco without understanding. He'd never asked him to do such a thing before.

"Which part of the question did you miss?"

"Can't you ask Deruta?" he said with a smile.

"No. I'm asking you. Wait a second!" He turned to Alberto. "Do you want something to eat, too?"

"No thanks, just coffee."

"So just two espressos, Italo. Don't take forever, though," he warned, then closed the door.

He went back and sat down across from Fumagalli. "Well, what did you find out?"

"First, tell me why you're not in a meeting with the police chief. Your officer told me that he'd dragged you into one."

"True. But in the end I managed to get the matter taken care of because I knew you were coming."

"Let's run the numbers. It took me less than ten minutes to get over here. And you were having a meeting with the police chief. Then you had enough time to smoke a joint; let's say that took another five minutes. But to judge from the faint aroma in here, I'd say you finished that joint at least seven or eight minutes ago. Therefore you started smoking that joint the minute Officer Pierron started driving over to get me. To complete my thought process, you had a conversation with the chief of police that lasted, if it ever took place at all, less than a minute. So you know what I think? I think that you never even laid eyes on the police chief, that you just dreamed up an excuse not to have to come see me. And in summation, I would say that you're a lying liar, barefaced and shameless. QED."

ANTONIO MANZINI

"Are you done?"

"Only if you tell me that I was right."

"You were right. Shall we move on to the things that matter?"

Alberto nodded. Then he pulled a notebook out of his pocket. He opened it. He checked his notes. "Listen carefully. We're talking about Esther Baudo."

"Go ahead."

"I sent all the documentation to the judge, but I'm talking to you about it directly. There's something that doesn't add up."

Rocco pulled a cigarette out of the pack on his desk.

"It bothers me if you smoke."

"You bother me if I don't. Go on. What doesn't add up?"

"The fractures."

Rocco's face became a living question mark.

"Not the fractures associated with the blows to the cheekbone; you remember, right? No. I'm talking about old fractures. I found one to the ulna and one to the radius of her right arm. A couple of cracked ribs, and that's old stuff too. And then there was her right cheekbone. It shows an old fracture, from . . . I'd say, roughly, a few years ago."

Rocco took a long, slow puff. He exhaled the smoke toward the ceiling. "So you're saying?"

"One of two things: either the woman practiced extreme sports . . ."

"No, I don't think she did."

"In that case, there's nothing left but a car crash. Otherwise, I wouldn't know to explain it to you. I mean, that kind of damage to her bones."

Rocco stubbed the cigarette out in the ashtray. He stood up and walked over to the window. But he didn't look out at the landscape. He put one hand over his eyes. "This is a terrible thing, you know?"

"You think so?"

"I do."

Italo Pierron walked into the room with two small plastic cups. He set them down on the desk. "How much sugar?" he asked Alberto with an ironic smile, but the medical examiner said nothing and just tossed back the espresso in a gulp. The officer realized that the silence, like a highlighter on a blank page, pointed to something very important that had just happened. "What's going on?" he asked, glancing at Rocco.

"Come with me, Italo." Then the deputy police chief looked at Fumagalli: "I'm going to have Deruta take you back to the hospital. Thanks, Alberto, you've been very helpful. Like always." And as he walked past him, he gave him a slap on the back.

"Aren't you going to drink your coffee?"

But Rocco had already left the room, followed by Italo. The medical examiner tossed back the second cup of coffee too.

"WHERE ARE WE GOING?" ASKED ITALO.

"Charvensod, to pay a call on Patrizio Baudo's mother."

"What's going on?"

"A lot of things don't add up."

"No, I didn't mean that. What's going on between you and me?"

Rocco smiled. "Why would you ask me that?"

"Because you're being strange."

"Ah, I'm being strange? You've been fucking Rispoli and I'm being strange?"

"No, wait, what does Rispoli have to do with this?"

"I saw the two of you in the passport room."

Italo downshifted and then hit the accelerator. "So?"

"Italo, you know I had my eye on her."

"So what, you have some kind of *jus primae noctis*?"

"So what if I did?"

They drove in silence through a few more curves. "It happened when we were staking out Gregorio Chevax, the other night."

"Did you start it or did she?"

"Let's just say that I arranged for her to start it."

"I want the details."

Italo took a deep breath. "Well, I started things, I guess. I said to her: What if Chevax sees us? And she answered: impossible. So then I said: Should we do like in the movies? We could pretend to be a pair of lovers making out, and that would allay all suspicions. She looked over at me and then said: oh heavens, I'm pretty sure I just saw Chevax's shadow! And she threw her arms around me. And we kissed. And we laughed."

"And that's all?"

"And that's all."

"Goddamn," Rocco said, "that took some imagination.

Technically you brought up the subject, but she took the initiative."

"Yes, but I knew she liked me. I'd known it for a while."

"Well, would it have killed you to tell me?"

Italo pulled up in front of Patrizio Baudo's mother's house. Rocco opened the door. "Anyway, don't get too comfortable. I'm still going to make you pay."

"You're not very sportsmanlike," retorted Italo, getting out and following him.

"Whoever said I was?" They started walking toward the house when the door opened and Signora Baudo emerged. She had seen them coming. Her face was worried. She was holding a dish towel and clutching it to her belly. "Dottore, has something happened to my son?" were the first words out of her mouth.

A pile of snow beside the sidewalk reached out and nipped at the deputy police chief's left Clarks desert boot.

"Goddamn it . . . no, Signora, as far as I know he's fine. Why do you ask?"

"I'm so anxious. He went up to Pila this morning on the cable car and he's had his cell phone turned off ever since."

"He went to Pila?"

"He said that he needed to get up into the mountains, and far away from this . . ." She swept her right hand in a circle to indicate everything around her.

"No, Signora, you'll see, he must just have wanted a little time to himself. We came for another reason."

"Would you like to come in? Can I offer you anything?"

Italo was already heading for the house. Rocco threw

his arm out to block him. "Maybe you can tell us. It's just a question. Was Esther ever in a serious car crash?"

"Esther? No. One time she was in a fender bender, but they exchanged information and the insurance companies took care of it. But why? Is there some complaint from an insurance company?"

"No, Signora," said Italo, "don't worry about that."

"It was strictly a formality," said Rocco, looking down at his shoe, which had already changed color.

"Are you sure you don't want a cup of coffee? You ought to get yourself a pair of shoes that are better suited for the snow."

Rocco looked at the woman. "You know, Signora? You aren't the first person to give me that advice." Then with a smile he went back to the car. Italo snapped her a sharp salute in farewell, then turned to follow his boss.

"WHAT CAN I TELL YOU? I'D HAVE TO GO DO A SEARCH in the archives." The man was unhelpful, speaking quickly in an unmistakable attempt to dispose of that unexpected visit from the police as soon as possible. "Do you have any idea of how long that would take me?"

The hospital's administrative director looked like anything but the administrative director of a hospital. Crewneck cashmere sweater, dark blue corduroy trousers. He wore a pair of glasses with lenses tinted light blue, like a Hollywood movie star. His flowing white hair clashed with his chubby round face. He sat there, knuckles pressed down on his desktop, and he hadn't invited Rocco, much less Officer Pierron, to take a seat and get comfortable in either of the two leather office chairs facing his desk.

"Don't you have a secretary, Dottor Trevisi?" asked the deputy police chief.

"It's Wednesday. Wednesdays are always a nightmare. What with scheduled visits and walk-ins, you can't even imagine the rush. Listen, why don't we do this: you leave me the note and I swear to you that in less than"—he glanced at the clock—" six hours I can give you the information you need."

"Let's say three hours."

"Five."

"Four, and we have a deal!" said Rocco, extending his hand. The director took it and shook it without understanding why. He took a sheet of paper and started writing. "Now then, Deputy Police Chief, do me a favor and remind me . . ."

"Certainly. I want to know whether and when you hospitalized, or even just treated in an emergency room visit, a woman named Esther Baudo. Baudo was her married name. Her maiden name was . . ."

"Sensini," Italo put in promptly.

Trevisi was taking notes without looking up, whispering with his Cupid's bow mouth each word as he wrote it: " . . . emergency room, Sensini married name Baudo . . ."

"If you'll forgive me for putting in my two cents, I'd take a look under traumatology. I want to know how and why."

" . . . how and why . . . excellent!" The administrative director looked up. "Well then, if there isn't anything else . . ."

"No, actually there is one more thing."

"Go right ahead, Dottor Schiavone."

"You just try not getting back to me in four hours and I'll be back with a nice little document signed by a judge."

"And would you mind telling me what I'd find written in that document?"

"Dottor Trevisi, it's not as if I came to see you because I don't have anything better to do. This concerns a murder. I hope that I've made things clear once and for all. Have a good day."

He turned and exited the office, with Italo hard on his heels. Trevisi immediately picked up the phone: "Annamaria? Please come to my office . . . there's some research I need you to do . . . of course, right now; when did you think? At New Year's? Who the hell cares if it's Wednesday!"

"SHALL WE GO VISIT D'INTINO?" ASKED ITALO AS they walked down the hospital stairs.

"What is this craze everyone seems to have about going to visit him?"

"He doesn't have family here in Aosta. We take turns bringing him water and cookies."

Rocco stopped. "And do you usually go with Caterina or on your own?"

Italo blushed. "Listen, Rocco, this thing with Caterina . . ."

"You want the whole story? I originally planned to take some serious revenge. Like put a note of demerit into your file and ask the police chief to have you transferred. But then I took a good look at you. You're just a pathetic loser with a mouth that belongs on a piggy bank, and when are you going to find another girlfriend?"

"And so?"

"And so I forgive you. In the name of the Father . . ."

"Oh go fuck yourself, Rocco."

"But at least once you need to tell me what she's like in bed."

"That's personal."

"Have you ever heard of a place called Scampia? Or Macomer? How about Sacile del Friuli?"

"Shall I start from when we got undressed?"

"Good idea. While we head into town, because we have somebody to go see. And even if it's technically strictly a pedestrian zone, we're going to take the car. Are we or are we not the police, for fuck's sake!"

"You're not going to add a note of demerit to my file because without me who do you have left at headquarters?" said Italo, with a wink and a smile.

"Well, I'd have Caterina. And believe me, she'd be plenty."

"What a bastard."

"You have no idea. Come on, start talking. Let's start with her nipples."

OFFICER ITALO PIERRON WALKED INTO THE TOMEI clothing shop, following his boss like a bloodhound at the heels of a hunter. The only difference is that a bloodhound knows what it's doing; it knows its job. Find the birds and scare them into the air. Instead, all Italo could do was look around in bewilderment and check the price of a pair of Church's shoes.

In his impeccable Prince of Wales tweed suit, Signor Tomei, proprietor of the Very English menswear shop that bore his name, hurried toward the two policemen with tiny steps. "Dottor Schiavone! I'm so happy you dropped by. As I told you on the phone yesterday, my wife has something to tell you."

And with a theatrical gesture he brought his wife, Finola, onstage. A woman with the most prominent chin Rocco had ever seen. This wasn't a chin, Rocco thought: it was a downspout.

"*Buongiorno*, Commissario." The English accent gave away her origin.

"Deputy Police Chief," said Rocco.

"Yes," said the woman. "I wanted to speak with you. Because . . . I remembered a very important thing."

"I'm all ears."

"My husband told me . . . and I started thinking. I thought and I thought and in the end I remembered." She looked Rocco in the eye and delivered her showstopper, but in English: "*A tie!*"

"I don't understand."

"The lady that is dead . . . she came to buy a necktie for her husband. *A tie*. That's what was in the bag."

Rocco looked at Italo, who wasn't understanding much but who was pretending to take interest in the conversation. "Can I see one?"

"Certainly. She bought a regimental tie. A very nice one. Cashmere and silk."

"Correct me if I'm wrong, but are regimental ties the ones with diagonal stripes?"

"Exactly!" said Finola, who had in the meantime pulled three gleaming ties out of a display case. "You see? This is what they look like . . ."

"And if I asked you to identify that tie, would you be capable of doing that?"

"Certainly," Signor Tomei immediately butted in. "I could spot one of our ties from a mile away. You know why?" he smiled connivingly. He picked up one of the ties and turned it over. "You see? On the back we've added the logo of our store. Nothing could be easier!"

A small white label, also made of silk, was stitched to the back of the tie, and it bore the name "Tomei," embroidered in an oval of laurel leaves. "That's our trademark. These ties are exclusive to us. They come from Ireland. Oh, Lord, they're actually made in India, but the design and everything else is pure Irish."

"Wait, is Ireland part of Great Britain, or is it Ireland?" were the only words to emerge from Italo's mouth; it was unclear why he'd felt called upon to vocalize his presence, which was otherwise entirely unnecessary in the shop. All he got in response was a scornful glare from Rocco, and another equally contemptuous glance from Finola, who couldn't let the question go unremarked. "Ireland is Ireland, Officer, and it's officially called Eire. Ulster, that is, Northern Ireland, is part of Great Britain. The capital of Ireland is Dublin. For Ulster, it's Belfast. If you want to know more about it, you'd need to read a book about Michael Collins."

Rocco brought the conversation back to the tie. "One last thing. Can you tell me the price?"

"For that tie? It's not for the weak of heart . . ." said Signor Tomei.

"Well?"

"About seventy euros. But you know, it's made of silk and it's practically a one-off, handmade. You see, cashmere-silk blend is a process that requires . . ."

"You don't need to talk me into buying one, Signor Tomei. All I need is the information."

"Sorry. Force of habit."

"Don't think twice. Signora Finola, you've been extremely helpful."

Finola Tomei smiled and revealed a specialist array of teeth. Spacialist in the sense that in the upper arch a canine was missing, and in the lower arch, two incisors. If you added to that fact the consideration that her teeth were enormous and stuck into her gums with no particular rhyme or reason, Finola Tomei's mouth seemed like the result of a frontal collision with a trolley. Rocco stood there, captivated, gazing at her. It was Italo who brought him back to earth. "Very good, Dottore, shall we go now?" he asked, shaking Rocco by the arm. Rocco smiled, winked at the husband and wife, and left the shop, escorted by Officer Pierron.

• • •

"A GARGOYLE. DID YOU SEE THAT, ITALO? SHE LOOKED like a gargoyle, one of those statues on Notre Dame Cathedral in Paris."

Italo smiled: "Pretty amazing. But more than one of those gadgets, those gargoyles, if you ask me she looked like one of those deepwater fish, what do you call them, abyssal fish. You know the ones: translucent, with tiny bodies and huge mouths?"

"You know, you're right?"

"I've seen ones on Animal Planet that are truly frightening."

"It's true, an abyssal fish. This is the first time it's happened to me."

"What?"

"The first time I've found a resemblance between a woman's face and an animal. It's never happened to me before."

"That's because you've never seen my aunt," said Italo. "Someday I'll introduce you. But you'd better brace yourself. Just imagine: she's eighty-two years old and she hasn't left her house since 1974."

"Can't she walk?"

"No, no, she can walk, and how. It's just that one day she decided she didn't feel like going out anymore. She says that everyone out in the world is crazy these days. Aunt Adele, that's her name. She's four foot eleven and she only talks at night. One look at her and your jaw would drop."

"And why should I meet her?"

"Because there's no better cook in the whole valley, believe me!"

"Then you know what I say, Italo? I say let's go have dinner at the Pam Pam, you and me. It's my treat. And bring Caterina too."

"And just what reason do you have for being so generous?"

"Because I'm depressed, because it's March twenty-first, the first day of spring, and it's an important date and I don't feel like eating alone. Is that enough for you?"

IN THE END THIS IS HOW HE ALWAYS WOUND UP FEELING. Tired and disgusted. Dinner with Italo and Caterina hadn't helped much. He'd laughed, he'd drank, he'd done his best to take his mind off it. But it hadn't worked. When all was said and done, the vacuum of death weighed on him worse than any other preoccupation. Because by this point Rocco Schiavone knew who was guilty of the murder. It had taken him just a few days to figure it out, to chase down and catch the killer, the idiot, the person who had chosen to upset the natural balance of things. Who had extinguished a human life—for what? Personal conceit? Anger? Madness?

But in order to understand whatever it was—conceit, anger, or madness—Rocco had had to plumb the depths of it, the way a good actor does before portraying a character. And in order to enter into the role, he'd have to go into the diseased head of those people, put on their filthy flesh like an overcoat, camouflage himself, and drop into the depths, the sewers, searching with a flashlight for the most indecent, the filthiest parts of a human being. And he'd have to stay down there, in the sewers, in the swamp, lying in ambush until the murderer, the bastard wandered into range. Then he could finally surface into the fresh air and try to get clean again. Only to get all that filth off him, it would take days, even months. And some of it always stuck to his skin, impossible to scrub away.

He knew that if he continued in that profession, he'd never be able to get the filth off him.

"YOU KNOW WHAT? I WENT BY THE APARTMENT. THE furniture is all covered up. With sheets."

Marina laughs heartily. "The wood worms can get in all the same," she said and leaned against the window glass.

"And I even went to visit you."

She looks at me and says nothing.

"I brought you daisies. The big ones, the kind you like."

"You ran into them, didn't you?"

"Yes," I tell her, but after a while, not right away.

"Were they both there?"

"Both of them."

"They wouldn't speak to you, would they?"

"No, Marì, they won't speak to me. Or if they do, it's only to make it clear that they'll never speak to me again."

Marina nods and goes over to sit on the couch. "You have to understand them."

"Oh, I understand them. I'm not stupid. Still, I hoped. I mean, after five years."

"How was Rome?"

"I wasn't there long. I don't know. It stinks."

"What did you go there for?"

"There were problems with the accountant."

"How many times have I told you? You're good at spotting lies but terrible at telling them."

Really, can't I just once get away with hoodwinking Marina? "Well, okay, it was just something with work."

"The double life of Rocco Schiavone!" She burst out laughing.

"What kind of double life are you talking about? It's life, and nothing more, Marì." I pour myself some white wine. These days, since Ugo first let me sample it, all I ever drink is this Blanc de Morgex.

"How are Mamma and Papà?"

"Skinny."

Marina nods. "Just remind me of one thing. That July seventh . . . what time was it?"

"Three thirty in the afternoon."

"Three thirty. Was it hot out?"

"So hot. It was cloudy, but it was still terribly hot."

"And where were we?"

"On Via Nemorense, outside the pastry shop."

"And what were we there for?"

"To get a gelato."

She gets up off the couch and goes into the bedroom. "Marina?"

She stops. She turns around and looks at me. "I'll come to bed too. I don't feel like staying up."

"You won't get a wink of sleep."

"Then you just go on talking to me."

HE WAS TURNING OFF THE LIVING ROOM LIGHT WHEN his cell phone rang.

"Schiavone, this is Dottor Trevisi, at the Parini Hospital in Aosta. Sorry to call you so late."

"Don't worry about it. What time is it, actually?"

"It's midnight."

"And you're still at the hospital?"

"I told you that Wednesday is always a nightmare. Listen, it's not a simple matter. But here's what we were able to find out. If nothing else, we had Esther Baudo in the emergency room, twice in 2007 and once in 2009. The second time, she was admitted to the trauma ward."

"All right."

"Then in 2010, again in the emergency room, where she was given stitches on the inside of her mouth and . . . I read here that in 2011 she came in with a fractured cheekbone."

Rocco sighed. "And it never struck you as odd?"

"Look, I've only been here since 2010, and the truth is that the woman always explained these fractures as the result of car crashes. Except for the last time, which at least is filed as a result of a domestic accident."

"Domestic. Yes. That sounds like a pretty good description. Thanks very much, Dottor Trevisi. You've been very helpful."

"Don't mention it, it's my job."

"WELL? ARE YOU COMING TO BED?" MARINA ASKS.

Tonight I'm not going to get a wink of sleep. Like so many other nights.

THURSDAY

He found himself standing outside the Baudos' apartment. Someone had removed the seals from the door, which stood ajar. All Rocco had to do was push it open.

In the living room, squatting behind a sofa, his back to the door, was a man.

"Did you take the seals off the door?" asked Rocco.

The man turned around. It was Luca Farinelli, the deputy director of the forensic squad. "Actually, no. It must have been one of your officers."

"Or one of yours. My officers haven't set foot in this place since the first day."

Farinelli stood up, dusting off the knees of his trousers. "And it's a good thing!"

"Mind if I ask what you're doing here?" Rocco asked.

"I'm working. What about you?"

"I'm looking for a tie."

"My men took all the ties to Fumagalli."

"Then they must have been the ones who broke the seals."

"My men don't pull mistakes like that. That's the kind of thing your people do. When are you guys going to learn the basics of handling a crime scene?"

"How's everything going? Is your wife doing well?"

"Why do you ask about my wife every time I see you?"

"Because I'm hoping that one day you'll say to me: she's not my wife anymore. We broke up."

"That'll never happen."

"I wouldn't be so sure."

The whole question of Farinelli's wife remained a mystery to Rocco Schiavone. She was spectacular. When she walked down the street, every head turned—men and women. Luca was an unsightly toad, and the only thing he made turn was Rocco Schiavone's stomach, and the stomachs of all the officers who reported to him.

"What a mess you guys made in here . . ." said Farinelli. "Like always."

"I know you were looking for me. So get to the point because I have no time to waste and I don't like being in this place."

"I've got to hurry back to Turin. Double homicide, stuff that would make your hair stand on end."

"That is, if you have any . . ." said Rocco, looking at the clearly thinning hair that Farinelli had been battling for years.

"I dropped by your office. I left a box for you. Take a look, you might find something useful in there. I'll say only two things. First, you pulled down the corpse before my men got there, and you touched the cable without gloves. Someone even went into the bathroom and took a pee."

"How can you be so sure?"

"Because we tested the urine. This is the second time that we've run into Officer Casella."

That idiot, Rocco thought to himself. Already, the month before, up in Champoluc, Casella had marked a crime scene by pissing everywhere, like a German shepherd. "I know. Casella must have bladder problems or something. What's the second thing?"

"There was a cell phone, half-crushed. It's useless now. And we couldn't find the SIM card. Just think, it might be stuck to the bottom of one of your men's boots."

Rocco helplessly threw open his arms. "Give me a break!"

"You move through these crime scenes like a herd of rhinoceros."

"Anything else?"

"Yes. I intend to ask the police chief for permission to hold a three-day seminar for your men. I'm sick and tired of running around fixing the stupid mistakes they make. They don't have the first notion of how to work a crime scene."

"Are you going to teach the seminar?"

"Certainly."

"Consider me enrolled. Anyway, this case is cracked. There's just one missing detail."

"Mind telling me which?"

"A tie."

"That again? We took them all to Fumagalli."

"All but one."

Then Rocco looked at Patrizio Baudo's bicycle, the Colnago worth more than six thousand euros. He walked over to it. He stood there, looking at it.

"Are you looking for it there?"

"No. But . . . something occurs to me."

He turned the bicycle upside down. The rear wheel spun freely. Rocco stopped it. He carefully examined the structure, the brake pads, the seat. Then he stuck his hand in his pocket and pulled out his Swiss Army knife.

"What are you doing, puncturing his tires?" Farinelli asked.

The deputy police chief said nothing, focused as he was on selecting the right tool. Then he opted for the saw and set to work on the bicycle seat. He carved through the rubber. He pulled out a spring. Then a piece of padding and finally a small cloth label. With a smile he showed it to his colleague from the forensic squad: "Look at that!"

"What is it?"

Rocco handed it to him. Farinelli inspected it. It was a small white label, with a logo stitched on it: two laurel branches surrounding a name, Tomei.

"So?"

"Just a piece of luck, Farine'." And he took back the little scrap of fabric. "Well, take care of yourself. And thanks for your excellent work and blah blah blah."

Without shaking hands, Rocco walked past him, leaving the room without taking his eyes off the white cloth label.

Luca called after him: "Take a look at the things I left in your office."

"You can bet on it. Will you put the seals back in place, so I don't have to?"

ROCCO SCHIAVONE AND OFFICER ITALO PIERRON knocked on the door of the Baudo residence in Charven-sod, a handsome chalet with a chimney spewing gray smoke into a gray sky. A chilly wind had begun to rush through the valley, making the pine needles whistle and banging shutters. Patrizio Baudo's mother opened the door. "Deputy Police Chief . . . please, come right in . . ."

"I was looking for Patrizio," said Rocco as he wiped his feet on the doormat.

The woman smiled and nodded her head. "He ought to be down in the garage. He uses it as an office and ware-house. Can I offer you anything?"

"Absolutely not, thanks . . ."

The house smelled of furniture wax. "Please, make your-selves comfortable," the woman said, pointing to the leather sofas by the crackling fire. "I'll go get him right away." She moved off silently. She opened a door and started down a metal spiral staircase.

"Nice place," said Italo, looking around. The whole living room was lined with a wooden boiserie and on the walls hung strange paintings done with old lace. Cowbells and antique wooden skis, a couple of alpine landscapes, and a corner bookshelf mostly filled with cookbooks. There was a handsome wooden crucifix over the kitchen door and a painting of a Virgin Mary with Christ Child by the front door. "Come on, Italo, we're not here on a social call," Rocco said brusquely. And he went down the metal steps that led to a cramped little room full of jars and paintbrushes. There was a half-open door. Rocco pulled it wide and found himself in a cellar apartment, about a thousand square feet. Patrizio's mother was standing in the middle of the large room. "He's not here," she said. "He must have gone out."

That underground loft was full to the ceiling with athletic equipment. Hanging on clothes racks, wrapped in cellophane, were ski pants, trekking pants, sweaters, and windbreakers. Hanging on pegboards, on the other hand, was an assortment of mountaineering equipment. New items, on display. Climbing harnesses, ice axes, helmets, crampons, ropes, and carabiners.

"I just don't understand . . . I even looked in the garage. The car is still there," the woman went on, looking at the two policemen.

Rocco stepped closer to examine the merchandise.

"These are my son's samples. He put it all here because he didn't have room in his apartment." The mother continued to look around her. "Maybe he went for a hike. Have you tried calling his cell phone?"

"It's turned off," said Italo, standing next to a group of futuristic-looking bike tires.

"I wouldn't know what to tell you. Not half an hour ago he was down here organizing his samples. He'll be back at work tomorrow. Can I ask why you want to talk to him?"

"No," said the deputy police chief. "You can't. *Arrive-derci.*" He turned and went toward the spiral staircase. Italo told the woman good-bye and followed his boss.

IT WAS A WOMAN CLEANING THE ARRAY OF VOTIVE candles under the icon of the Madonna in the church of Sant'Orso who untangled the mystery. "No, Father Sandro isn't here. He went with Patrizio Baudo to the cemetery, to visit his wife's grave."

Snorting in annoyance, Rocco left the church. "This wild goose chase is starting to get on my nerves." Before leaving the house of Our Lord, Italo crossed himself. "You want to get a move on?" Rocco shouted at him.

IT WASN'T HARD TO IDENTIFY ESTHER BAUDO'S grave. It was the one covered with flowers and wreaths. It was heaped high. That was because Esther was a new arrival. That's how it always went. Fresh funeral, fresh flowers, and the legends on the purple satin with gilded edges still legible. Then with the passage of time the colors would fade, the flowers would wither, the wreaths would crumble, and the grave would become the same as all the others. A couple of flower stalks in the vases. Nothing more.

Patrizio Baudo just sat there, next to the priest, staring at the headstone. Rocco gestured to Italo, who understood immediately and stayed about thirty feet away. The deputy police chief went over to the bench and sat down on the widower's other side. He said nothing.

"Deputy Police Chief!" said Father Sandro.

"Can you leave me alone with Signor Baudo for a minute?"

The priest exchanged a quick glance with his parishioner, patted his hand, stood up, and went over to Italo.

Rocco waited for the other man to speak first.

"*Buongiorno*, Commissario," he said.

"I'm not a commissario and this isn't a particularly good day. Especially not for you."

Patrizio Baudo, the koala bear from Ivrea, looked at the policeman with his small, drab eyes.

"You don't understand, do you?"

"No. I don't understand."

Rocco stuck his hand in his pocket and pulled out a cigarette. He lit it. The sound of the River Dora flowing past was calming, as were the small cypresses running beside the lane. But what Rocco was carrying inside him was a tornado ready to splinter anything it touched. It had been building up all night long. "So tell me something," he began, after taking a first drag on his Camel, "did you enjoy beating your wife?"

"Me?!"

"No, my dick. Now let's see. How many times did you send her to the hospital? The way I read it, five. Correct me if I'm wrong." He pulled out a sheet of paper with his notes. "All right, I'll read you your resume. Your wife suffered a fracture to the ulna and the radius of her right arm. Then she broke her right cheekbone and two ribs." He folded up the sheet of paper and put it back in his pocket. "And that's just the fractures, the times you overdid it. I can just imagine the bruises and lacerations, no? You have a lot to learn. There are much more sophisticated techniques. For instance, there are ways of hitting that are incredibly painful and leave no marks. Have you ever thought of beating your wife on the soles of her feet with a club? Or even with a rolled-up phone book? Believe me, it hurts like a bitch and it never leaves a bruise. Or you could try with a wet washcloth. Use that on someone's legs and you might leave a faint red stripe, nothing more, but the pain is intolerable."

"I don't know what you're talking about."

"Ah, you don't? Would you mind doing me a favor? Take off your gloves."

"Why?"

"Just take them off. Since the first time I saw you, on Friday, I haven't had a good look at your hands. Let's say I'm a bit of a fetishist." He dropped his cigarette on the ground. Patrizio Baudo slowly took off first one glove, then the other.

"Let me see your hands."

Patrizio held out his hands, palms up. Rocco grabbed both hands and turned them over. There were cuts and bruises on the knuckles. One knuckle was actually black. "They still haven't healed from last Friday? Did you try using a little Nivea cream?" Rocco remained calm. But Patrizio was scared. More scared than if the policeman had started shouting.

"So now I'm going to ask you again, politely this time. Did you enjoy beating your wife black and blue?"

The man turned to look at Don Sandro. "Don't ask the priest for help. Look at me and answer my question!"

Still, the priest managed to read the look of alarm on Patrizio's face and hurried over to the bench. "Do you mind telling me what's going on?" he asked.

"Padre, do me a favor and butt out of this."

"Patrizio, tell me what's happening here."

But Patrizio had lowered his head.

"I'll tell you exactly what's going on, Don Sandro. This gentleman has spent the last seven long years amusing himself by beating his wife bloody, so badly that he sent her to the hospital more than once."

The priest's eyes opened wide: "Is . . . is this true?"

Patrizio shook his head no.

"Don't lie, Patrizio!" From benevolent and blue, Don Sandro's eyes hardened into a pair of razor-sharp arrowheads. "Not to me. Did you do what the deputy police chief is saying?"

"It didn't . . . it didn't always go that way. Sometimes I . . ." And with that he stopped.

"Go on. I want to hear. You what?" said Rocco. But Patrizio kept his mouth shut tight. And Rocco went on. "Now I'm going to lay the situation out for you, and you're going to listen quietly without interrupting, and if you do I'm going to break you in half right here and now, in front of your wife's grave and your spiritual father."

"Please, Dottor Schiavone . . ." the minister of God objected.

"Don Sandro, you can't even begin to imagine how hard I'm working to stay calm and collected. And just to put things into terms you'll find familiar, I think it's nothing short of miraculous that I'm not blowing my cool entirely and kicking this piece of shit's ass in. Now then," Rocco went, steadily raising the volume of his voice. "On Friday morning you beat your wife black and blue. Why, what had you found, some text message on her cell phone? Did you suspect she had a lover?"

"I didn't . . ."

Rocco let fly with the speed of an express train at full velocity; a straight punch knocked Patrizio Baudo's head around on its gimbals. "I told you not to interrupt me."

"Dottor Schiavone!" shouted the priest as the widower put a hand up to the cheek that the deputy police chief's hand had just stamped, leaving a mark like a decal on window glass. "No interruptions, I believe I just told him. Let's go on."

"Dottor Schiavone, I'm not going to let you—"

"Padre, stay out of this. This isn't one of your little lost sheep. This is a vicious coward who's always gotten away with it. Am I right, Patrizio? Then let me continue, and don't try to interrupt again. On Friday morning you beat your wife silly, she still had the marks on her face. You went overboard and you killed her."

"I told you that—"

This time it was Rocco's elbow that smashed into Patrizio Baudo's cheekbone. The impact snapped the man's head around 180 degrees and a spurt of blood shot out of

ANTONIO MANZINI

his mouth and stained the gravel at the priest's feet. "Oh
sweet Jesus!" he said. "Dottor Schiavone, I'm going to let the
authorities know . . ."

"Silence!" Rocco shouted, with foam on his lips. "Shut
the hell up."

Italo had come over. What looked like a peaceful conversation, at least from where he'd been standing, was suddenly deteriorating into something terrifying. He knew that
he needed to be ready to intervene as needed.

Deputy Police Chief Schiavone went on talking, calmly,
while the widower spat out a mouthful of red saliva. "And
all that happened in the kitchen. You strangled her with the
tie. The necktie that your wife gave you for your name day.
So you decided to stage a suicide. But first you drew the curtains and then—still worried someone might see something,
some chance observer, someone from across the street—you
actually lowered the wooden roller blinds, and that was your
mistake. In part because there's no one who can see into
your windows from across the way. No one lives across from
you, hadn't you ever noticed that? But you were in a hurry,
you knew that Irina would be there at ten, you didn't have
much time to think, so you lowered them. Then you went
out for a bike ride. If I were to ask you, would you be able to
come up with anyone to confirm your alibi? Did anyone see
you out riding? What do you have to say for yourself?"

Patrizio said nothing.

"Now is the time to talk. I asked you a question. Did
anyone see you on your bike?"

The widower shook his head no.

"Excellent. Then you got rid of the necktie, which was the murder weapon. You went home and you put on the whole charade. You kept your gloves on all morning, you never once took them off. And even when I came to the church to show you the brooch, do you remember? You were still wearing your gloves. Just like you are now. You were afraid to let anyone see your hands. You were afraid to show those hands, hands that had beaten someone. Specifically, your wife, Esther."

Patrizio had pulled out a handkerchief to wipe his lip. "I didn't kill her. I didn't kill her."

Rocco looked at him. He needed to clench his teeth and ball his fists as hard as he could to keep his impulses under control. He stood there, glaring at the man's jugular. He'd have happily ripped it open with his teeth.

"Esther and I . . . we fought, it's true. She . . . she just knows how to make me see red. I swear it, when she acts a certain way I just go blind with rage. She wanted to go away, she wanted to go to live with that bitch, Adalgisa!"

"Patrizio . . ." said the priest. "Patrizio, I'm begging you. Come back to your senses."

"What senses do you want me to come back to?" The koala's eyes widened, spreading like an inkblot on a sheet of paper. Now those eyes were completely dark and the white seemed to have vanished entirely. "She didn't understand, Padre. I loved her but she was constantly testing me. Every blessed day. Every day was an ordeal. She'd send texts and then erase them. Who was she texting? I had to know. I was her husband. Jesus Christ on a crutch, did I or did I not have the right to know?"

The priest raised both hands to his face. Patrizio went on: "Last year, I went and stayed with my mother for two weeks. And do you know what Esther said to me, Padre? Do you want to know? The happiest two weeks of my life! Her exact words. And the same thing with her cell phone. Text after text to that bitch Adalgisa, all of them saying: the happiest two weeks of my life! But still, she wanted money, fine lady that she was. Boy, did she want money! What about me? It was my job to work like a slave to make sure she had a credit card and plenty of cash to pay for her ridiculous whims."

"Why didn't you ever come talk to me about it? Why didn't you ever say anything?" asked Don Sandro.

"What could you understand about it, Padre? What do you know about having a wife? Have you ever had any experience in that area?"

"You're right, I don't know anything about having a wife. But I know a little something about the human soul," Don Sandro replied.

"All you've ever been able to tell me is: confide in Christ. Confide in Christ. But where was Christ for the past seven years? Where was He? Let me tell you where He was, Padre. Somewhere else. And you know when Christ came back? When I punished her. That's right, that's when peace returned, let me tell you. And believe me, I'm not ashamed to say it, bending her to my will was the only solution. Even if sometimes that was painful to me."

"You were breaking her bones!"

Patrizio's bloody smile seemed like a mask of horror. "Sure, that happened once or twice. Maybe even a few times . . . but you see? I might not have meant to, but sometimes all it took was a little bit of force and *crack!*" He snapped his fingers. "She broke like a twig. Not that I wanted it, but it would just happen . . . she had brittle bones, evidently. I bet if I'd never broken anything, we wouldn't be here arguing right now, would we?"

Rocco got to his feet. Patrizio was still talking to the priest, and by now it seemed that there was no way of stopping him. Usually a priest hears confession in secret, Rocco thought to himself. And also, maybe he wasn't remembering the details exactly, but wasn't there supposed to be the sign of the cross and some other kind of religious formula before you can start pouring your shit into the priest's ears?

"I knew it the whole time, but there always has to be someone at home who gives the orders and someone else who obeys them. And if that means that sometimes I had to resort to physical discipline, well then, Padre, what can I tell you? I resorted to it. Don Sandro, you can't imagine what it's like to live with a woman who might decide, from one minute to the next, that she wanted to go out and do who-knows-what with who-knows-who. I caught her red-handed, you know that? I caught her red-handed with a coworker of mine. In a café. Drinking a *granita di caffè*. With whipped cream. In February!"

"You . . . you did this to your wife . . ." said Don Sandro with his eyes fixed on the ground. Patrizio Baudo went on shouting, his teeth stained with blood as hysterical tears rolled down his cheeks. "She'd snicker behind my back every time we went out. Even in church, Don Sandro, even there. One time, you know what she said to me? That it was a pity that you'd become a priest, because it was such a waste of a handsome man. So what's the explanation? You must have had impure thoughts about my wife, that's it, isn't it? Tell the truth!"

"Patrizio, you need to calm down!"

"Why, are you saying you wouldn't have taken a piece of her?"

Don Sandro's right hand shot out with an astonishing agility and left a bright red mark on Patrizio's cheek.

"Padre," Rocco said. "Please. Control yourself."

Don Sandro was having difficulty breathing and he kept his eyes glued on Patrizio Baudo's face. The hand that had slapped him was bright red. "What have I done . . ." said the man of God, "what have I done . . ."

Rocco glanced at Italo, who was standing a few yards away from the bench. The officer read an unequivocal message in his boss's glance. So he stepped toward Patrizio Baudo while pulling a pair of handcuffs out of their case.

"But afterward, Esther understood!" Baudo was whispering to Don Sandro as Italo fastened up the cuffs around his wrists. "She'd understand and ask me to forgive her. And if I did what I did to her, it was out of an overabundance of love. That's right, it might seem hard to believe, but it's true."

With a mighty yank Italo tried to drag Patrizio away

from the bench and guide him, handcuffed, toward the car. But he went on talking. "And then she'd understand, Padre, you hear me? And she'd come to bed with me. And she'd be sweeter and more womanly than ever before. Why didn't she ever report me to the police? Eh? Answer me that, why not? You tell me why, Dottor Schiavone. Did you ever see her at police headquarters?"

By now Patrizio and Italo were about fifty feet away. The policeman was having a hard time dragging the man away. "Because deep down she was fine with it. She liked it that way! It was my way of showing her my love. And she was fine with it!"

"Get moving, god damn you to hell!" Italo shouted. But Patrizio paid him no mind.

"It was just a matter of calibrating my strength. I didn't know how to control myself. That's all. But she was perfectly happy with it!"

"I'm going to kick your ass right over to the car if you don't get moving!"

"But you have to believe me, everything I ever did to her, Esther deserved it. She practically asked for it!"

"God damn it to hell, now you've gone too far!" Italo hit him hard with his shoulder. Patrizio fell to the ground, kicked frantically, and then got back to his feet. "I didn't kill Esther. I only punished her, and she deserved it. I was her husband, I had the right to do it, and it was my duty. It's written in the books, Padre. It's written in holy scripture!"

At last Italo managed to drag the man away and they

vanished behind a cypress tree. As if by magic, his screams were swallowed up by the silence of the cemetery.

Rocco and Don Sandro found themselves face-to-face. A pair of survivors in the wake of a cyclone that had left nothing standing but them.

"So, next time, shall I hold him and you can hit him, Padre?"

Don Sandro collapsed onto the bench. "I . . . I can't believe it. I'd known them for all these years. And all this was happening right before my eyes."

"Right before your eyes, right before the eyes of their neighbors, the eyes of the whole city, of the hospitals and even the police. Don't blame yourself. You're not the only one at fault."

"How can you say such a thing? This certainly is my fault. If not, what are priests for? If a priest can't even intervene to rescue a family?"

"Because the only way of rescuing that family was something that you, Padre, will never be able to accept. It's called divorce."

"You see, Dottor Schiavone? What God has joined together let no man put asunder, and this I know. But sometimes God has joined together absolutely no one at all. And so there's nothing there to put asunder."

JUDGE BALDI WASTED NO EXTRA TIME SIGNING THE WARrants. He was clearly delighted that the case of Esther Baudo's death had been disposed of in just a few days. "You're a lightning bolt," he'd told Rocco. "Now, if you'll excuse me, I'm in the middle of nailing one of the largest cases of tax evasion in the history of Val d'Aosta." Together with the two members of his police escort, he took off at top speed, leaving the DA's office and heading for Courmayeur. Suddenly Rocco Schiavone found himself with nothing at all to do. He went strolling down the halls of police headquarters with his hands clasped behind his back, like a pensioner roaming the streets, supervising road repairs and construction sites. He'd bought a couple of coffees from the vending machine, along with a chocolate bar, and even a snack. Of course, he'd spat everything—coffee, chocolate, and snack material—into the plastic rubbish bin that some wise soul had placed right next to the vending machines. For the first time since he'd moved to Aosta, he'd gone home after lunch. Stretched out on the sofa with a blanket over his legs, he decided to do a little reading. He chose a book of short stories. If he wanted to start reading again, he'd have to treat it the way you would a sport, or jogging. After a long period of neglect, you can't go out for an hour-long run. Your muscles aren't in shape for that. Likewise, he was in no condition to start a novel. He lacked the stamina to run, and he lacked the concentration to read. If he fell asleep while reading a short story, he'd be able to pick up the thread again without much trouble. He happened to choose a book of short stories by Chekhov. When he got to the fifth Russian name, Olga Mikhailovna, his eyelids slid shut like a pair of roller shutters.

It was the police chief who woke him up. He'd taken advantage of the resolution of the case to hold a press conference, confident for once that he could dominate the questions from the news vendors. Rocco had been summoned to attend. He was dreaming of the Russian steppes, rubles, and versts of land. Without an excuse ready to hand he'd capitulated. So he'd be unable to avoid that pain in the ass that he'd promoted that very day to the ninth degree of objectionability.

HE FOUND HIMSELF SITTING AT THE BIG CONFERENCE table in the meeting room at police headquarters, looking out at a pack of reporters armed with notepads, cell phones set to record, and TV cameras on tripods at the far end of the room. Chief of Police Andrea Corsi had been speaking without a break for fifteen minutes now, and Rocco was lost in his thoughts, though he was careful to look out at the press with a good imitation of a focused, interested expression. It was an old trick of his, and he'd used it to make it through all those years of high school. It was enough to put both elbows on the table and place his hands in front of his mouth, narrow his eyes, and nod from time to time, in a slow, profound, thoughtful manner.

But actually his thoughts weren't there in that room. His mind was elsewhere. Again he had that uncomfortable sensation of having forgotten something.

"For that matter, my deputy police chief, Dottor Schiavone, can confirm this," said Corsi.

And suddenly he was the center of attention. "Certainly," he said, without the faintest idea of what he had just confirmed. All eyes were on him. Even the police chief's. He knew he needed to add something, but he didn't know what. The general topic had to be Patrizio Baudo's arrest, but he hadn't the slightest idea of what specific angle they were discussing. So he stalled for time. "Certainly, that's in line with the typical case studies we've seen," he said.

"What case studies?" asked a reporter with curly hair.

"The ones that line up with the statistics gathered by police headquarters," said Rocco.

Error. He saw the reporters' faces twist in confusion.

"Excuse me," asked a young guy with white hair, "but what are you saying, that the police are keeping an eye on the prices of racing bikes?"

What the fuck are they talking about now, goddamn it to hell? thought Rocco. Go on lying, never own up to the truth. "Certainly. Among other things. You should understand, my good man, that it's from details like this, apparently insignificant details like the price of a racing bike, for example the price of a Colnago, which can range around six thousand euros, that we can figure out an amazing array of things. Let me give you an example. Our man, Patrizio Baudo, was jealous of his bike, and he treated it as if it were his daughter. This jealousy of his ensured that the racing bike in question ultimately became a Trojan horse, because it was under the bicycle seat that he hid the necktie that had been the murder weapon. But the shop label got tangled in the seat springs and tore off."

They all went on looking at him, in utter silence. He was tempted to ask the police chief under his breath what the hell they were talking about, but he knew that such a question would be transformed into a dressing-down lasting at least an hour in Corsi's office, and he knew that his nervous system was in no shape for such an ordeal.

"I can't quite see what any of this has to do with the Aosta–Saint-Vincent–Aosta race," said the curly-haired reporter.

A lightbulb flashed on in Rocco's head. They were talking about that fucking amateur charity bike race, the Aosta–Saint-Vincent–Aosta, the weird obsession that had come over the Aosta region's governor.

"It has more to do with it than you realize, clearly," said Rocco, in a desperate bid to make sense. "Because it helped me to focus on the Baudo case; I believe that Baudo was planning to compete in that race and was training for it on a daily basis."

"But we were just talking about the bicycle that was going to be given as a prize to the winner!" blurted out an elderly journalist who, in spite of her age, seemed to be pregnant.

"And I'm here to confirm that it's going to be a Colnago racing bike worth six thousand euros," Rocco said with grim determination. Corsi looked over at him, openmouthed. "It is?" he asked.

"It's an idea of mine."

The police chief took back the floor in a frantic bid to salvage the situation. This time Rocco decided to listen. Once

again, the topic was Esther Baudo's murder. The questioning
had begun with a well-dressed and rather aggressive young
woman who asked: "So are we seriously going to waste our
time here today talking about this bike race and ignoring yet
another case of femicide?"

The room had burst into a roar of frantic talk. Corsi was
helplessly trying to keep up with the reporters' questions.
"Why don't the Aosta police get organized and set up a task
force to work on this social blight?" "Why should a woman
have to be driven to this point before anyone will listen?"

Corsi had done plenty of homework, and set out to prove,
with facts and statistics, that the Aosta police force had in
fact frequently intervened to stop the mistreatment of women
within the family setting, and was working in close collab-
oration with a number of regional associations. The police
were well informed and on the alert.

"Then why is Esther Baudo resting in peace in the cemetery now?"

"We have no record of any complaint from Signora
Baudo. Unfortunately that's the real problem with domestic
violence. Unless somebody says something we're helpless,
because we have no information."

"Holy Christ," the dark-haired woman cried, "a woman
is hospitalized five separate times, I say, and the police don't
even have an inkling of suspicion?"

"But, Signora, you see—"

"You can call me *dottoressa*, not *signora*," said the
journalist. Corsi turned red as an apple. He corrected himself. "Dottoressa, unless we receive reports from the health

authorities, which means an administrative director or a head physician, or even just a call from a doctor, there are certain things that we have no way of knowing."

"And yet I'm well aware of cases that have been reported and never investigated. Is it true that unless the husband beats his wife to a bloody pulp there's nothing that the police can do about it? That first a woman has to wind up in the hospital and only then are you willing to listen? Have any of you ever heard of psychological violence?"

Rocco plunged back into his thoughts. He still had that same sensation, the feeling that some detail had eluded him. Some fragment. A name. Something. Then he saw a familiar face in the room. She'd just sat down next to the TV cameras. It was Adalgisa, Esther's friend, and she was trying to catch his eye. She smiled at him ever so faintly, the corners of her mouth rising slightly. Rocco replied with a tiny tilt of the head. Adalgisa's eyes were glistening and a sweet smile lit up her face. She was thanking him.

"That man, Patrizio Baudo, beat his wife bloody for years, and she never worked up the courage to go to the police or to the Carabinieri. I'm just trying to understand how such a thing could happen in the year 2013."

Corsi held both arms out wide: "Dottoressa, I can't answer you that. All I can tell you is that my men and I are doing everything within our power to make this city a better place."

"Perhaps one of your men could speak to this question?" asked the journalist who looked pregnant.

"But without bringing in the issue of bicycles," added the curly-haired reporter, and everyone burst out laughing.

Touché. The deputy police chief could only shrug and move on.

"So what is the specific question?" asked Rocco, as he twisted open a bottle of water. He had no interest in making an even worse showing on his second appearance.

"Why does it seem to be impossible to put a stop to these violent and destructive dynamics in the context of family life?"

"That's a very good question, Signora." And he poured himself a plastic cup full of water. "But you need to understand. I'm not a sociologist, much less a psychiatrist. I'm just a humble deputy police chief. A cop, as they say on TV."

"But what's your experience? What have you seen? You work in the field, you're not a pencil pusher," the elderly journalist insisted.

Rocco took a sip, then set down the cup. "There are two types of criminals. There are hardened criminals, and they're not hard to deal with. And then there are people like Patrizio Baudo. Normal people, people you might work with and see at the office every day. Then they go home and beat their wives or molest children. If you ask their neighbors, they're good citizens. But they're actually the worst. Respectable people are the ones I fear the most. I'm not afraid of hardened criminals; I'm afraid of respectable citizens."

"As a great American writer once said: 'Beware the average man, beware his love, for it is average and it seeks average.'"

This time it was Adalgisa who had spoken, and everyone had turned to look at her.

"You kind of modified the exact quote to suit your purposes, but let's agree, that's the basic concept," Rocco added with a smile.

Corsi broke in abruptly. "Now, before this press conference turns into a symposium on world literature, are there any other questions?"

Three more arms shot up. "Do you think Patrizio Baudo will be able to plead mental infirmity?" It was the young man with white hair.

"That's something you should ask the judge and the criminal psychiatrist."

"In that case, what kind of questions should we ask you, excuse me very much?"

"You can ask us how we caught him, when we caught him, and what evidence we used to nail him. Concerning Patrizio Baudo's mental illness we have nothing to say; that lies outside our jurisdiction," the police chief replied.

Rocco leaped to his feet. "I hope you'll all excuse me. I'm having trouble breathing, and I'm afraid it may be a panic attack. I have to go."

"Are you all right?" a reporter asked in an alarmed voice.

"Let's just say that I'm sick and tired of being here."

He hurried down the steps so he could get outside and fill his lungs with fresh air. Even if it had started raining again, it was nothing but a fine, tolerable drizzle. In any case, better than going to the office to listen to Deruta's whining or the case history of D'Intino's ribs or the fabulous love story between Italo and Caterina.

"Dottor Schiavone!" A woman's voice made him spin around.

It was Adalgisa. "Dottor Schiavone, just a moment."
She caught up with him.

"Weren't we once on a first-name basis?"

"You're right, Rocco. I wanted to thank you, for real. And I'm feeling terrible."

"Why?"

"Because of things that were said in there."

"Are you talking about the bicycle?"

Adalgisa smiled. "No. But can I buy you an espresso?" She opened her umbrella. Rocco took it, the woman locked arms with him, and together they strolled toward the nearest bar.

THE COFFEE WAS DECENT, AND EVEN THE CONSOLA-tion biscotto wasn't bad. Too much butter, but every now and then Rocco needed a little hypercaloric filthy excess. It helped him to put up with a day that had been hard enough to take and a sky that had been vomiting rain for months now. Whether cool or icy, it was all just water.

"I was the one who should have done something. Because I knew, I knew everything, and I never lifted a finger."

"What did you know?"

"That Patrizio beat Esther. Hospitalized five times! Is that really true?"

"I'm afraid so."

"I only found out about it when she went in because of her arm. She told me she'd fallen downstairs. Once that bastard started beating on her, she wouldn't call me for weeks. I told her a thousand times: Esther, let's go report him to the police. You can't go on like this. But she always stood up for him. He was just jealous, she'd say, and also Esther was afraid."

"Afraid of what?" Rocco asked.

"Afraid of being left to fend for herself. She had no work. And maybe Patrizio would have come after her. I don't know, Esther's parents were dead and her only family was a sister in Argentina—they hadn't spoken in years."

"May I?" Adalgisa nodded and Rocco scarfed down the woman's biscotto as well. "Why didn't you tell me anything?"

"I've thought about it plenty of times. I could have told you these things about Patrizio, but then what if it turned out that Patrizio was innocent? That would have been a terrible thing. To accuse a person of murder is no joke."

"When we talked earlier you said it was bound to happen, sooner or later, and you were talking about Esther's suicide."

"She was just falling apart. We'd practically stopped talking to each other. She no longer told me about herself, about the life she led. She spent her days at home, watching TV or cooking for her husband. Every time she went out, he grilled her relentlessly. He didn't kill her last Friday, Rocco. He killed her for seven long years."

"Seven years of agony. Not something you'd wish on your worst enemy."

The woman picked up the valise and set it on her lap. "I have something for you." She pulled out a small black notebook. She handed it to the deputy police chief.

"What is it?"

"Something Esther gave me. Thoughts, a diary—I'd like you to read it. But only if you promise to give it back when you're done."

"Why do you want me to read it?"

"Because now that I know you better, I'm sure I can give it to you and not worry. Because you'll find Esther in that notebook. Because you never knew her. But what you did for her is more than anyone else ever did."

"I didn't do anything for her at all."

"That's what you think, Rocco. But you've done a great deal, I assure you."

WHEN ADALGISA LEFT, SHE'D GIVEN HIM A KISS ON the cheek. Sitting in the bar, he'd ordered another espresso. He had Esther Baudo's black notebook in his hands. He opened it. He started to read.

WHAT A STRANGE, ODD THING TIME IS. YOU CAN *measure it with a clock, a calendar, or a chronometer. But it's relative. While you look out the window and watch a snowflake fall, not even a minute has gone by. Nothing. A minute of nothing. That same minute for a newborn baby is the beginning of a lifetime. For someone swimming, that minute amounts to years of training. For me, it was just a snowflake falling. And I wonder what my minute is. My hour. Or even my day. There are people whose day consists of sitting in front of the television and watching the Home Shopping Network. For a dog, it's his two daily meals. For a prison inmate, it's just one day checked off his sentence. But for me, it'll be the day that changed my life. And when will it come? And what will it be like? Sunny? Will the sun be out, or will it rain? It's a safe bet that it will rain. I've never been very lucky.*

BOOK CLUB. WE TALKED ABOUT "MURDERS IN THE RUE Morgue." Only an orangutan could have committed the murder. Fantastic. Adalgisa and her literary byplay. I don't like detective stories. She explained them to me, showed me how to appreciate them. She works so hard. Is it worth it? To someone who can't even bring herself to get out of bed this morning? Maybe not. Still, I like her project. Sure, it's pure fantasy, but Adalgisa has a brain that travels at the speed of light. If you really could turn an orangutan into a murderer . . . impossible though. Impossible? Why? It just depends on the orangutan.

FIRST DRAFT OF AN AUTOBIOGRAPHICAL NOVEL. I'D like to call it Penelope.

She was falling slowly, gliding toward the bottom as the air exited her lungs with a hiss. Behind her eyelids, nothing but red, and the noise of her heart pounding more and more slowly in her ears. She fell as slowly as a red oak leaf in autumn, fluttering lightly before touching earth. She could no longer open the fingers of her hand, and everything was calm. Quiet and lovely. It was like falling asleep. Or the way it was after making love with Enrico, when they were still in love, when they were young and it felt as if they had all the time in the world at their disposal. But now time was running out. And that wasn't really such a bad thing, after all. The street noises were muffled. Her muscles relaxed and nestled against the ceramic sides of the tub. A sudden chill. Then one last tiny gasp, the last heartbeat, fainter than a canary's. And everything ended . . .

. . . IT'S NOT ME THAT I THINK ABOUT AT NIGHT. AND IT'S not him either. He's not much more than a digestive tract. But I mustn't defile these pages by writing about him. It's a waste of paper . . . I think about Adalgisa's games. Hmmm. Could that be the solution? I can't see any others.

A BOY IN THE STREET LOOKED AT ME TODAY. HE MIGHT have been twenty years old. And I looked away. He went away. I saw my reflection in the glass of the front entrance. There I was. Two groceries bags in each hand. My hair tangled like a bunch of spinach. What did he see? What was he thinking when he looked at me? Probably pity. A bottomless sense of pity. What do I think when I look at myself in the *glass of my front entrance? Is this my life? Is this what I wanted for myself? Is it worth living for thousands of days like this one?*

ON SUNDAY I WENT TO CHURCH. I DIDN'T WANT TO HEAR *Mass. I just wanted to look at the church. But I got there at the wrong time. I walked in right in the middle of Mass. The priest read Genesis, 2:21–23. I reread it at home. It says: "So the Lord God caused a deep sleep to fall upon the man, and he slept; then he took one of his ribs and closed up its place with flesh. And the rib that the Lord God had taken from the man he made into a woman and brought her to the man. Then the man said, 'This at last is bone of my bones and flesh of my flesh; this one shall be called Woman, for out of Man this one was taken.'"*

It got me to thinking. According to the Bible story, woman was born of man; in fact, woman is a part of man. And the man goes crazy for the woman and loves her. But in reality all he loves is himself. He loves a piece of himself, not someone different from him. He lives with himself and has children with himself and makes loves to himself. A love focused on his own person, a love that has nothing to do with real love. I believe it's the most perverse thing I've ever read in my life. The man is in love with himself and nothing else. And that's according to Sacred Scripture. The inferiority of women is just a side issue. It's just a fig leaf to conceal all the rest.

Ownership. One person belongs to another, is owned by them. By divine decree. Which means my life has value because it belongs to a man. Beasts of burden, houses, farmland, women. All chattel. All possessions. They belong.

. . . I'LL NEVER HAVE A BABY.
Because she'd be born a girl.
And she doesn't deserve that. Her mother would already have suffered through that.
Wherever you are, daughter of mine, please forgive me. Forgive your mother. She never felt up to it. And she never will. Never . . .

. . . I'M NO LONGER MYSELF. I'M NO LONGER MYSELF. I'M no longer myself.

. . . IT'S A MECHANISM THAT REQUIRES OILING, IT NEEDS to be fine-tuned. But if the trick works . . . there are no alternatives. I have no alternatives.

AT THE CENTER OF THE LAST PAGE, THERE WAS A phrase from the Brothers Grimm: *"Hansel and Gretel didn't give it overmuch thought, because they were sure they could find their way home by the breadcrumbs they'd dropped."*

• • •

ROCCO SHUT THE NOTEBOOK. AND ONLY THEN DID IT dawn on him what was wrong. What he'd overlooked. What the detail was that kept nagging at him, that lurked in the folds of his mind. When everything became clear, it was like being punched in the solar plexus. Powerful, sudden, the kind of thing that takes your breath away and makes your legs turn to rubber. He had to rush right over to headquarters. "It was too easy," he said, pushing open the café door as he left. "It was all too easy. Idiot, idiot, idiot!"

HE THREW OPEN THE DOOR AND LUNGED INTO THE office. On his desk was a note from Italo listing all the calls he'd received: three from the police chief and, most important of all, the three calls from Luca Farinelli. Next to the note stood a cardboard box. The deputy chief of the forensic squad had left it for him. Inside were plastic bags containing various scraps of paper. On the box was a note:

All of these are things that were on the floor in the
room with the corpse. See if any of it can prove useful.
After you've looked it over, please give me a call and
I'll file it away in the archive.

HE STARTED SORTING THROUGH, PLASTIC BAG BY PLASTIC bag. A couple of restaurant bills, shopping lists, a gas bill to pay, a parking lot receipt. Nothing much. But his eye had recorded something that his mind took a few extra seconds to register. He picked up the parking lot receipt again.

Parini Hospital. Departure time, 8:10 A.M. On Friday, March 16.

Who left the parking lot of the Parini Hospital at 8:10 on the morning that Esther died? And why was that receipt in the room where the corpse was found?

"A necktie . . ."

The clouds parted and a shaft of sunlight shone through. "The light!" shouted the deputy police chief.

Italo Pierron came running: "What light? What's happening?"

"I'm an idiot, Italo, a blundering idiot! Shut the door."

The officer immediately did as he was told. Then he sat down across from the deputy police chief: "What's going on? Can you explain?"

"Esther Baudo. She sent me exactly where she wanted me to go."

"What are you talking about?"

"I hadn't figured out a fucking thing! Now, Italo, listen carefully. We think it was the husband, right?"

"Yes, and he strangled her with his tie and then staged the hanging with the clothesline off the lamp hook."

"And already there's one thing that doesn't add up. The light. Remember? When we walked in I flicked on the light switch and there was a short circuit. What does that make you think?"

"I don't know."

"We'd already figured it out, idiots that we are! It's obvious that the killer closed the shutters afterward. And he left the room. She hanged herself with the tie, the cable came later. Do you remember what Alberto said?"

"No, I wasn't there in the autopsy room. I was outside throwing up."

"He said that there was one bruise about two finger breadths in width that was from the object that actually strangled the victim, which is to say the tie, and then a smaller one around her neck that was the mark of the cable. Now, we've said that her husband, after strangling his wife, hauled her up as if with a pulley by using the lamp hook. Then he supposedly tied the cable around the leg of the armoire, closed the shutters, and left. You with me?"

"And that's exactly what happened, right?"

"No! Because *we* caused the short circuit, when we turned on the light. So what does that mean? That the wires were exposed and were touching, and the minute we flipped on the switch, the power went out. The cable was attached to the ceiling hook of the lamp fixture; it didn't even come close to touching the wires. So how did these blessed electric wires come into contact? During the first hanging."

"The first hanging?" asked Italo, openmouthed.

"That's right, the first hanging. Exactly. When Esther took her husband's tie, twisted it into a noose around her neck, and let herself drop into thin air."

"I'm not following you. What about the cable?"

"Someone stepped in after her death. And you know

how? By wrapping the clothesline around her neck, loop-
ing it over the lamp hook, cutting away the tie, and leaving
Esther Baudo to dangle there."

"Someone did that? But who?"

"An ally. A girlfriend? A person who left the parking lot
of the Parini Hospital at eight ten?"

"So someone helped Esther after she was already dead,
do I have that right?"

"Exactly right. It's a mechanism that Esther and her
girlfriend had fine-tuned over time. The perfect murder. Perhaps at first it was nothing but a mental parlor game. How to
commit suicide and pass it off as murder. What would they
plant? They'd plant the shopping bag from the store, with the
sales receipt, and the gift card for her husband, pointing to
the idea that that necktie, the name day gift, was the murder
weapon. And in fact, we never do find that tie. All we find
is the logo of the 'Tomei' clothing store on the cloth label,
right under the seat of Patrizio Baudo's bicycle. And that was
already an odd coincidence. She never gave her husband
that gift. He never laid eyes on that necktie. All that mat-
tered was that we see it, you get that?"

"Wait, Rocco, wait a sec, I'm not sure I follow you. Let's
start over again. Esther and Patrizio have a fight."

"Let's just say that Patrizio that morning threw a fit
and really gave her a beating. Anyway, it all happens in
the kitchen. That's why the place was such a mess. Esther
decides she can't take it anymore and this is the right day.
They've long ago organized everything down to the last
detail, she and her girlfriend. All they need now is the right

occasion. So she calls her ally—and unfortunately we never found Esther's SIM card. Only her cell phone smashed to smithereens. It must have been a surreal phone call. Just try to imagine it! She tells her ally: The time has come. I'm doing it today. You know what to do next! And at that point, what had been nothing more than a literary plaything suddenly turns into something terribly real!"

"And she commits suicide. That is, to be more accurate, she hangs herself with the tie . . ."

"Exactly. Now the ally arrives, loops and secures the clothesline, cuts and removes the necktie, and then Esther's dead body drops in the noose of that metal cable securely anchored to the armoire. The ally lowers the blinds, shuts the door, and leaves."

"The ally lowers the blinds but doesn't turn on the light?"

"No. The light stays off. I told you that. The short circuit took place either because in the first hanging the wires pulled by the necktie were exposed and came into contact, or else the electrical problem was caused by the ally, the accomplice, precisely in order to signal to us: It's a murder! No one hangs themselves in the dark. Get it?"

"The ally is clever."

"No, the ally is a cretin. Because she thinks we're going to fall for this crudely staged murder. The ally and Esther were crude in their belief that we'd swallow it, hook, line, and sinker."

"Not really, Rocco. You threw the husband straight into jail."

Rocco pretended he hadn't heard, but Italo had just spoken a blessed truth. "A murder disguised as a suicide by hanging. You see that, Italo? She passed it off as a murder disguised as a suicide by hanging. But there was a mistake. Her ally was clearly upset, she did it all in a state of grief and horror, and overlooked one precious detail." Rocco held out the envelope containing the ticket from the parking lot. "Something crucial, you see? Proof that she was there, in the apartment. Then she left without being seen. And you and I turned the light on a few hours later."

"So anyway, Esther and her ally left you a series of clues . . ."

"To ensure her husband would be arrested. To punish him. Do you know the fairy tale of Hansel and Gretel?"

"The story about the breadcrumbs?"

"Exactly. That's what they did to us."

"So who's the ally?" asked Italo Pierron.

"Someone who goes to visit her mother with a broken hip at the Parini Hospital every morning. Someone who wants to become a writer."

"And who's that?"

"Adalgisa Verratti. Esther's only friend. Who's so confident that their plan will work that she never says a single word about Esther's appalling relationship with her husband. She leaves that to us. She knows that sooner or later we'll nail him for it."

"So you're saying Patrizio Baudo is innocent?"

Rocco looked at Officer Pierron. "Technically, perhaps. He didn't murder his wife. Or at least he didn't on March sixteenth."

"But he'd been murdering her for the past seven years, is that what you're trying to say?"

"Yes. That's what I'm trying to say."

"What are we going to do?"

The deputy police chief got up from his chair. He went over to the window and looked out. Then he rested his forehead against the glass.

"Seven years is a long time."

"Seven years is a fucking long time, Italo."

"Well . . . is it? That depends. But yes, it's a long time."

The deputy police chief hurried back to his desk. He pulled the receipt from the hospital out of the plastic bag. He looked at it.

"What are you going to do, Rocco?"

He took out his lighter and burned the receipt in the ashtray. The thermal paper turned black with a sudden flare, and nothing was left of the evidence but a flake of carbon in the midst of a desert of stubbed-out Camel and Chesterfield butts.

"*Te l'appoggio . . .*" said Italo, using a distinctly Roman expression. "I'm with you on this." He'd started picking them up by now. "*Te l'appoggio totalmente.*"

But Rocco said nothing. He closed the cardboard box. "We can give this back to Farinelli. So he can file it away."

Italo took the box and headed for the door.

"Italo?"

"What is it?"

"Only you and me."

"Like always, Rocco. Like always." And he left the office.

Rocco sat down as his desk. He pulled open a drawer. He looked at the joints, lying ready. Then he closed the drawer again.

HE WENT WALKING THROUGH THE CENTER OF AOSTA without any particular destination. He found himself almost entirely by chance in front of Adalgisa's bookstore. He'd seen her not even an hour before, but maybe it was time to settle the matter and prevent any further complications. He went in.

He searched through the shelves. And he found the book he was looking for, in the children's section. He went over to the cash register. There was a man with a beard.

"Is Adalgisa here?"

"She didn't come in today. That'll be ten euros fifty."

Rocco paid and left the bookshop.

He walked the three hundred yards that separated the bookshop from Adalgisa's apartment building. There were various surnames on the intercom. But not Verratti. He pushed a button at random.

"Yes?" asked an elderly voice.

"Mailman."

The buzzer buzzed and the door swung open. He examined the mail slots. There he did find the surname Verratti. Apartment 6. He looked up at the landing. There were three apartments. He did some quick mental arithmetic and climbed up to the third floor. The door to Apartment 6R was open. Rocco pushed it gently. Coming down the hall toward him was Adalgisa, a roller suitcase in her right hand and her purse slung over her left shoulder. As soon as she saw the policeman she turned pale.

"Going somewhere?"

The woman swallowed uneasily. Rocco closed the front door behind him. He looked at the hallway. White. With a bookshelf loaded down with books. "There's no need," he said to her. He put his hand in his pocket and handed her Esther's notebook.

"Did . . . did you read it?"

"Enough to understand."

The woman tucked Esther's diary into her purse.

"I passed by the bookstore. Look what I bought." He showed her the book of fables. "I decided to start reading again. I'm starting from square one, a nice fairy tale. That's a good method, don't you agree?"

Adalgisa shifted her weight onto her right foot. Her hand let go of the suitcase handle.

"What's your favorite fairy tale, Adalgisa?"

"I couldn't . . . really say."

"Mine is Hansel and Gretel. The one with the breadcrumbs. To find their way home. Sometimes it's breadcrumbs, sometimes it's pebbles. And sometimes it's neckties."

Adalgisa gulped.

"Don't worry. I just wanted to tell you that we've found the way home. Thanks in part to you."

"And what are you planning to do?"

"I don't know. Take a walk. And try to figure out if the work I do still has any meaning."

"I don't—"

"You know what?" Rocco interrupted. "When I was talking with you I had the distinct sensation that I was under a microscope. You were very good. I really should have been studying you. But you were more skillful than I was. And you know why? Because you put your heart into this thing. I was just being a professional."

"That's not true. Face it, you do have a heart."

"Still, there is one thing that hurts my feelings. You assumed that I was an idiot. And that I'd go for it hook, line, and sinker." Rocco started laughing softly. It was a hiccupy laugh, the kind that's contagious, and in fact Adalgisa indulged in a smile, along with him. "And my assistant, Officer Pierron, has a point. Deep down, I am an idiot, because I did fall for it. I fell for it because I was blind, my friend. Because I listened to my nerves, not my brain. Frustration instead of calm and cool deliberation. And you knew that. If you ask me, you knew that in the presence of Esther's corpse, something would snap inside me. Something that would blind me. You know me much better than what you read in the newspaper. It's crazy that you figured all this out just from a short conversation in a bar. If you write the way you study up on people, then you have a brilliant future ahead of you. How did you manage to identify my weak point?"

"Are you talking about your wife?"

Rocco nodded.

"I asked around. At police headquarters too. I have a friend who's a cop."

"It wouldn't be Deruta, would it?"

"No. His name's Scipioni."

"Take care of yourself, Adalgisa, and don't worry, you can stay in Aosta. No one's going to come bothering you."

"*Grazie*." The bookseller's eyes were wet.

Rocco turned and made for the door. But when he got there he seemed to change his mind. He turned back around and spoke to Adalgisa. "Two things. Throw away your keys to Esther's apartment. You don't need them anymore. And when you take police seals off the door, make sure you put them back afterward. Otherwise you're leaving indelible evidence. Remember that in your next detective novel." And with that he left the apartment.

HE'D BEEN USED. MOVED HERE AND THERE LIKE A puppet on a string, by a dead woman and her good friend. A woman who had found in that suicide one last extreme act to complete her life and to punish once and for all the man who had destroyed that life.

A parlor game that moved from the world of fantasy into real life, the deputy police chief thought to himself.

How many times had he played those parlor games with his friends? Like: You're all alone on an island populated by rats and seagulls. You have no weapons. How do you survive? What do you do?

He could just see them, Adalgisa and Esther at their book club, planning a fake suicide, with plenty of details. Who knows, maybe just to make the game more interesting, more realistic, they had even set it on the stage of Esther's home.

And then they'd actually put it into practice.

Rocco had never glimpsed such extreme despair, such desperation. Total, with no way back. To reach this point involved a plan so absurd and complicated that only a woman could have come up with it. Only a woman could have implemented it.

And who was he to ruin that plan? No one, nothing, a pawn. A puppet, in fact.

He walked past Nora's shop. He stopped about thirty feet away and just looked. She'd changed the window display. Now there was a severe, very elegant wedding dress, a little bit in the style of Grace Kelly. He heard a peal of laughter echoing off the walls. He recognized it. That was Nora. She was on the other side of the street and was walking toward her shop with Anna and the interior decorator Bucci-something something. They were laughing loudly and eating gelato. A gelato in that cold, Rocco mused with a smile. He turned up his coat collar. They saw him. All three stopped short in the middle of the street. Nora's eyes were big and round. Anna had a half smile on her lips. The interior decorator was waggling his eyebrows, clearly ill at ease. Rocco leaned against the wall. A little boy riding a bicycle with training wheels went by, brow furrowed in concentration, followed by his father. Nora broke away from the trio and walked toward the deputy police chief. Rocco turned and vanished around the corner, mentally wishing her all the best. She deserved it.

IN SPITE OF THE COLD, HE WAS SITTING AT ONE OF THE tables outside the chalet bar in the Piazza dell'Arco di Augusto. The bar was closed. He just sat there, in silence, listening to the sound of the wind and the few cars going by. He thought about Rome, his dusty apartment with its ghost furniture. He looked at the sidewalk wet with the rain that had just stopped falling. The mountains all around, still garbed in winter. The clouds rushing past, every once in a while having a little fun by offering a clear view of the snowcapped peaks. The occasionally hasty pedestrian turning the corner toward Sant'Anselmo.

"THERE'S NOTHING TO CELEBRATE, YOU KNOW," MARINA tells me.

"What are you doing here?" I ask her.

"I'm enjoying the sunset."

"What sunset? It's too cloudy to see anything."

"Have a little faith. It's a cold city. But a pretty one."

"True. It's pretty."

"You're a cop, not a judge."

She's never been so direct. "I know. I'm not a judge."

"You can't always just do what you want."

"I know that too."

"So you're going to leave things the way they are?"

"I'm going to leave things the way they are."

"Don't you think he's innocent?"

"No, Marina, he's not."

"Look!" says Marina. "There it is. It's like the diluculum.

The first light. The gleam of hope. So you see, sooner or later it's bound to come?"

RIGHT THERE, IN THE MIDDLE OF THE SKY, THE clouds had parted. A ray of sunlight had shot down through that quilt of shadows and pierced the Arch of Augustus, illuminating the piazza and the street.

Rocco stood up. Slowly, he walked out into that narrow shaft of bright light. He was going to follow it, without thinking, at least this once, wherever it took him.

Maybe it would take him home.

ACKNOWLEDGMENTS

First of all, my sincere thanks go out to Piero and Luciano of the Aubert bookshop in Aosta. Your kindness and generosity have touched me deeply.

Then, thanks to Paola and her "tips."

I cannot fail to thank Mattia for his attachment to Rocco Schiavone, as well as Maurizio, Floriana, Francesca, Marcella, and the Sellerio publishing house as a whole.

A huge thank-you to my family, which surprisingly continues to stay with me: Toni "if-there's-one-thing-that-gets-on-my-nerves," Giovanna "check-and-make-sure-you-got-back-in," Francesco "I-was-robbed," Laura "hold-on-a-sec-lemme-put-in-my-earbuds," Marco "what's-the-word-from-parliament," Jacopo "A-plus-plus-plus," Giulia "Idefix," and last but only because he's the youngest, Giovanni "teach-this-year-I'm-definitely-passing-the-class!"

A wholehearted thank you to Fabrizio, who by now knows Rocco better than I do.

ACKNOWLEDGMENTS

To Nanà, Smilla, Rebecca, and Jack Sparrow, who was a "guest" at my house, bringing a breeze of love.

Thanks from the heart.

As of November 21 in 2013, the year I wrote this book, there were 122 cases of femicide in Italy.*

Until that number drops to zero, Italy won't be able to call itself a civilized country.

A. M.

---

* Source: Casa Internazionale della Donna in Rome.

ABOUT THE AUTHOR

Born in 1964 in Rome, Antonio Manzini is an actor, screenwriter, director, and author. He studied under Andrea Camilleri at the National Academy of Dramatic Art and made his debut in fiction with a short story he cowrote with Niccolo Ammaniti. He is the author of three murder mysteries that feature Deputy Police Chief Rocco Schiavone, a cop who thinks outside the box and disrespects both his superiors and police department regulations. *Adam's Rib* is the second of these novels to be translated into English.

THE ROCCO SCHIAVONE MYSTERIES BY
ANTONIO MANZINI

"Fans of Andrea Camilleri's Sicily-set 'Inspector Montalbano' series will enjoy this debut mystery for its sly humor, vividly drawn characters, and amusing cultural clashes between rugged mountaineers and the more urbane southerner." —*Library Journal*, starred review

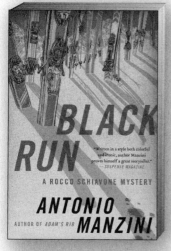

BLACK RUN
A Rocco Schiavone Mystery

After getting into serious trouble with the wrong people, Deputy Police Chief Rocco Schiavone is exiled to Aosta, a small, touristy alpine town far from his beloved Rome. When a mangled body is discovered on a slope above Champoluc, Rocco immediately faces his first challenge—identifying the victim, a procedure complicated by his ignorance of his new home. Proud and undaunted, Rocco makes his way among the ski runs, mountain huts, and aerial tramways, meeting instructors, alpine guides, the enigmatic folk of Aosta, and a few beautiful locals eager to give him a warm welcome. It won't be easy, this mountain life, especially with a corpse or two in the mix. But then there's nothing that makes Rocco feel more at home than an investigation.

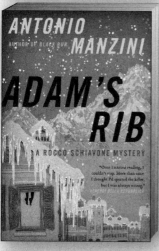

ADAM'S RIB
A Rocco Schiavone Mystery

Six months after being exiled from his beloved Rome, Deputy Police Chief Rocco Schiavone has settled into a routine in the cold, quiet, chronically backward alpine town of Aosta: an espresso at home, breakfast in the piazza, and a morning joint in his office. A little self-medication helps Rocco deal with the morons that almost exclusively comprise the local force, especially on a day like today: Rocco's about to stumble on a corpse. It begins when a maid reports a burglary, but there's no sign of forced entry. Something is off about the carefully ransacked rooms, and that's when he finds a body: a woman, the maid's employer, left hanging after a grisly suicide. Or is it?